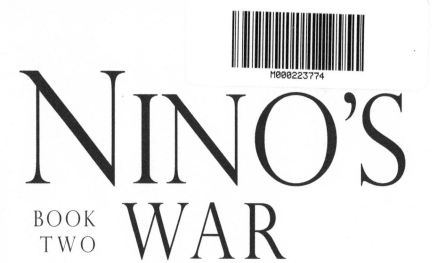

NINO'S

BOOK TWO

WAR

NINO'S

BOOK TWO

WAR

J.D. KEENE

Published by JDKeene Publishing

www.jdkeene.com

ISBN: 978-1-7330881-3-8

Cover Design by Dawn Gardner / dawngardnerdgee@gmail.com

Interior formatting: Mark Thomas / Coverness.com

To my sisters, Elizabeth Gassoway and Mary Durr,
and my brothers Andy Keene, Evan Keene, and Mark Keene.
You are the best.

And as always, to my wife Katie who is a constant source of wisdom a
encouragement.

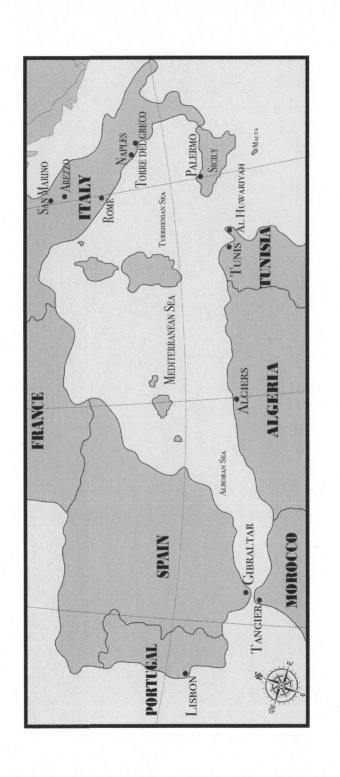

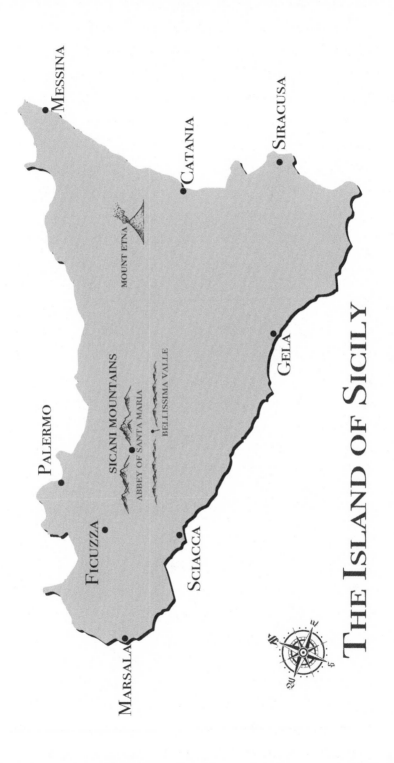

The Island of Sicily

CAST OF CHARACTERS

Fictional Characters -America

Servidei Family

> Nino
>
> Hannah, Nino's wife
>
> Lilia, adopted daughter
>
> Solomon, infant son

DiVincenzo Family

> Salvador, Nino Servidei's father, New York City crime
> boss
>
> Maria, Salvador's wife, Nino's mother
>
> Angelo, Nino's brother

Other Characters

> Father Nunzio, Nino's priest and boyhood mentor

Fictional Characters — Sicily

> Alfonso DiVincenzo, *Capo di tutti capi* (Godfather) of
> Sicily, Nino's grandfather
>
> Pierre Morneau, Alfonso's house manager
>
> Madam Lucia, brothel proprietor, Palermo Sicily
>
> Gabrielle Fontaine, prostitute
>
> Hortense Vernier, prostitute
>
> Father Russo, the Abbey of Santa Maria

Leone Family

Bruno, grandfather, and patriarch of the Leone citrus
dynasty, Italian partisan

Lorenzo, Bruno's son, Italian partisan

Aldo, Lorenzo's son, Italian soldier

Isabella, Lorenzo's daughter

Roseman Family

Manuel, owner of the Roseman cameo shop, Italian
partisan

Olivia, Manuel's wife

Fictional Characters — Axis Military

Generalmajor Richter, German Wehrmacht commanding
general of western Sicily Italian 6th Army.

Maggiore Brambilla, Italian officer, Generalmajor
Richter's interpreter

Carporale Vito Bianchi, Italian soldier, Nino's best friend.

Historical Characters — Allied Powers

Franklin Delano Roosevelt, President of the United
States.

William J. Donovan, Director of the Office of Strategic
Services.

General Dwight D. Eisenhower, Supreme Commander
Allied Expeditionary Force of the North African
Theater of Operations.

Father Felix Morlion, Belgian Dominican priest, founder
of the Catholic intelligence organization known as
pro Deo (For God).

Historical Characters — Axis Powers

General der Panzertruppe Fridolin von Senger und Etterlin, German Liaison Officer to the Italian 6th Army.

CHAPTER 1

Nino studied his wife from across the room. She was magnificent. To him, she was the most beautiful woman in the world, and he adored her. Hannah Servidei stirred a pot of bean soup at a cast-iron stove. With a playful grin, she glanced over her shoulder. Nino drew near. From behind, he moved her sandy blonde hair to the side and kissed her neck. "That glorious scent of pinto beans you are wearing excites me."

She moved the pot to the side and turned to face him, resting her arms around his neck. "Everything excites you. That's why I have a little version of you growing inside of me."

"That's what you get for being so beautiful."

"That's what I get for marrying a man twelve years younger than me who can never get enough."

"I'm guilty. I admit it. I can't keep my hands off you."

She kissed his lips. Not just a peck, but a prolonged, passionate kiss.

Their adopted daughter, Lilia, entered the kitchen. Speaking in Italian, she said, "Will you play with me, Papa?"

Nino turned to her and knelt. "What would you like to play?"

"Piggly Wiggly. I'll go get it."

Hannah said, "No sweetheart, your grandmama will be here soon. I've already set the table. I'm going to the bedroom to rest until she arrives. You come with me and we'll nap."

"But—"

Nino interrupted her. "Listen to your Mama."

"Okay, Papa."

"I'll wake you when she arrives," Nino said.

Their apartment was on the third floor of a forty-year-old, six story building. There were two narrow rooms, the kitchen, which also served as the entranceway for the lone external door, and the bedroom behind the kitchen. Each floor had six apartments that shared the same toilet and bath at the end of the hall. Outside of the kitchen window was a fire escape. Both the building heat and cast-iron stove required coal.

Nino put on his coat, opened the window, and climbed out on the fire escape. It was his private retreat. Hannah referred to it as his den.

The afternoon sky was clear, and the gusts of wind across his face were cold. He enjoyed an occasional brief blast of chilly air. It energized him.

Nino inhaled several deep breaths, blew them out, then watched as they crystalized in the air. Other than a group of boys throwing snowballs in an alley, there were few people out.

His mother usually arrived by taxi, but since it was Sunday, he thought his father might have his driver bring her in his Cadillac Fleetwood.

Across the street, he saw the two Jenkins boys running in a full sprint before soaring from the sidewalk, first Jed, then Frank. They flew over six steps and landed at the top near the entranceway of their apartment. With a blaring horn, a car pulled up to the adjacent building. The driver parked, and he too sprinted into an apartment building.

In the street below, a cab arrived. His mother paid the driver and approached his apartment. Nino rose to let Hannah know she had arrived. He paused. His brother Angelo's car raced down the street. It stopped abruptly at the curb. Angelo got out and said something that caused their mother to step back and cover her mouth. They turned and at a hurried pace made their way toward the entrance of his building.

Nino yelled into the bedroom. "Hannah, Mama is here. Angelo is with her."

"Angelo too? We should have plenty of soup."

Nino listened for their footsteps. When they arrived at the landing, he opened the door. Their faces were red.

"Is something wrong?" Nino asked.

Upon entering, Angelo said, "You haven't heard, have you?"

"Heard what?"

"The Japanese have bombed some place in Hawaii called Pearl Harbor. Where's your radio?"

"It's in the bedroom. Follow me."

Nino entered the room with Angelo and his mother Maria trailing behind him.

Hannah sat at the edge of the bed. "What is all the excitement about?"

Without answering, Nino turned on the radio.

"... heavy shooting seems to be (break in the transmission) We cannot estimate just how much damage has been done, but it has been a very severe attack. The Navy and Army appear now to have the air and the sea under control.

We repeat, Hello, NBC. Hello, NBC. This is KTU in Honolulu, Hawaii. I am speaking from the roof of the Advertiser Publishing Company Building. We have witnessed this morning from a distant view, a brief full battle of Pearl Harbor and the severe bombing of Pearl Harbor by enemy planes, undoubtedly Japanese. The city of Honolulu has also been attacked and considerable damage done. This battle has been going on for nearly three hours. One of the bombs dropped within fifty feet of KTU tower. It is no joke. It is a real war. The public of Honolulu has been advised to keep in their homes and away from the Army and Navy. There has been serious fighting going on in the air and in the sea. The heavy shooting seems to be (break in the transmission) We cannot estimate just how much damage has been done, but it has been a very severe attack. The Navy and Army appear now to have the air and the sea under control.

Hannah struggled to stand from where she was sitting on the edge of the bed. "What does this mean, Nino?"

"I don't know."

Angelo said, "I hope it means we are going to war. If so, I'm enlisting. I'm going to fight."

Maria said, "Don't act so hastily, Angelo."

Nino turned and looked at Hannah.

"Don't look at me like that, Nino. You have a five-year-old

daughter and a child due next month. You aren't going to war and leaving me a widow."

Angelo said, "She's right, little brother. You have a family. Let us single guys take care of the Japs. We'll whip 'em. It will be over before it gets started."

Nino looked at Hannah, then to Angelo. "Don't worry. I have no intention of going to war. War is foolish."

* * *

The aroma of fried eggs and bacon hovered in the air. With a steaming pot in hand, the waitress approached their table. "More coffee?"

Nino waved her off.

Angelo mumbled, "Yes ma'am." The crumbs of the toast he was eating fell into his lap.

They looked through the diner window at the military recruiting office across the street.

"I need to get over there." Angelo said. "The line is wrapped around the building, and they don't open for another hour."

Nino said, "I've heard it has been like that every day since Pearl Harbor."

"And it will stay like that now that the Germans and Italians have joined forces with the Japanese. They picked the wrong country to fight with."

"I wouldn't be so confident. I know little about the Japs, but I saw the German Army firsthand when I was in Italy. They have rolled over everyone who has gotten in their way."

"They haven't fought any Americans yet."

Nino shook his head.

Angelo continued. "You need to keep a close eye on those spies you are guarding on Ellis Island."

"Those people aren't spies. They are families who came here to get away from the fascism in Europe. I don't blame them. I saw it myself. It is evil."

"How do you know they aren't spies? They are Germans and Italians, aren't they?"

Nino laughed and leaned forward. "We are Italians, Angelo."

"We are Americans. You and I were born here."

"Should Mama and Papa be incarcerated? They weren't born here."

"You are twisting things," Angelo said. "Mama and her parents came her to escape Mussolini. So did Papa."

"Papa came here to avoid a murder conviction in Sicily."

"Those people you are guarding got here after the war broke out in Europe. I'm sure most of them are innocent, but I can also guarantee you that there are some spies mixed in with that bunch. If you were a spy, what better way to disguise yourself than as a family?"

"I'm not having this discussion, Angelo."

They eased the brotherly tension by returning to their breakfast.

Nino said, "Are you prepared to kill another man?"

"I'm looking forward to it."

"Be careful what you wish for."

"What's with you. Aren't you pissed off that the Japs attacked us?"

"I'm just warning you that once you…" Nino paused and looked down. He got a lump in his throat.

Angelo asked, "Once I what?"

"I've heard that once you take another man's life, something inside you changes."

"That's the ex-priest coming out of you."

"I was only studying to be a priest. I never actually became one."

"Same thing."

Nino wrapped his hands around his cup and smirked, then turned his attention to the young men waiting in line.

"Angelo!" a voice from across the restaurant shouted.

Nino turned to see a chunky, redheaded young man approach them.

Angelo addressed him. "Hey, Red. Are you joining up?"

"I am." He nodded across the street. "It looks like every man in New York is waiting to join the army."

Angelo said, "That little one in the plaid cap is Smithy's little brother. They won't take him. He's only fifteen. But I give him credit for having balls."

Nino took a sip of his lukewarm coffee. He noted the camaraderie between Angelo and Red. He then focused his attention on the fifteen-year-old boy Angelo had pointed out. Nino thought of Hannah and Lilia, and his little one who wasn't born yet. He knew his obligation to provide for them would protect him from the draft under the class III-A exemption. His job working security at Ellis Island would also provide an exemption.

Angelo snapped his fingers in front of Nino's face. "What were you daydreaming about?"

"Nothing," Nino said.

Red said, "Angelo, now that the Germans and Italians have joined the fight with the Japs, you might be fighting your relatives if we get into a scuff with Italy."

"It doesn't matter to me. I'm an American first and an Italian second."

Angelo rose from the table. "I have to get in line, Nino. I'll let you know when they tell me I leave for training."

Red said to Angelo. "Let's get over there."

As they left, Angelo shouted back, "Tell Hannah I said hello."

Nino waved his hand and watched them leave. He followed their path across the bustling street. There were young men everywhere blocking traffic. Dressed in overcoats and fedoras, flat caps and coveralls, they came in all shapes and sizes.

Nino's mind wandered to Italy. And although he held him in contempt, he thought of his Sicilian grandfather, Alfonso DiVincenzo. The head of the Sicilian Cosa Nostra.

THE ISLAND OF SICILY
FICUZZA
LA FORESTA
ALFONSO DIVINCENZO'S COMPOUND

The sun was high, yet the canopy of tall trees engulfing the property created a soothing darkness. He had strong-armed the previous owner to sell to him thirty years earlier for a quarter of what the estate was worth. The eighteen-room, one story stucco home, occupied the middle of seventy acres, known as *La Foresta*. A six-foot wall guarded the perimeter of the house. Behind the home was a stable for his black stallion, Hercules.

Alfonso DiVincenzo stepped onto his back patio and lit a cigar. Although not tall, his girth, along with his reputation, created an intimidating presence.

His house manager strode from the kitchen and onto the patio, where he placed a tray on a wrought iron table. "Your breakfast, Mr. DiVincenzo."

Alfonso said, "Thank you, Pierre. I hear the telephone. Go answer it, please."

"*Si, Signore.*" Pierre turned and ran.

The Italian army had drafted the youngest of the armed thugs Mr. DiVincenzo employed. The other dozen still with him were in their forties or older and had been with him for a decade or longer. Employment, other than farm labor, had been sparse in Sicily. Working for Alfonso DiVincenzo—the *Capo di tutti capi*, or godfather of Sicily, paid well and was viewed by most as a position of prestige.

From the house, Pierre yelled, "Mr. DiVincenzo, it is Enzo. He is at the northern guard shack. A column of military vehicles—both German and Italian—is making its way up the drive."

"Let everyone know. Have them grab their weapons and take their positions."

"Si, Signore."

Alfonso made his way through his spacious home before exiting the double oak doors at the entrance. The surrounding wall encircled a courtyard. Within the courtyard was a shallow pool filled with leaves and twigs that had fallen from branches high overhead. An aroma of pine lingered in the air.

He puffed on his cigar and listened to the vehicles approaching over the horizon. The sound of trucks reverberated under the shelter of trees. He looked north to the distant crest of his narrow driveway. The first to appear was a Mercedes—a black staff car, followed by two *Kübelwagens*. Bringing up the rear were four troop carriers. The staff car rolled through the opened gate of the courtyard, while the others halted outside the wall.

Alfonso stood tall and proud as the Mercedes halted in front of him.

The driver opened the rear door and a German generalmajor emerged. He was tall and slim, with a pencil thin mustache which held a hint of gray, as did his short-cropped hair. He appeared ten years younger than Alfonso's sixty-six. With him was a young, tall, Italian *maggiore* who approached Alfonso. "Good morning, Mr. DiVincenzo. My name is *Maggiore* Brambilla, and this is Generalmajor Richter of the German Wehrmacht. General Richter would like to speak to you. I will serve as his interpreter."

"I don't recall scheduling an appointment with General Richter. Perhaps he should return after arranging something with my house manager."

Maggiore Brambilla turned to Richter and relayed the information. Richter laughed, and in German, said something to Brambilla.

Brambilla said to Alfonso, "General Richter said that he has no time for appointments, and that you will meet with him now or we will conduct our business with or without your permission."

Alfonso turned, entered his home, and gestured for them to follow him into his den. He made his way around an oak desk and motioned for the two men to sit in the leather chairs facing him.

"How may I help you, gentlemen?"

Brambilla said. "You are a loyal Italian, and believe in the Axis cause, do you not?"

Alfonso smirked. "Go on."

"As I'm sure you are aware, the British have begun a

bombing campaign. It started with a few sporadic attacks in the port of Palermo. This has recently expanded to our airfields, fuel depots and base camps."

"What does this have to do with me?"

"Tall trees to hide large numbers of military vehicles from the air are few."

"And you want to use my property."

"Your estate is centrally located so that our vehicles and troops can move swiftly to get where they are needed."

Alfonso leaned forward, cigar in hand. "Do I look like I have shit for brains? Why would I put a target on my property so the British can drop bombs on it?"

"We will be careful. We will only move the vehicles in and out at night. During the day, all the enemy will see is a patch of tall trees. Besides, so far the Luftwaffe and Italian air force have repelled many of the British reconnaissance planes."

"So far?"

"We are confident we will continue to have success."

"*Maggiore*, let me make something clear, and feel free to share this with Generalmajor Richter. Twenty years ago, your precious Mussolini sent Cesare Mori here to Sicily to destroy me and everyone like me. I have associates imprisoned on the islands of Lipari and Salina because of Mussolini. Now he sends you and this German here to ask for my help? Mussolini can kiss my Sicilian ass."

Sensing the conversation was not going well, Richter asked Brambilla for a translation. After receiving it, Richter stood and made his way around the desk, and hovered over Alfonso. "Tell this 'Sicilian' he has no choice. Tell him I have four troop carriers of foot soldiers who are waiting for my orders to take command of every acre of this property if he doesn't cooperate."

Alfonso looked to *Maggiore* Brambilla. "He doesn't look happy."

Brambilla informed Alfonso of Richter's statement.

Alfonso rose from his chair and looked Richter in the eye. "Tell Generalmajor Richter here, that he has no idea who the hell he is dealing with, and if he doesn't leave my property now, I will kill him."

Maggiore Brambilla said, "I strongly suggest you withdraw that statement, or I will throw you in prison."

"What did he say?" Richter asked.

Alfonso glared directly at Richter.

Brambilla said, "I'll ask one more time, Mr. DiVincenzo. Do you withdraw your statement?"

Alfonso took a puff of his cigar and smirked. "I want to be paid for the use of my land, and with *Deutsche marks*, not the useless Italian shit that Mussolini prints."

ELLIS ISLAND, NEW YORK

Nino disembarked from the ferry, signed in at the guard shack and entered the immigration detention area. It was a warehouse with brick walls, a concrete floor, and a musty smell that lingered in the damp, frigid air.

He walked past the German detainees, most of whom were in the few beds and wooden benches made available to them. Wrapped in winter coats, they huddled near a coal heater in the corner. He then entered the registry room, where they detained the Italians.

Even before the declaration of war against America, the

roundup of those referred to as *enemy aliens* had been going on for weeks. On December 12th, the day after Germany and Italy declared war on the United States, the arrests of recently landed German and Italian immigrants accelerated. Ellis Island housed many of those from New York City.

Dressed in a port security uniform and wearing a billy club at his side, Nino worked a twelve-hour evening shift, arriving at 6:00 pm. His job was to walk the floor and keep order. But to the desperate families who lay huddled under blankets, on cots and on the chilly floor, Nino was viewed as a friend.

"Nino, were you able to locate my son?" an elderly man shouted from behind a row of huddled families.

Nino approached him. "*Si*, Mr. Lupo. He asked me to give this to you." Nino handed him a letter. "He is being held at the 43rd precinct in the Bronx. I informed him you were here and that you are safe. I have contacted my priest, Father Nunzio. He is with the local Catholic diocese. He is working on getting your son an attorney. I see Father Nunzio often. I will continue to update you as I find out more information."

"Bless you, Nino."

Another man shouted. "Nino, Sofia is sick. We think she has a fever."

Nino approached the man and his wife, who were sitting on a wooden bed. The mattress was stuffed with straw. He sat down next to the wife and looked at the sleeping girl. Her face was ashen. She was only five, the same age as Lilia.

After feeling her forehead, he said, "She is burning up. How long has she been like this?"

"Since this morning when she woke up," her father replied. "I asked the other guard to help, but he didn't speak Italian. He didn't understand and just laughed at me."

Nino said, "Mr. Cremonesi, wrap her up in a blanket and follow me. I will escort you to the infirmary. It is on the other side of the island, and it is bitter cold outside."

As they approached the exit of the registry building, another guard spotted them. "Where do you think you are going with them, Servidei?"

"I'm taking them to the infirmary. Their daughter is sick."

"You don't have that authority. You need to get permission."

"There won't be anyone authorized to give me permission until the morning. We aren't waiting that long."

"Servidei, I'm warning you. If you leave here with them, I'll be forced to write you up."

As Nino opened the door and led the family out, he said, "Do what you have to. This little girl is too sick to wait any longer."

CHAPTER 2

THE BRONX NEW YORK
THE APARTMENT OF SALVADOR AND MARIA
DIVINCENZO

Maria DiVincenzo stood at the entrance of her husband's den. "Your pride is costing you the opportunity to see your granddaughter."

Salvador leaned back in his leather chair and puffed on a forty-dollar cigar. "What are you talking about? She ain't my granddaughter. She's Nino's Jew kid he adopted with his Jew wife."

"Don't be so disrespectful. Hannah is a wonderful wife and mother, and Lilia is a precious little girl, and they adore Nino. They make him incredibly happy."

"They don't even share my name. Nino fixed that when he changed his last name to Servidei. Why the hell should I care about his wife and kid?"

The live-in maid, Elsa, approached Maria from behind. "Here is your coat. Elwood just buzzed. Your cab is waiting downstairs, Mrs. DiVincenzo." She then held the coat up for Maria to slip her arms through the sleeves.

Maria thanked Elsa and returned her attention to Salvador.

"Nino has been home from Italy for two months and you have made no attempt to see him."

"He knows where we live."

"You threw him out of the house seven years ago. Do you really think he feels welcome here?"

"He betrayed me."

"Salvador DiVincenzo, one day you will lie on your deathbed and there will be nobody by your side because you have burned so many bridges."

"What the hell will I care? I'll be sick. I probably won't want nobody around, anyway."

"You're incorrigible."

"I don't even know what the hell that means. How can I be something I don't even know about?"

Maria shook her head. "I'm going to pick up Nino, Hannah and Lilia. We are going to the church. They are having a special Mass for the soldiers and sailors going off to war."

Salvador shouted back, "I probably won't be here when you return. I have things to do."

ELLIS ISLAND, NEW YORK

"How is Sophia, Mr. Cremonesi?"

"She is still at the infirmary, Nino."

"It's been two days."

"She still has a fever. They let us see her earlier today for an hour but made us return here to the registry room. We have received no information since then. Will you check on her?"

"Please help us, Nino," Mrs. Cremonesi said.

"Don't worry. I'll check on her."

As Nino walked away, Mr. Cremonesi said, "Are you in trouble, Nino?"

"Trouble—what do you mean?"

"There is a rumor you are under investigation and there will be a hearing. You won't lose your job because you helped us, will you?"

"I have heard nothing of a hearing."

"We will pray for you, Nino."

"Thank you, Mr. Cremonesi."

Nino approached a group of children playing jacks in the corner. When they saw him, they shouted, "Nino, do you have chocolate today?"

He reached into his pocket. "I have a little. But not enough for everyone. You must share."

Nino pulled his collar around his face and neck and stepped into the cold. He cut across the large, grassy area that separated the registry building from the infirmary. Mr. Cremonesi's comment about an investigation unsettled him. He knew from experience that rumors passing among the detainees often proved to be accurate.

By the time he reached the infirmary, his face was numb from the frigid wind. He entered and approached a nurse. "Excuse me, nurse. I came by to check on the little girl I brought in two days ago. The Cremonesi girl. How is she doing?"

"We were going to get her parents in the morning." She looked at the floor.

"What is it?" Nino asked. "What is wrong?"

"The girl passed away an hour ago."

THE BRONX NEW YORK

Lilia ran to Nino after he closed the door. He knelt on the kitchen floor to embrace her. "Did you have fun while I was at work, my sweet?"

"*Si* Papa. Grandmama came over. She brought me a new coat."

She struggled to release his grip. "Let me get it."

Nino released her, then watched her run into the bedroom.

Hannah was frying eggs. Nino moved toward her from behind and wrapped her in his arms. "How are you feeling?"

Caressing her stomach. "I'm ready for this little one to come out."

"Are you sure Mrs. Rhodes knows what to do?"

"She has borne three of her own children by herself and has helped two other women in the building give birth to theirs. They have told me I'm in expert hands. She lives right below us."

"If it happens at night while I'm at work, how will you contact her?"

"Your mother comes by every evening."

"She isn't here all night. What if you and Lilia are here by yourselves?"

"We have a plan. I'll beat on the floor with a broomstick, and Lilia will run down and knock on Mrs. Rhodes' door in case she doesn't hear me."

"That's not a plan. That's a Laurel and Hardy routine. Mrs. Rhodes doesn't speak Italian. How will she know what Lilia is saying?"

"Lilia's English is getting better every day. Stop worrying."

"Lilia is five. You are counting on a five-year-old who only knows seven words of English to run and get help for you. I just hope it happens during the day while I'm here."

"Sit down for breakfast," Hannah said as she set the table.

As he did, Lilia entered the kitchen wearing her new coat. "Look, Papa."

"That's beautiful. You look so elegant."

"My arms are too short for this coat, but Grandmama said it will soon fit me when I get bigger."

"You look like a princess." Nino said.

"Put your coat back and come sit down," Hannah said.

As Lilia left the room, Nino said, "Sophia died. I didn't get her to the infirmary on time."

"Oh, Nino, I'm so sorry."

"Her parents..."

Nino paused to regain his composure.

"... they are devastated."

There was silence in the room, before Nino said, "I may lose my job."

"Why?"

"Before I took Sophia to the infirmary, I was supposed to get permission, but there was nobody there authorized to give it to me."

"I don't believe they will fire you for trying to save a little girl's life. If they do, something is wrong."

"They don't like me there, Hannah. They say I don't understand my job. I'm supposed to guard them, not help them. They think I have gotten too close to the detainees. They call me Father Servidei."

Hannah laughed. "Do they know you were once in Rome studying for the priesthood?"

"I never brought it up."

"Even if you lose your job, you'll figure something out. You always do."

"I wish I were that confident."

"Nino, how many times have we been through this? It is the same pattern with us every time. Something bad happens, you worry yourself sick, while I think nothing of it. And why do I think nothing of it? Because I am married to Nino Servidei. The same Nino Servidei who rescued me from a Jewish internment camp. The same Nino Servidei who safely smuggled me and Lilia out of Italy. And you know what, Nino? During that entire adventure, I never doubted that you would do it. Lilia and I just went along for the ride, trusting you would keep us safe. And here we are. I stand here as your wife, with no concern that you won't provide for us." She then approached and embraced him. "You are my hero. You always have been, and you always will be."

He kissed her. "I hear once the war effort ramps up, the docks will be hiring. We will need to ship troops and supplies overseas."

"Your father controls the docks. Would you be willing to work for him? You said you would never work for the mafia."

"I know what I said. He would never hire me, anyway."

ELLIS ISLAND

"Have a seat, Nino."

Nino sat but kept his coat on. Like every other building on Ellis Island, the administrative building was cold, dank, and smelled of mold.

"This is really hard for me. I went to bat for you. You are getting a raw deal."

"What are you talking about?"

"The board met. You have been terminated. They determined you broke protocol when you escorted that family to the infirmary."

"The girl died. She should have been taken earlier in the day."

"I know that."

"What was I supposed to do?"

"This isn't about what you were supposed to do. I'm going to share something with you, Nino. I don't like it and I don't think it's fair, but a member of the board found out your father was Salvador DiVincenzo. He bent the ears of the other board members weeks ago about getting rid of you. He convinced them you may not have America's best interest in mind because you have family connections in Sicily."

"That's ridiculous. There are hundreds, if not thousands, of families in New York with family in Italy. Why is mine different?"

"Look, Nino, you know the deal with your father. He's a gangster who has a lot of shady dealings and has hurt many people."

"That has nothing to do with me."

"Actually, it does. I'm sorry. But today is your last day."

"I have a family to feed and rent to pay. Do you know how hard it is to find a job?"

"That won't be the case much longer. There are several factories that will ramp up soon to support the war effort. You can go to work for one of them. Maybe you could work for your father."

"That won't happen."

"You can always go join the army like all the other young men your age."

THE BRONX NEW YORK
THE CHURCH OF OUR LADY OF MERCY

The wooden bench was harder than he remembered. Nino thought back to the many times he had sat on the bench outside of Monsignor Nunzio's office, waiting for him to return—never knowing when he would.

Other than his mother, Monsignor Nunzio had been Nino's greatest friend during his childhood. A childhood immersed in trauma and loneliness.

With his head bowed and hat in hand, Nino waited patiently. He heard footsteps before the rotund, elderly priest appeared around a corner. "Nino, my friend, it is always good to see you. What gives me the pleasure of your visit?"

"Do you have a moment, Monsignor?"

"For you, I always have time."

Nino followed him into his office, making his way to the same high back leather chair he always sat in. It had aged from when he was a boy. He sank deep into the worn cushion of the tattered chair.

"How may I help you, Nino?"

"I don't know that you can. I'm in a jam, and I just need to talk to someone."

"You have been in jams before and have always worked your way out of them. Why is this one different?"

"Because now I have a family to feed."

With a lump in his throat, he paused.

"I lost my job."

"Does this have something to do with the sick girl? The one who passed away."

"How did you know about her?"

"Father Bartoli visited Ellis Island early this morning. The immigrants talked to him. You are a legend among the Italians. 'Their hero,' is what some of them have said about you."

"I try to do my part."

"This is unfortunate at so many levels. You are a good man with a family to care for. But also, from what I hear of the mistreatment of the refugees, they need an advocate like you inside those walls with them."

"So, besides my family, I guess I let them down too."

"You have let no one down. The world would be a much better place if there were more Nino Servideis in it."

"I don't know what to do. Hannah and Lilia count on me. I'm frightened I will fail them. The baby is due next month..." Nino bowed. "How will I support my family?"

Monsignor Nunzio rose and sat in the chair next to Nino's. "Where is your faith? This isn't the Nino I have always known."

"Losing my job isn't the only thing weighing on my mind."

"What else is it?"

"It's the war. Angelo leaves in a few days for training. Every young man I know is enlisting, or already gone. I feel like a coward for not joining the fight."

"As you just said, you have a family. No one will judge you for wanting to stay and take care of them. There is a reason they let fathers with young families stay behind."

"I know of many men who have families who have

volunteered. Why should I be any different?"

"We are living in difficult economic times. Many of them joined because..."

"Because they needed a job. Is that what you were about to say? They joined because they needed the money. Well, I need the money too. The army doesn't pay much, but it pays enough to feed my family and keep a roof over their head."

"Nino, you are a man of God, you aren't a soldier. And you most certainly are not a killer."

Nino paused and looked down at the ground. "I wish that were true."

"What do you mean?"

"I've told you very little of my time in Italy."

Monsignor Nunzio leaned back in his chair and remained silent.

"When we were in Italy, the Carabinieri arrested Hannah. While the police held her, they..."

"Yes, Nino."

"They molested her. There were two initially, then a third."

"My dear God, I'm so sorry, Nino. That must have been awful for Hannah."

"Hannah is a strong woman. She appears to have moved on from the incident better than me. I've always felt guilty because I wasn't with her when they arrested her."

"You mustn't blame yourself. What happened to Hannah was not your fault. You are always too hard on yourself. When you were a boy, you lived with guilt because your father was a murderer, however you have murdered no one."

Nino took a deep breath, then exhaled. "I wish that were true, Monsignor. Shortly after I learned of Hannah's assault by the police; we boarded a train from Rome to Torre del Greco. My friend Vito Bianchi had given me a gun. I foolishly accepted it. We were traveling in the middle of the night and were the only ones in the train car. A policeman boarded and wanted to see our passports. Hannah and Lilia were asleep. I showed him mine, but he insisted on seeing Hannah and Lilia's too. I knew that if he saw their papers showing they were Jewish immigrants, he would arrest them. When I turned and saw my precious Hannah and Lilia sleeping peacefully, visions of Hannah's assault raced through my head, and it enraged me. Determined to protect them, I pulled the gun on the officer and escorted him to the rear of the train. When we were on the platform, he said he would have us arrested at the next stop."

Nino turned his head from Msgr. Nunzio. "After he said he would arrest us, I pointed the gun at his heart and pulled the trigger. I shot him in cold blood, then watched as he clutched his chest and fell from the speeding train into the dark of night. I murdered him."

Msgr. Nunzio sat back in his chair, gripping the ends of his armrests. "There have always been debates among men of faith about the justification of taking another man's life. It's not something I could do. That's not why God put me on this earth. However, what I know about you, Nino, is that you love Hannah and Lilia deep into your soul. Just as I feel God's purpose in my life is to serve my fellow man through the church, you feel God's mission for your life is to protect your family. Whatever you feel you needed to do to accomplish that is not for me to judge. That is between you and God."

There was silence in the room. Nino continued to avoid eye contact with Msgr. Nunzio.

"Nino, do you pray for the man you shot?"

"Many times per day."

"And his family?"

"Of course. I have visions of small children about Lilia's age who waited for their papa to come home, yet he never did because of me."

"Don't do that to yourself. You don't know if he had children. Continue to pray for him and his family. I too will pray for them. But most of all, I will pray for you, my son. I will pray that God will grant you peace. You are not a murderer, Nino—you are not. Don't tell yourself that you are. You are a protector of those you love. That is how you must see yourself."

"I try Monsignor, but I can't get the image of the policeman out of my head. It is ever present."

"When you see his image, replace it with an image of Hannah and Lilia. You saved them, Nino. And I know you well enough to know that if you had it to do over again, you would protect them the same way."

Nino nodded. "You are right, Monsignor. I would."

"So, move on. Live your life in peace. As for you wanting to contribute to the war effort as a soldier, that doesn't surprise me. All I ask is that you pray deeply before making such a decision. In the meantime, I will see what I can do about helping you find a job."

THE BRONX NEW YORK

A gust of wind forced him to pull his collar up and place his hand on top of his cap. The flurries blew horizontally. It had been a long walk from The Church of Our Lady of Mercy. He remembered that even as a boy, he frequently walked home after his conversations with Msgr. Nunzio. Here he was, years later, doing the same.

When he got to his building, he glanced up at his third-floor window. Hannah wouldn't be expecting him. She was used to him walking in the front door right after the sun came up. Not at this late hour of the evening. Lilia would be in bed.

Upon entering the first floor, the warm air of the building comforted him. He brushed off the snow and made his way to the stairwell, looked up and hesitated before making the climb to his apartment.

At the top of the stairs, he stared at his door. When he entered the little kitchen, his eyes locked onto Hannah, who sat at the table with her sewing kit mending one of Lilia's dresses.

As he closed the door behind him, Hannah said, "Why are you—?"

He looked down at the floor.

She set the dress down, crossed the room, and embraced him. "It's okay, Nino. You will find another job. I have faith in you."

DiVincenzo Compound

Alfonso woke to the sound of vehicles. Engines revved and brakes squealed. Large pieces of machinery were surrounding his house. He glanced at his watch. It was 01:37 am. He put on his robe and made his way to his front courtyard. Pierre and two of his other men had arrived before him. They watched a convoy of motorcycles, trucks and tanks. Halftracks were pulling mobile artillery units. The vehicles circled his home. They parked outside of the wall, while others continued their journey deeper into the forest.

Two dozen motorcycles came into view, followed by Generalmajor Richter's staff car. Richter's car entered the circular courtyard and halted at Alfonso's front door.

Richter and *Maggiore* Brambilla got out of the vehicle. His driver removed two suitcases from the trunk.

"What the hell is this, *Maggiore* Brambilla? The agreement was that you pay me for the use of my land. You said nothing about Richter staying in my home."

"It will only be four days per week. The generalmajor will spend his weekends in Palermo."

Richter said something in German.

Brambilla said, "The generalmajor would like to thank you for your hospitality. He is assuming you have two guest rooms for us."

Alfonso rolled his eyes. "Pierre, take them to the two rooms at the rear of the house. Keep them as far away from me as possible."

1942

CHAPTER 3

Young men waiting for their day of departure leaned against the bar, their boisterous laughter creating white noise. Destined for the army, navy or marine corps, they filled the corner booths and wiped tears from the faces of their sweethearts.

Sipping his beer, Nino sat at a distant table, studying their expressions, pondering who among them would never return.

Glancing at the corner entrance, Nino noticed Angelo brushing the snow from his hat and coat. To catch his attention, Nino raised his hand over his head and waved.

Angelo approached and embraced him, patting his back multiple times. "Any luck finding a new job?"

"I just left the Navy Yard. In the next few weeks, they will hire hundreds. I put in my application. I should know soon."

"Papa has some clout at the Navy Yard. If you want to—"

"No way, Angelo. I don't want any job that has anything to do with papa. If I get it, I'll get it on my own."

"I hear ya."

Nino said, "So, this is it. Our last beer together before you go. Only two more days. Take care of yourself, Angelo."

"It's a shame how this all worked out. You were in Italy for three years, you get home, now I'm going off to war. We sent you off to Rome to become a priest, and you came back three years later with a wife and an adopted daughter. I still can't believe my little brother has a family."

"Sometimes I can't believe it myself."

"I told Papa that you met Grandpapa in Italy."

"What did he say?"

"You know Papa. That jackass barely acknowledges you exist."

"Do you know it's been seven years since I've spoken to him?"

"He hasn't changed. The only good thing about this war is it is getting me out of the family business. It is dirty, Nino. I've seen things, and I've done a few of them too. Things I'm not proud of. I did them simply because papa ordered me to. Papa is a thug who only cares about himself. He has hurt people. He has hurt some people really bad. I'm glad to be getting away from him. I wish mama would leave him."

"Once I get on my feet and can get a bigger apartment, I'll have mama come live with Hannah and me."

"She'll never leave papa. She's too loyal."

Angelo motioned to the waitress for a beer. "How's Hannah? That baby will pop out any day now, won't it?"

"She still has a few weeks."

"Nino, I'm tellin' ya. I've never seen Mama so happy. When you showed up, she not only got her favorite son back, but she bagged a daughter and granddaughter with the same shot. Once that other kid drops out of Hannah, she'll have another to slobber all over. She loves those two—Hannah and Lilia. I think she loves them even more than you. I never thought I would say that. She don't even care that they're Jews."

"They are Catholics now."

"They may attend Mass with you, but they are still Jews."

"Sometimes I think you run your mouth just to get under my skin."

"It really doesn't matter, does it?"

"Not to me and Hannah."

Angelo laughed. "I'm sorry, Nino, but I never met no one more Catholic than you, and you end up marrying a Jew. I think it's hilarious."

"Stop, Angelo."

The waitress brought Angelo his beer. Nino asked for another one for himself.

"After you leave Fort Jackson, where will they send you?"

"I don't know. I guess infantry school someplace. They don't tell you much until you get there. I'm hoping to get into the Army Air Corps. I want to fly."

"A pilot?"

"I'll take anything. My buddy Jim told me they need everything from tail gunners to pilots. I don't care. Just get me in the air."

"Are you scared?"

"Of what?"

"Getting killed."

"A little. But I know you and Mama will pray for me."

"I didn't think you believed in God."

"I don't, but you and Mama do. I'm counting on you to pull some strings."

Nino laughed before they both sipped their beers.

Angelo asked, "What is Italy like?"

"It depends on where you are. Rome differs from Naples. Sicily differs from Rome and Naples. They're all beautiful in their own way."

"Do you ever want to go back?"

"Maybe. We have friends there. The Roseman's—Hannah's in-laws from her first husband. They helped me smuggle Hannah and Lilia out of Italy. One day I would like to see them again. My best friend in the entire world is Vito Bianchi. He was my roommate in college."

"Is he the one who helped you bust Hannah out of that internment camp."

"That's him."

Angelo chuckled, "If they send me there to fight the Italians, I'll look them up."

"Just be safe, Angelo."

THE ISLAND OF SICILY
CALTANISSETTA
ITALIAN 213TH COASTAL DIVISION

Caporale Vito Bianchi knocked on his commanding officer's door.

"Enter."

He approached the desk and stood to attention.

"Caporale Bianchi, I am not pleased. I am not pleased at all. Why do they keep sending me troublemakers like you? Who have I pissed off? That is the question I keep asking myself."

As he turned through the pages of Vito's service record,

he said, "Let me make something clear, Bianchi. I've already figured you out. You are a non-conformist. You have a track record of staying out all hours of the night, missing roll call, and it says here your previous command busted you down to Caporale because they caught you in a compromising position with a *generale di brigata's* daughter. What the hell is wrong with you?"

"You should have seen her, *Primo Capitano* Bonetti. She was magnificent. One of the most beautiful women I have ever encountered."

"She was sixteen."

"Oh, but she did not look sixteen. She was a goddess."

Returning to the files, the *primo capitano* said, "It says before you were drafted into the army, the polizia caught you with a cache of firearms in your college dorm. Why aren't you in prison?"

"My father is a Doctor near Milan. He has connections."

"At least you admit it. I'm assuming it was your father who pulled a few strings to get you here instead of the front lines in North Africa."

"No, sir, I don't believe he did that for me."

"Don't talk back."

"I meant no disrespect, sir."

The primo capitano closed the file, set it aside, and looked up at Caporale Bianchi.

"What is your job, Caporale? Has your *sergente maggiore* assigned you your duties?"

"No sir. I arrived three days ago. I haven't received an assignment yet."

"Your profile says you used to race motorcycles."

"*Si*, Primo Capitano. I have ridden since I was a boy. My father bought me my first Benelli when I was twelve."

Laughing, "I'm sure your father has purchased many nice toys for you."

Vito remained silent.

"How is your night vision?"

"My vision is perfect. Day or night."

"Good. We have three messengers assigned to our command. One of them had a fatal accident yesterday. Because of the recent air strikes, you will need to use your vehicle headlights sparingly. I am working on a report you must deliver to *comandante Giordano* in Gela tomorrow. It is a three-hour journey round-trip. I expect you back before nightfall. I don't want you driving over a cliff like the other guy."

He reached into his desk drawer, removed a notepad, then scribbled on it. "Take this to the motor pool. It is a note informing them I have made you the new messenger. Besides me, you will transport messages for other officers here at the command. The motor pool will issue you a motorcycle. It is for official military business only. When we send you somewhere, you are to come right back, do you understand?"

"*Si*, Primo Capitano."

* * *

"I'm here for a motorcycle. Primo Capitano Bonetti gave me this note."

The kid behind the desk said, "How the hell did *you* get this job? I put in for it."

"Is it a good job?"

"It is the best. There are six field commanders on this post who are sending documents to units all throughout this island.

You messengers are constantly on the road—gone all day—with little accountability. It's not fair."

"But at least you stay dry. Me, *Mi Amico*, I will be wet and cold when it rains."

With a smirk, the clerk said, "Follow me."

Vito trailed behind the Caporale to the back where two mechanics were working. One had the hood open on a troop carrier and the other was gassing up a Moto Guzzi motorcycle.

"Are you the new messenger?" the mechanic asked.

"That is me. I am Caporale Vito Bianchi."

"Do you know how to ride, or are you just another green kid like the last guy?"

"My skills are legendary in the hills of Milan. Although I would prefer my Benelli rather than a Moto Guzzi, it will do."

"It will have to. We are running out of parts, so don't wreck it."

"Your machine is safe with me."

The mechanic finished fueling and replaced the nozzle. Vito approached the bike, threw his leg over and jumped hard on the kick starter. The engine roared to life.

"Be careful" the mechanic said. "I just rebuilt the engine. It will hum. These winding mountain roads are dangerous."

Vito revved the engine several more times before cutting back on the throttle. "You are clearly a master mechanic. And you need not worry. These narrow mountain roads will not be a challenge."

* * *

Vito flew through the Sicani mountain range with the throttle wide open. There were twists and turns, and when he arrived at the top of a hill, he pulled back on the front of the bike, went airborne, and landed hard on the other side. Occasionally he would turn off the road and cut through open areas and slalom between trees, leaning hard left, then right, then left again. In the distance, he saw a steep hill, raced up the slope, then flew high into the air, not knowing what was on the other side. After landing, he dashed to the highest point of the next hill. When he arrived, he stopped and put his feet on the ground. He looked north to rich greenery, olive groves and citrus farms. To the south was the southern coast of Sicily—Gela in the distance. With his left hand on the clutch, he revved the engine; it was music to his ears, reminding him of his youth.

A German convoy snaked up the mountain, maneuvering around a series of hairpin bends. Four vehicles in all. A troop carrier in the front and rear, and two flatbed trucks in the middle. The trucks each held aerial antennae.

He remembered the documents in the leather satchel slung over his shoulder, and off he went, his rear tire spitting dirt into the air.

CATANIA SICILY
THE OFFICE OF THE GERMAN LIAISON OFFICER

General *der Panzertruppe* Fridolin Rudolph von Senger und Etterlin had been a Rhodes scholar. In addition to his native German, he was fluent in both French and English yet had to rely on his translators to communicate with his Italian military counterparts. After spending the winter of 1942 on the Eastern front, he welcomed the warmer climate and thus far peaceful existence of his current command. He now served as the German Liaison Officer to the Italian 6th Army in Sicily.

"How concerned should we be, Generalmajor Richter?"

"I hope my fears are unwarranted, general, but from what I have seen in the field, we are overly optimistic that we can count on the Italians to defend this island," Richter said.

"You are not the only field general who has been in this office expressing that same trepidation."

Richter said, "Many of my men have reported derogatory comments coming from the Italian foot soldier against both Mussolini and our Führer."

"Are there consequences? Is anyone ever reprimanded?"

"We have brought it to the attention of Italian field generals. They pretend to be concerned, but in the end, nothing changes."

Richter continued. "They are often under-manned during drills and their vehicles, particularly tanks, are frequently out of commission because of limited parts."

"I have been made aware of this, General Richter. Their tanks are French. I have contacted Oberst Schwartz in Vichy, asking to put pressure on the French government to send us more parts."

"And the response from Oberst Schwartz?"

"He says there are limited parts on the way, but little of what we actually need."

"Is there any chance of us getting any more of our own forces here?"

"The eastern front has taken priority. You know that."

"The motivation of the Italian soldier was a concern of mine from the beginning, general."

"Mine too," said General von Senger und Etterlin. "And we are not alone. Mussolini dragged the Italian people into this war. Their heart was never in it. Now their wounded soldiers are returning from North Africa and eastern Europe with stories of defeat. The Italian people are war weary."

Von Senger und Etterlin added, "I meet with general Guzzoni of the Italian sixth army next week. I will bring it to his attention and demand he do something about it."

"Will it work?"

"I will remind him of the obvious, that Sicily is Italian soil, not German, and he must do something about the morale of his men, or Sicily will be lost to the Allies."

CHAPTER 4

———

"Grandmama," Lilia shouted as she ran toward Maria. "It's good to see you, Maria." Hannah closed the door. "Thank you for coming."

"You never have to thank me for watching Lilia," she said as she knelt to embrace her granddaughter.

Maria looked up at Hannah. "How are you feeling?"

Hannah caressed her stomach. "I've had a little pain this morning."

"What does it feel like?"

"Just a little tightening in my lower stomach."

"Are you sure they aren't contractions?"

"I've felt this before. Besides, it's too early. I still have over a month."

"Where is Nino?"

"He's out looking for a job."

"What about the Navy Yard?"

"He still hasn't heard from them."

"He'll get something soon."

"I hope so, I've never seen him like this."

"What do you mean?"

Hannah said, "Lilia, go into the bedroom and play. I'll let you know before I leave."

"But I want to—"

"Don't argue with me. Get in there and close the door."

Lilia pouted as she entered the room, pulling the doorknob behind her.

Hannah turned to Maria. "Please have a seat. Would you like some coffee?"

"That would be lovely."

As Hannah poured, she said, "I have never seen Nino so down. It's as though he has lost his confidence. It's not like him."

"He worships you and Lilia. And now with the baby coming, he probably feels like he failed his family when he lost his job."

"He lost his job helping a sick child."

"And if he had it to do over, he would help her again," Maria said. "That's how Nino is."

Hannah sat next to Maria. "Is Salvador still ill?"

"Yes. Elsa is tending to him. I'm glad you sent for me. I needed a break. He is not a good patient. I've tried to get him to go to the doctor, but he says he doesn't trust them. He doesn't trust anyone."

"Is he in bed?"

"Heavens no. He is not one to stay in bed all day. He is in his den working on his ledgers." Maria chuckled. "I'm sure he has two sets."

Hannah glanced at her watch. "I need to get going. I'll be back after I complete my errands. It should only take a few hours."

She opened the bedroom door. "Lilia, Mama is leaving. I'll be back soon."

Hannah slipped her coat on.

She bent down and kissed Lilia. "Be good for Grandmama."

"She's always well behaved for me," Maria said.

Looking down at Lilia, Hannah said, "How come you aren't always well behaved for me?"

Lilia shrugged her shoulders. "I don't know, Mama."

* * *

Her nerves were on edge as the taxi came to a stop in front of Hoffman towers. She paid the driver and looked up at the seven-story structure.

Hannah wished her first visit here would have been with Nino so he could show her the apartment he grew up in.

She walked through the double glass doors and entered the lobby. Dressed in white gloves, and a long coat, a dark-skinned doorman answered the door.

"May I help you, ma'am?"

"I'm here to see Salvador DiVincenzo."

"Is he expecting you, ma'am?"

"He is not."

"I'm sorry, but Mr. DiVincenzo doesn't see callers without an appointment."

"You must be Mr. Elwood Jackson."

"Yes, Ma'am, I am. Have we met before?"

"We haven't. My name is Hannah Servidei. I am Nino's wife."

"Oh, my... I should have known. You are just as Mrs. DiVincenzo said you were. She is very fond of you. And she loves little Lilia. Whenever she is with her, she returns with a big grin on her face and tells me how wonderful her precious Lilia is."

"Maria is a blessing to all of us."

"I always ask her about Nino. I've missed him so. There is nobody like him. To most who live in this building, I am just the doorman. I have worked here fourteen years, yet some of the long-time residents don't even acknowledge me when they pass. They have never even asked me my name. But that was never Nino. I remember my first day on the job, Nino came sprinting down the stairs and said, 'I'm Nino, what is your name?' He was only seven years old yet wanted to know all about me.'"

"That sounds like Nino."

"I'll ring up to Mr. DiVincenzo and let him know you are here to see him."

Hannah felt a sharp pain in her lower back as the elevator ascended. When it reached the seventh floor, she took a deep breath and turned her chin up, holding her head high.

When the elevator opened, an elderly woman appeared at the double doors, holding one of them open for Hannah to enter an elegant foyer.

"May I take your coat, ma'am?"

"No, thank you. I don't believe I will be here long. You must be Elsa."

"Yes, ma'am, I am," she said as she closed the door. I'll inform Mr. DiVincenzo that you are here. He is in his den."

Hannah soaked up the opulence of the foyer.

Listening to her heels click on the marble floor, she took a few steps toward the back hallway. Nino had told her his room was there. She smiled, envisioning Nino as a little boy, running through the apartment.

She glanced up to see a chandelier. She remembered Nino telling her Salvador imported it from South America.

"Mr. DiVincenzo will see you now."

The den was located off the foyer. Hannah followed Elsa in. Wrapped in a gold silk housecoat and wearing a black ascot around his neck, he rose, removed the cigar from his mouth, and coughed while pounding his chest. Elsa closed the door behind them, and Hannah remained in the center of the room, waiting for Salvador's coughing to cease.

Salvador pointed to one of the two chairs in front of his desk. His coughing continued. Hannah sat. Salvador took a large swig of something in a flask and had a seat himself.

After placing his cigar in the ashtray, he said, "So you're Hannah."

"I am."

There was an uncomfortable silence. Salvador glared as if he were studying her.

Hannah sensed it was an intimidation tactic that Salvador had used many times. She held her ground, staring back at him, never breaking eye contact.

Salvador smiled. "They were right—Maria and Angelo. You are beautiful."

In a cool tone, Hannah said, "Thank you."

He laughed. "That boy, Nino. He travels to Rome to become a priest and instead, comes back with a beautiful Jew wife and kid."

Hannah remained stone faced.

"How old are you, Hannah?"

"I'm thirty-three."

"And Nino. How old is he?"

"He's your son, you should know."

Salvador shook his head. "You have a little fire in you, don't you?"

"Nino is twenty-one."

Salvador puffed on his cigar, then removed it from his mouth. "So, you seduced my baby boy."

"I did, but he has never complained."

"I like you."

She shrugged.

"Maria told me how Nino rescued you from an internment camp, then smuggled you and Lilia out of Italy. I'll admit, that took a lot of balls."

"Nino is a wonderful man. He would do anything to protect his family."

"Has he found another job yet?"

"No."

"That's why you are here, isn't it? You want me to hire Nino."

"He would never work for you."

"Then why are you here?"

"I'm here because I have something to say to you, and you are going to listen."

Salvador coughed once, then said, "I ain't done nothin to you."

"It's not about me. It's about Nino. He doesn't know I am here, by the way. If he did, he wouldn't be happy."

"Go on."

"There is no finer person in this world than Nino Servidei. He is a sweet, kind and wonderful man. I couldn't ask for a better husband and father for my children."

"What does that have to do with me?"

"I look at him sometimes, and I wonder how he can be the extraordinary man he is after what you did to him. You abandoned him. You kicked him out of his home when he was only fourteen years old. How could you have done that?"

Salvador leaned back in his chair and crossed his arms, saying nothing.

"You hurt him. You broke his heart."

Salvador coughed uncontrollably before taking a swig from his flask.

Hannah stared back at him, believing her words were meaningless to the murdering crime boss she was addressing.

He stood and paced the room. "I know I hurt him. That's not easy to live with. Nino probably believes I never think of him. I think of him every day."

"What do you think about?"

"Many things. When he left for Italy, I questioned why he wanted to be a priest, yet I admired his courage for going to Rome."

"Do you have regrets?"

"I don't waste time on regrets. I can't fix regrets; they are the past."

"You cheated yourself, Salvador. You cheated yourself out of a life with an exceptional son who would have made you proud."

"He has made me proud. You are the only person I have ever said that to. I have never even told Maria that I am proud of Nino."

"You need to say it to him."

"Nino will never speak to me. He hates me. He hates me so

much he changed his last name to his Mama's maiden name just to let me know he no longer wanted anything to do with me."

"Nino would forgive you. I know he would."

Salvador coughed once, took another swig, then strolled to the window overlooking the Bronx. "What you don't understand is I am who I am. I have done a lot of bad things in my life. I have hurt many people. Yes, I believe Nino might forgive me for kicking him out of the house, but he will never forgive me for what I have done to others."

"That doesn't mean he won't speak to you."

Salvador turned to face Hannah. "Maria told me you were special. 'A blessing' I believe, were the words she used. I'm not a religious man, but I agree. If there is a God, he blessed Nino by putting you in his life. It took a lot of spunk for you to come here. Most people fear me and do their best to keep their distance. You, on the other hand, love my son so much that you came here to chew my ass. Does Maria know you are here?"

"I told her I had errands to run. I didn't tell her I was coming here."

"She loves little Lilia."

"Lilia loves her."

"I would like to meet her."

"That would be up to Nino."

Salvador returned his gaze to the window and shrugged his shoulders. "Do you think you could talk him into... you know, meeting with me?"

"Is that really what you want?"

"Look, this ain't easy. I have never discussed this kind of stuff with nobody before. As I stand here, I don't know why I'm spilling my guts to you. You've caught me at a weak moment. Maybe it's all this whiskey I've been guzzling every time I cough. By the way, don't go tellin' nobody what we've been talkin' about. This is just between us—you got it?"

Hannah fought the urge to grin. Salvador had allowed himself to be vulnerable in front of her, and he was regretting it.

"It would be meaningless for me to tell Nino of your true feelings for him. He needs to hear all this directly from you, not second hand from me. So no, I will not make him aware of this discussion. And I will try to convince him to meet with you. But you must promise me that when you do, you will tell him what you have told me."

Salvador chuckled, coughed, took another swig, then chuckled again before puffing on his cigar. "I need to hire you. I need you to negotiate my union contracts. Those union bosses would melt in front of you."

Hannah smiled. "I love being a wife and mother. You couldn't pay me enough to give that up."

"I like you," Salvador said. "Nino hit the jackpot when he found you."

Hannah said, "I believe I need to get back home."

"Let me walk you to the door."

As Hannah followed Salvador to the French doors, she held her abdomen. "Oh God"

"What's wrong?" Salvador asked.

With a grimace she said, "The baby. I think it's coming."

Salvador looked down to see Hannah standing in a puddle of water. "What the hell is that?"

"My water broke."

"What do we do?"

"I need to get to the hospital."

Salvador shouted. "Elsa! Elsa! Call DeFazio. Have him bring the car around front. Tell him to hurry."

* * *

"Forget the red lights, DeFazio. Just slow down, make certain nobody is coming then roll right through them."

"Yes, Mr. DiVincenzo."

Hannah was in the rear seat behind the driver. There was enough room for her to slouch down, spread her legs, and press her knees against the back of the driver's seat.

"How much farther?" Hannah shouted.

"We still have several blocks, ma'am."

"Please Hurry. This baby wants out."

Salvador was also in the back seat on the passenger side.

"Damn it, DeFazio. Step on it. There are five hundred bucks in it for you if you get us there on time."

"I'm doing my best, Boss. The closer we get to the center of town, the heavier the traffic is."

"You need to figure out how to get us there," Salvador said.

"Do you want me to drive down the sidewalk, Mr. DiVincenzo? There are a lot of people out today. I would hate to hit them."

"No, don't drive on the sidewalk. I can't believe this. I've spent my whole life trying to avoid cops, now I need one, and they ain't around."

Salvador looked at Hannah. She was taking quick breaths, stopping only to yell out in pain.

"Ya gotta hang on, Hannah. This ain't no place to have no kid. Lay on the horn, DeFazio," Salvador said as another coughing fit started. He reached into the inside pocket of his overcoat and took a swig of his flask.

"Oh God! The baby is coming. Please hurry."

"What the hell are you going to do?" Salvador asked.

Hannah turned her legs to Salvador. "Pull my undergarments off."

"I ain't doin that. DeFazio, I'm warning you. You damn well better get us there quick."

Hannah said, "There is no time, Salvador. You must help me."

"Jesus Christ, why is this happening now." Salvador blindly reached under Hannah's dress, slid his fingers into the top of her panties and pulled until they were past her knees and feet. He threw them in the front seat, then looked away from her.

"Can you see the baby's head?" Hannah shouted.

"You want me to look up in there?"

"Just do it. Tell me if you see the head."

He lifted the hem of her dress and peeked in. "Oh shit, I think I see it."

"The head?"

"Yeh. I see the top of the kid's head."

"How much of it is out?"

"Nothin yet. I only see the top. I see it through the hole."

Hannah grunted, held her breath, pushed, then screamed. "It's coming out. Guide the head but be gentle."

He looked Hannah in the eye. "I ain't doin that."

"Please, Salvador. I need your help."

"DeFazio, pull over so you can do this."

"We are almost there, Boss."

Hannah reached up and pulled on the back of DeFazio's seat, and screamed, "It's coming!"

Salvador removed his overcoat and fedora, then flung them into the front passenger seat. He reached under her dress then between her legs. "I feel the top of the kid's head."

He looked back through the windshield, hoping they had arrived at the hospital.

Hannah shrieked. "Oh god, it hurts."

"How far to the hospital, DeFazio?" Salvador shouted.

"Only a few blocks, but there are cars sitting at a red light. I can't get past them."

"Lay on the horn."

Salvador peeked between her legs again. "The head is coming out."

He glanced at Hannah. Sweat poured from her forehead. Her hair clung to her face. Salvador looked up to see a blocked intersection, then peeked under her dress. "Keep pushin'. It's coming."

Hannah's screams intensified, becoming louder and more frequent.

"The head is out!" Salvador shouted.

He shifted his gaze from the baby to Hannah's face. Her complexion was red, her teeth clenched. She stared back at him. The monograms on the cuffs of his tailored shirt were splattered in blood.

"The shoulders are out now," he said. "The kid is sliding right out. Just a little more."

"I can see the hospital, Boss," DeFazio shouted. "It's three blocks away."

Salvador didn't respond. He gently placed his hands under the baby's skull. "The shoulders are out. The kid is just sliding into my hands."

Hannah took several deep breaths, groaned one last time, and pushed. The baby wailed.

"It's out. What do I do now?" Salvador yelled.

Hannah reached out but said nothing. Salvador extended his arms, placing the baby on Hannah's chest. She cradled it. The umbilical cord, still attached, lay across her belly.

"You have a grandson, Salvador."

Salvador reached into the front seat, retrieved his overcoat, and laid it over Hannah and the baby to keep them warm. He looked down at the seat of his Cadillac, his shirt, and hands to see he was now wearing Hannah's blood. Turning his gaze to the front windshield, he saw DeFazio laying on the horn as he pulled up to the hospital.

ISLAND OF SICILY
THE DIVINCENZO COMPOUND

Alfonso entered his library to see *Maggiore* Brambilla asleep in a corner chair. His legs lay extended and crossed; his leather knee-high boots rested on a small table. Alfonso approached and slapped his feet, causing the maggiore to wake.

"Get your feet off of my table."

Brambilla remained seated. He rubbed his eyes.

"Where the hell is Richter?" Alfonso said.

"It's Saturday. He is in Palermo with his whores."

"Why aren't you with him?"

"He doesn't need me. All of his whores are French. He speaks French better than I do."

"Doesn't he share them with you?"

"He has. But I need a break from him."

"So, *I'm* stuck with you."

"You are pressing your luck with Richter, Mr. DiVincenzo. He doesn't like you."

"I don't give a shit who likes me or doesn't like me."

Brambilla crossed the library. At a wet bar, Alfonso poured him a glass of cognac.

"I don't know why, Mr. DiVincenzo, but I like you. Everyone else hates you, but I don't."

"I'm overjoyed to have your affection."

Brambilla laughed. "You know we will win the war, don't you? Then whose side will you be on?"

"I'm not on anybody's side. I just want Mussolini and Hitler to get their vehicles of war off my property."

"And if they don't?"

"Oh, they will leave. One way or the other, they will leave. Even if it means setting every acre of my property ablaze, they *will* leave."

THE BRONX NEW YORK

"Can I hold him, Mama?"

"Take your shoes off and climb up in bed with us, Lilia."

Nino and Maria were on either side of the hospital bed. Nino picked Lilia up and laid her next to Hannah, who held little Solomon. He kissed Hannah, then kissed Solomon's forehead. "He's beautiful like his Mama."

Lilia looked up at Maria. "Grandmama, do you know why his name is Solomon?"

"Yes, you have told me. It is a wonderful story."

"It's because a man named Solomon took us for a ride in his boat and saved us."

Hannah said to Nino. "He looks like you. He has your nose and dark hair."

"Who do I look like?" Lilia asked.

Nino and Hannah laughed at the statement by their adopted daughter. Nino said, "You are beautiful, just like your mama."

"Where is Salvador?" Hannah asked.

Maria said, "He is on his way."

Hannah addressed Nino. "When he arrives, will you speak to him?"

"I have no interest."

"I understand how your father hurt you. But he helped bring your son into the world. You should at least thank him."

"I owe him nothing."

"Use it as an opportunity to mend old wounds."

Maria said, "It's okay, Nino. You don't have to speak to him."

Perturbed, Hannah looked at Maria, who shook her head, hinting for Hannah not to push the issue.

Hannah said, "Well, at least *I* would like to thank him when he gets here."

* * *

Nino had taken Lilia across the street for ice cream when Salvador entered the hospital room. He looked down at Hannah, who was holding Solomon.

Salvador said, "He's a cute kid."

"He looks like Nino," Maria said.

"Yeah, I guess he does," Salvador replied.

Hannah said to Salvador, "Thank you for helping me."

"What choice did I have?"

"I ruined your coat and shirt."

"You should see the back of my car."

"I'm sorry."

"Forget about it. I got a guy who is an expert at cleaning up blood."

The statement caused an uncomfortable silence.

Hannah said, "Nino took Lilia for ice cream. They will be back soon. You said you wanted to meet Lilia. Now is your chance."

"Look, I'm glad the baby looks good, but I got things to do. I got to go. Congratulations on the new kid, Hannah. Maria, I'll see you at home later."

As Nino made his way down the hallway, thirty paces away he saw Salvador leave the hospital room. It was the first time he had seen his father since the old man had sent him to a boy's home years earlier. After an initial step toward Nino, Salvador stopped. Their eyes locked momentarily, then Salvador turned and darted in the opposite direction and hurried down a flight of stairs. Nino's stomach turned at the sight of the man who had rejected him.

When Nino entered the room, Hannah said, "You just missed your papa."

"I saw him, and he saw me."

"Did you speak?"

"No."

"How come?"

"Drop it, Hannah. Please just drop it."

Maria said, "Nino, you don't look well. Are you okay?"

Nino gazed back at Hannah; her smile lit up the room as she

sat up in the bed feeding baby Solomon. "I'm fine, mama. I've never been happier."

The nurse arrived with a wheelchair. "Are you ready to go home?"

Nino said, "I need to telephone a cab."

"That won't be necessary," Maria said. "Your papa sent one of his men to take us home. He is waiting downstairs."

Nino raised his eyebrows. "He *did*?"

Maria pulled him out into the hallway and whispered, "And you don't need to worry about the hospital bill. He paid that too."

CHAPTER 5

H is appearance was not of a man who had spent the past decade tormenting Nazis. Father Felix Morlion was bald, wore thick glasses, and had a substantial waistline.

"The Director will see you now," the aide to Mr. Donovan said.

Entering the office, Father Morlion approached the man President Franklin Delano Roosevelt had handpicked. "Thank you for seeing me, sir. I wasn't certain if you would."

Pointing to a chair in front of his desk, Donovan said, "Have a seat, father."

Sitting down behind a desk that occupied significant floor space, Donovan said, "I found your letter to be both intriguing and timely. We have had success, although limited, in recruiting missionaries in Europe and North Africa to help us gather intelligence. However, more so with Protestants, than Catholics, a strategy we have been looking to expand."

"I believe I can help."

"Yes, father. After reading your dossier, I believe you can.

The anti-Nazi propaganda campaign you ran in Europe is impressive. The number of underground contacts you have throughout the continent is extraordinary. That is exactly what we need. Do you think you could deploy them on our behalf?"

"I have connections throughout the European Catholic community, even within the walls of the Vatican. I know who we can trust and who we can't. I still have open methods of communication with a few of them, and, with your help, I believe I can reestablish contact with many of the others."

"Tell me about these communication methods."

"It's complicated, Mr. Donovan. It's a slow process. A message from me to one of my contacts may take weeks—months even. But my network is like a string of pearls. One pearl makes a telephone call to another, who passes a coded note to another, who steps into a private confessional with another."

"And you trust these...'string of pearls,' as you call them?"

"It's far from perfect, but it is how we have informed the world of the evil of Nazi Germany."

Donovan glanced out of the window of his office. "Can you recruit agents here in the United States?"

"Agents, sir?"

"Yes. American Catholics," Donovan said.

"I don't understand."

"My plan is to enlist American citizens—Catholics of course—who are bilingual. I want to send them to Europe and place them undercover among the ranks of the everyday citizens. They will hide in plain sight among their peers. As I said, we have had limited success doing this with Protestant missionaries, particularly in North Africa. The intelligence they have gathered has been invaluable. However, we are just now building a European strategy with Catholics. That's where you come in."

"You want me to recruit American Catholics to go undercover in Europe?"

"That's what I'm asking, yes. Once they arrive in Europe, they will be the ones connecting with your people on the ground. The ones you said we can trust. I would like Americans to be part of your 'string of pearls,' as you refer to it."

"That's risky."

"Not doing everything within our power to stop the evil blanketing Europe is far riskier."

Donovan added, "Before we get too far, there is something I need to make clear. It is something you may already know. Although most of the operatives you recruit on our behalf will be simple observers, gaining intelligence, we may require others to do more—much more."

"What do you mean, Mr. Donovan?"

"We may need to ask some to kill. Either indirectly, by guiding airstrikes, or directly, by assassinating military or political leaders. This job won't be for the faint of heart."

"I understand that."

Taking a deep breath and leaning back in his chair, Father Morlion continued. "Mr. Donovan, I have lived my entire life in Europe. I was born in Belgium. It is my home. I have spent more than a decade witnessing and reporting on the human atrocities perpetrated upon God's children by the Nazis. It is a level of barbarism that I have found difficult to put into words. I have seen innocent people beaten in the streets, received reports from trusted colleagues of others loaded up in cattle cars and taken away to God knows where. Others have been executed in front of their families. The numbers of my contacts who have reported these events are too many to count. Yes, I am a peaceful man of God. But I say without hesitancy, that our Father in heaven is on our side, and I am confident He will accept whatever means we feel necessary to put an end to this work of the devil."

THE BRONX NEW YORK
HANNAH AND NINO'S APARTMENT

Nino entered the apartment and closed the door behind him.

"Any word from the Navy Yard?"

Nino hung his coat on a hook, pulled out a chair. "Not yet."

"You need to swallow your pride, Nino. Your father will hire you. I know he will."

"I've told you. I will never work for my papa. His wealth is blood money. It's dirty. How can you expect me to work for him?"

"Don't look at it that way. You could ask him to work at the docks until you hear from the Navy Yard. I know that would make you feel better about not going over..."

"Over to fight? Is that what you mean? Like Angelo and the other American boys? Nino seized his coat and made his way to the door. I don't need you to patronize me, Hannah. Every day, I know that I'm here while American boys are overseas fighting and dying. I don't need to be reminded of it."

"That's not what I meant, Nino..."

Her voice trailed off as he sprinted down the stairs.

ISLAND OF SICILY
SICANI MOUNTAIN RANGE
ABBEY OF SANTA MARIA

The south side of the structure overlooked the valley. An eight-meter-high wall surrounded the Abbey of Santa Maria.

Lorenzo Leone drove his cargo truck through the gate, where he saw Father Russo in the courtyard speaking to Sister Anna.

Within the walls of the abbey was an orphanage, which comprised a school, living quarters for the children who lived there, and a chapel.

Lorenzo parked in the center of the courtyard and leaped from the cab.

"Bruno couldn't make it?" Father Russo asked.

"He is helping Isabella. One of our mares is about to give birth. They are experts with such things. I for one can't stomach it. I'll fill him in when I get home."

The Leones owned the most prosperous citrus farm in the central region. They called it *Bellissima Valle, and* it had been in the family for nine generations. Lorenzo lived there with his daughter Isabella, and his Father Bruno. Their ancestry was a mixture of Greek and Arab and was evident in their olive skin and dark features.

"Do you know if Manuel is coming?" Father Russo asked.

"He'll be here."

Father Russo turned to Sister Anna. "Have you put the children to bed?"

"Tucked in tight. A few of the boys still have excess energy and won't stop talking."

"They will fall asleep soon. You get to bed too."

Lorenzo and Father Russo turned to see Manuel Roseman's Fiat sedan enter the gate. He pulled beside Lorenzo's truck, then climbed out of the vehicle. The three men crossed the courtyard and approached Father Russo's office.

"How was the drive, Manuel?" Lorenzo asked.

"Too many German vehicles. But otherwise, good."

Manuel addressed Father Russo. "Do you have any more flyers, Padre? I'll stop in Morssomeli on my way back to Palermo and post some more."

Father Russo said, "We must cease with the flyers for now, Manuel. The *Carabinieri* came by again last week. They were asking questions. Particularly if I knew who was posting antifascist propaganda. We may have better things to do, anyway."

"What do you mean, father?" Lorenzo asked.

"Step inside. I'll explain."

Father Russo's office had a desk, a row of bookshelves against one wall, and two wooden chairs that faced the front of the desk. There was a small fire in the corner fireplace.

"I would offer you something, but all I have is a cold pot of coffee that was prepared this morning."

"Do you have a pitcher of spring water?" Manuel asked. "There is nothing like it after a dusty drive up the mountain."

"I'll be right back, gentlemen."

As Father Russo left the office, Lorenzo asked, "How are you making out with the coastal bombing, Manuel?"

"It is sporadic. The Brits target ships in the harbor. Unfortunately, they aren't always accurate, and their bombs occasionally fall inland. Four days ago, they wiped out an entire city block and killed six civilians. But so far, they are only hitting us about once per week."

"Have any bombs landed near the cameo shop?"

"The ground has shaken a few times and we occasionally lose electricity, but so far we have been lucky."

Father Russo returned with a pitcher of water and three tin cups.

"Thank you for coming, gentlemen. Although, I wish Bruno were here. He holds a lot of influence on this island and knows who we can trust and who we can't."

Lorenzo and Manuel looked at each other. "Trust, father?" Lorenzo asked. "What do you mean?"

Father Russo paced his office. "Gentlemen, as I have discussed with you before, I have a connection. I can't tell you who, only that he is a Catholic, an antifascist, and sympathetic to our cause. He has contacted the American government. They are looking for our help."

"Help with what?" Lorenzo asked.

"German and Italian force strength and troop movements."

Lorenzo and Manuel looked at each other.

"They want us to spy?" Manuel asked.

Lorenzo spoke up, "That is taking our cause to a whole new level, father. Printing antifascist and anti-Nazi flyers and posting them on signposts and buildings is one thing. Reporting troop movements that may get our Italian soldiers killed is something completely different. It has only been two months since my son Aldo was killed in Ethiopia. Now you are asking me to spy on the Italian army, so another father may lose his son to the British. I don't think I can do that."

"I understand, Lorenzo."

Manuel spoke up. "Lorenzo, I say this with respect to Aldo. I don't see that we have any choice. Aldo went to war because they forced him to. He told you himself, he fought because of a brotherhood with his unit, not for Mussolini. He hated Mussolini as much as we do. I must tell you that as a Jew that sees what the Italian government is doing to my people, my loyalties are to old Italy, not fascist Italy."

Father Russo added, "As a man of God, I too am conflicted. I did not become a priest to choose sides in war. But I know things, Lorenzo. I have heard of the firsthand accounts of the atrocities committed by Hitler. My thoughts are that, because Mussolini has allied himself with Hitler, Italy too has blood on its hands. I can't sit back and do nothing while the devil himself spreads his evil throughout Europe."

Lorenzo looked at Manuel, then back to Father Russo. "I will not be committing to this without speaking to my Papa."

* * *

Bruno was wiping his hands and Isabella was watching the foal struggling to stand when Lorenzo entered the barn.

The eighteen-year-old Isabella said, "Look at him, Papa. Isn't he beautiful?"

"He is wonderful. What are you going to name him?"

"Sampson."

Lorenzo looked at the mare resting in the hay. "How is Sophia?"

Bruno said, "She appears to be doing well. She only lost a little blood. It was one of the simplest births I have witnessed. Your mother had a harder time with you."

Lorenzo turned to leave the barn. Still wiping his hands, Bruno followed him.

"Why did Father Russo call the meeting?" Bruno asked. "Did the *Carabinieri* pay him another visit? He needs to be careful with that printing press."

"It was about something else that I need to discuss with you."

After entering the side door of the house, Bruno filled two glasses with limoncello.

Lorenzo pulled up a chair. "Do you remember when Father Russo told us about a contact he had in Belgium? The one who runs the network."

"The one who told him of the Jewish slave labor camps?"

"Si, that's the one. Father Russo said he recently heard from him again. Apparently, he is in America. Now that the Americans are in the war, he is working with them."

"What does that have to do with us?"

"They need our help."

"Doing what?"

"Spying on our own army, as well as the Germans. They want us to report troop movements."

Bruno raised the glass to his lips, downing the limoncello in one swig, then reached for the bottle to pour more.

"This is good."

"The limoncello?"

"No, that the Americans want our help."

"Why do you say that, Papa?"

"Because that could be the beginning of the end for Mussolini and Hitler."

"But we would give them information that will get Italian soldiers killed. British artillery killed Aldo. Why would I help them break the heart of another Italian father? I don't have that right."

Bruno downed another swig.

"Lorenzo, as long as Mussolini and Hitler are in power, innocent people will continue to die in the name of fascism. Don't bury your head in the sand. I fought for this country in the Great War. I did so proudly. But the Italy of today is not the Italy I fought for. Our economy is in ruins, they treat Jews like second-class citizens and anyone who speaks out against Il Duce gets arrested or worse. In Rome, the black shirts are raining terror down on subversives. They have forced them to drink castor oil."

"That's a rumor."

"It is true. I spoke to Giovani Concepcion two days ago. He had just returned from Rome and witnessed it himself."

Lorenzo said, "If Aldo were still alive and fighting, we wouldn't even be having this discussion."

"But Aldo isn't alive. You blame the British for Aldo's death. I blame Mussolini and Hitler. They are one and the same and they have dragged Italy into this war. Somebody needs to drag us out of it."

"By helping the Brits and the Americans kill Italian soldiers?"

"No Lorenzo, by helping the British and Americans give our country back to us."

THE BRONX NEW YORK

His eyes burned from the cigarette smoke hovering in the air. Nino tipped his glass to drain the last few drops of his third round. "Give me another beer."

A mirror occupied the wall behind the bar. He had been glancing at it for the past hour, watching the yard workers spill in from the rain. It was late afternoon, and their shift had just ended.

A gentleman pulled out the bar stool next to Nino's and sat down. He appeared to be in his fifties, average height, had gray hair, and was thick around the middle. Most of the men in the bar wore a dirty hat. Those behind him wore flat caps like Nino's. The man next to him wore a fedora.

"Bourbon on the rocks," the man shouted with a raised hand.

The bartender slid Nino's beer to him, then turned around for a bottle of Jim Beam.

As the bartender placed the man's drink on the bar, a younger man approached from behind and slapped the older man on the shoulder. "What the hell are you doing here, Dugan? Don't you get enough of us working men during the day? Now you're coming into our drinking hole?"

"If you blokes would do what I'd tell ya to do, I wouldn't need to drink."

"Ha... All you guys in management ever do is complain. When's the last time you got your hands dirty?"

"I had my time getting my knuckles busted up. Now I prefer to be the boss."

The man turned and shouted back, "Enjoy your beer and leave us be, will ya?"

The older man turned to Nino. "You see the crap I tolerate? Most of these guys in here work for me. Some are decent blokes, but for most, if I don't watch everything they do, they will turn slack. When I ride em, they hate me. Not a single one of these guys in here is management material. Most are like Randolph there. All they do is complain. I can't trust none of 'em."

The older man reached his hand out to shake Nino's. "I'm Jack Dugan by the way. You are dressed too good for a yard worker. You must work in the big office where they keep track of the numbers."

Nino shook his head. "No, I applied at the Navy Yard weeks ago. I haven't heard back. I stopped in again today to check."

"Don't worry. Rumor has it that because of the war, the floodgates for hiring will soon open."

"I've been praying."

"So, you aren't working now?"

"No, sir. I had a job at Ellis Island but... I won't get into it."

"What'd you do before you worked at Ellis Island?"

"I was in Italy studying to be a priest. I met a girl there and got married."

"Really? An Italian girl?"

"She's American. I met her over there."

"A priest you say?"

"Yes."

"I bet I can trust a priest. Do you think you could help me keep these guys in line? I need an assistant foreman."

"Yes, sir. I'm willing to do whatever it takes."

"What did you say your name was again?"

"Nino—Nino Servidei."

Jack Dugan handed Nino a napkin and a pen. "Write your name down here."

As Nino wrote, Dugan said, "It will take me some time to have the ladies in the office pull your application. But once they do, I'll force it to the top and get you hired. Today is Wednesday. I want you to meet me at gate four of the Navy Yard at 07:00 am on Monday. When you show up, I'll have a job for you."

Nino shook Dugan's hand. "Thank you, sir. I will work really hard for you, I promise."

"I know you will, kid. But I'm warning you, these guys ain't going to like me bringing in an outsider to supervise them. They will be rough on ya."

"Mr. Dugan, I have a family. I'll do anything to provide for them. Harsh words and bad attitudes aren't anything I can't handle."

* * *

Jack Dugan turned to watch Nino leave the bar, waited three minutes, then swallowed back the last of his bourbon.

There was still a cold, light drizzle when he stepped onto the sidewalk. He pulled his fedora over his eyes and flipped his collar up. He walked two blocks north, then turned right, before knocking on the back window of the Cadillac Fleetwood.

After he slid in, Salvador DiVincenzo puffed on a cigar. "Well. What happened?"

"Your boy starts Monday morning."

Salvador stared at him momentarily before saying, "That pleases me. You just saved your brother's life. I won't kill him. But that doesn't mean he is off the hook for the money he owes me. Last I checked, it was up to fifty-four hundred dollars with interest. I can't just let that slide."

"He knows that. He's working on getting you the money. Times have been hard since his wife took ill."

"Send him a message for me. Tell him since you got Nino a job, I'll spare his life, but if he doesn't start making payments, he might end up with a few injuries."

"I'll tell him, Mr. DiVincenzo. I'll call him as soon as I get home."

"You better treat my boy right. Now get the hell out of my car."

* * *

Nino sprinted up the stairs and flung open the door to the apartment. Hannah and Lilia were eating dinner.

"Sorry we didn't wait for you, Nino, but we didn't know when you would get home. Where have you been all day?"

"Hannah, I have great news. I went by the Navy Yard to see if they had started hiring. They hadn't. I was feeling sorry for myself, so I went to the bar across the street."

"You promised you were going to stay away from that place."

"It's a good thing I broke my promise, because while I was there, I met this man by the name of Jack Dugan. He's one of the lead foremen at the yard. He sat next to me and we started talking. When he found out I had been in Rome studying to be a priest, he must have liked that. He said that means he could probably trust me. Anyway, I'm to meet him at gate four on Monday at 07:00 am. He's going to hire me as his assistant."

Hannah rose and embraced him. "That's wonderful, Nino. You see, I told you everything would work out."

ISLAND OF SICILY
ABBEY OF SANTA MARIA
SICANI MOUNTAIN RANGE

"I received another letter last week," Father Russo said. "This one was from the Vatican. They want to know our commitment. I have thirty days to send them a coded message by wire."

"The Vatican?" Manuel asked.

"The holy church is walking a tightrope," Father Russo said. "Publicly they are neutral to appease the fascists. Some within the walls of the holy city even support Mussolini. Others are working behind the scenes to defeat him."

"And the pope?"

"He is the most skillful tightrope walker of them all."

"If we move forward, father, are you concerned about the children in the orphanage?" Bruno asked. "If we get discovered, what will happen to them?"

"Other than me, nobody here will know of our plan. I must have faith that if the authorities discover what we are doing, they won't punish the nuns and the children."

"Is it fair to take that risk?" Lorenzo said. "They are innocent."

Father Russo said, "So are the millions of children throughout Europe who are suffering under the iron fist of fascism."

"I agree," Manuel said. "I am concerned for my fellow Jews, especially the children. If the fascists win this war, the freedom of every Jew in Europe will be at risk. Possibly even our lives."

"I need to know that we are all in agreement," Father Russo said. "Are we all willing to help the allies as they have asked?"

"I'm in." Manuel said.

"Me too." Replied Bruno.

Lorenzo hesitated, then looked at Bruno. "I'm in, but we keep Isabella out of this. She must never know. I don't want her involved."

"Of course," Bruno said. "She will never know."

Lorenzo looked to Father Russo. "Isabella volunteers here three days per week. You must promise me you too will keep her out of this."

"Of course, Lorenzo. You have my word. Isabella will never know we are helping the allies."

Lorenzo shook his head and turned away.

Father Russo said, "I will travel to Messina tomorrow to send the wire to Rome."

THE BRONX NEW YORK
HANNAH AND NINO'S APARTMENT

Hannah placed a slice of bread on Lilia's plate. Nino was sitting across from her holding baby Solomon and making faces to make him laugh.

"Your Mama came by this afternoon," Hannah said.

"Why didn't she stay for dinner?" Nino asked, as he twirled spaghetti around his fork, careful not to drop Solomon.

"She said your father was taking her out to dinner."

Nino smirked. "She used to complain that he never took her out."

"She said he has been sweet with her recently."

Nino shook his head before sipping his wine.

"Why are you so cynical about your father?"

"Because he is just going through a phase. He'll be his old mean self again soon."

"Do you think you will ever speak to him again?"

"Not if I can help it."

"How was work today?"

"Work was wonderful."

Hannah grinned. "You always say that. How can work be wonderful every day?"

"Work isn't always wonderful but having a job and coming home to you and these two little rascals is wonderful."

Hannah said, "Oh, how could I forget? Your mama said that

they accepted Angelo into the Army Air Corps. They will train him to fire machineguns out of airplanes."

ISLAND OF SICILY
ABBEY OF SANTA MARIA
SICANI MOUNTAIN RANGE

Sister Catherine entered Father Russo's office. "A truck has just arrived. The driver said he needs to speak to you personally."

Entering the courtyard, he approached the driver. "May I help you?"

The driver said, "Father Russo, I have supplies for you." He lowered his voice. "They are from the Vatican. May we speak in private?"

They proceeded to Father Russo's office.

Upon entering, the driver said, "I am a British agent. I filled the back of my truck with vegetables, and clothing for the children. At the bottom of the clothing is a wireless. I need to show you how to use it, then we need to hide it someplace where only you can find it."

Father Russo rubbed his chin momentarily while looking down at the floor. After a moment of pondering, he said, "Follow me."

As they entered the chapel, the driver followed him to the rear of the altar where Father Russo knelt and removed a sliding door. Inside were two brass candelabras and a communion set.

"Will it fit in here?" asked the padre.

"Perfectly," replied the driver. "Now, let's go get it, and I will show you how to activate it, but more importantly, *when* to operate it."

CHAPTER 6

NORTH AFRICA
ALGIERS

Her code name was Cobra. She glanced to her right, then her left. A German staff car approached the sidewalk and halted. The officer in the back seat addressed her in unintelligible French, although his demeanor was of a man believing himself to be charming. She waved him off and stepped back from the curb. He stared at her with a scowl before tapping on the driver's seat. The car sped off.

Within minutes, a black sedan approached and stopped. The license plate ended in the number four and there was a scratch on the right front fender adjacent the headlight. She flicked her cigarette to the ground, picked up her suitcase, and climbed into the passenger seat. The driver was overweight and appeared two decades older than her twenty-four years. They didn't speak during their journey, and as always, their destination was unknown to her. They headed north toward the coast. When possible, the driver traveled through back alleys. After turning onto a main road, they saw a Vichy checkpoint in the distance.

"Stay calm," the driver said.

"It's only a checkpoint. I have nothing to hide. I am a French citizen. I'm assuming by that accent, you aren't."

The driver ignored her comment. He slowed as they approached. There was a sentry on either side of the vehicle. Gabrielle and the driver handed over their papers.

The guard on the passenger side looked at her, then at the driver, then back to her. "Why are you with him? Is he your father?"

"No. He's rich."

Both sentries laughed, then waived them on.

Gabrielle and her driver entered the warehouse district. After several turns, they arrived at the rear of a dilapidated stucco building. The driver got out and looked around before opening the carriage doors. After the car drove in, a thin man in a white suit opened her door. She got out of the vehicle and waited for instructions.

The thin man said, "This way."

Although uncertain who her father was, her mother assumed by her daughter's dark complexion and sultry exotic features, that it was one of the Arab men she frequently entertained. These traits allowed Gabrielle Fontaine to charge top dollar in her chosen profession. She had also been working for the American government for two years. Mainly as a transfer handler for couriers, but also gathering intelligence from German, Italian and French officials who paid for her intimacy.

They entered a shabby office in the back of the warehouse.

The man behind the desk lit a cigarette but didn't stand. "Have a seat, Gabrielle."

She did as instructed. In English she asked, "Do you have another cigarette, Mr. Jacobs? I'm out."

He reached into his desk and tossed an unopened pack of Lucky Strikes on the desk. "Here, have the entire pack. It may be a while before you get anymore."

"Are you testing me?"

"What do you mean?"

"American cigarettes. I must not be going anyplace too dangerous if you are giving me these."

He reached back into his drawer and tossed her a pack of Macedonias.

Gabrielle said, "So I am going to Italy? Where in Italy?"

"Sicily—Palermo."

"My Italian is limited, but I'll make do."

"You'll be targeting a German."

"Why another German? I've told you, I speak French, English, and a little Italian. I know forty or fifty words in German, but I can't have a conversation."

"It doesn't matter. The generalmajor you will target, Richter is his name, speaks French exceptionally well. He likes French women."

"What makes you think he will like me?"

Jacobs laughed. "What man has ever resisted your charms?"

"There was one once. You sent him to me to pick up an envelope."

"He must have preferred men."

"No—married. He wanted to remain faithful to his wife."

"After all the men you have been with, you remember that one?"

"He was special. Handsome, and funny with a boyish charm. His name was Nino. He told me how beautiful his wife was, and he could never be unfaithful to her. I remember being jealous, wondering why she got to spend her life with him while I spent my life pleasuring dirty sailors, soldiers and old businessmen."

"She made different choices."

"You think I live this life by choice?"

"I don't have time for your sad life story, Gabrielle. Neither do you. You need to catch a train to Tunis."

"I hate Tunis."

"You won't be there long. You will arrive in the morning."

He reached back into his drawer and removed an envelope, then made his way around the desk. After handing it to her, he sat on the edge and crossed his arms. "When you get to the pier, look for a fishing boat by the name of *Libertà*. There is a small crew. The captain goes by the name of Jacopo. He is expecting you."

"A fishing boat. I'm supposed to travel to Sicily on a fishing boat?"

"German and Italian patrol boats don't make a habit of harassing every fishing boat they see. There are too many of them."

"What happens when I get to Palermo?"

"There is a brothel near the docks. The address is in that envelope. When you arrive, you will ask to speak to Madam Lucia. Tell her you just arrived from France. It will be less suspicious than telling her you were here. Let her know you need a place to earn a living."

"I don't work brothels anymore."

"You do now. Generalmajor Richter orders his entertainment from Madam Lucia."

"What do you mean by orders?"

"He doesn't go there personally. Once a week he sends his aide there to pick up a few companions for the weekend."

"Does this Madam Lucia know I'm coming?"

"No. The presence of the German and Italian armies in Sicily has made her prosperous. She would betray you in an instant."

"What information are you looking for from this Generalmajor Richter?"

"Just like the others, anything of value. Work the pillow talk. Treat him like a king and make him believe he has impressed you with his rank. See if he will spill his guts."

"If I uncover something, who should I pass it onto?"

"We have been working with a network. They will contact you."

"How?"

"They will request your services at the brothel. Once you are alone with them, they will tell you that you look familiar and ask if you have ever been to Venice. You will reply that you have been, but you were a child at the time, and they must have you confused with someone else. They will reply by saying, 'I too was there as a child. We may have met at that time.'"

"Are you sure I can trust them?"

"For the past few months, this network has been providing the British with information. Although the Brits have found it to be limited, they say it has been reliable and the network can be trusted."

"When will I be returning to Algiers?"

"When you are more valuable here than in Sicily."

"What about my apartment?"

"We'll keep paying your rent. Everything will still be there when you come back."

THE ISLAND OF SICILY
PALERMO

Manuel opened the door of the Roseman Cameo shop. It was late in the afternoon and the sun shining through the plate-glass window illuminated the front display case, yet the back of the store remained dark. As he closed the door behind him, he heard his wife Olivia's voice from the back office.

"Is that you, Manuel?"

"Si."

Olivia entered the showroom. "Did they say when we would have electricity again?"

"At least two more days."

"We can't run a business like this. We didn't have a single customer today."

"It will get better."

"Not until this war is over."

"We need to be glad the bombs have missed this block. I could take you four kilometers east of here and—"

She interrupted him. "I know, Manuel. You have shown me. You don't need to remind me how British air raids have destroyed Palermo."

He approached her, and they embraced.

"Are we really doing the right thing, Manuel? Every time Father Russo sends a message, bombs drop on Sicily."

"Not every time, and we only inform them of German positions, not Italian."

"You are fooling yourself."

"No, we were fooling ourselves when we thought Italian Jews would be safe under Mussolini. Our Jewish friends can no longer teach school or work for the government. Hell, we can't even swim at a public beach in the summer. Do you really think I care if a few Italian soldiers die in order to get our freedom back?"

"That's a terrible thing to say."

"I know. I'm sorry, but there is no perfect war. Someone must die, and everyone does their best to make certain it is someone other than themselves or their family."

The front door opened, and Lorenzo Leone entered.

"We weren't expecting you, Lorenzo."

"Father Russo received a wireless message yesterday," Lorenzo said. "The Americans are sending an agent. A girl. They want us to contact her. She will be here in Palermo and Father Russo thought you could be her point of contact."

Olivia said, "I don't like this. We went from posting anti-fascist flyers, to reporting troop and ship movements. Now they want us to contact other agents on the ground. We are getting in way over our heads."

Manuel turned to Olivia. "I'm not having this discussion with you. If you don't want to take part, I understand. But I've made up my mind. I refuse to sit back and do nothing while I lose my country to evil."

"I didn't say, I wouldn't help you. I was reminding you of what's at stake."

"I don't need to be reminded."

Lorenzo asked, "Would you like me to return to share the details?"

"No, we are fine. Go ahead, Lorenzo," Manuel said.

"Her name is Gabrielle. She will work in a brothel on the waterfront."

"A brothel." Olivia said. "The Vatican and Father Russo are entangled in a brothel?"

Lorenzo laughed. "I asked the same thing of Father Russo. He said, the Vatican is no longer involved. They were just the initial messenger. We are collaborating with the Americans on this one."

"Are we still working with the British?" Manuel asked.

"We are all on the same side."

"What is the plan?" Manuel asked. "What is my role with this agent, Gabrielle? Do I contact her, or does she contact me?"

"You'll contact her."

"Where?"

"At the brothel."

Olivia said, "So, Manuel is supposed to just stroll into a brothel and ask for this, Gabrielle. The brothel is near here. We are well known in this neighborhood. Isn't there a better way to do this?"

"I only need to go in there once," Manuel said. "After I make contact, I'll tell her to report to me here."

"So, a prostitute will come into our store?" Olivia asked.

Manuel said, "Technically, it's not our store. We had to sell it to Lorenzo because of the racial laws, remember?"

"Don't change the subject."

Manuel asked Lorenzo, "How will she know to trust me?"

Lorenzo handed him a note. "Memorize this exchange about meeting her in Venice."

A bell over the door rang and an Italian naval officer entered as Manuel slipped the paper into his vest pocket.

Lorenzo turned to the door. "I'll return."

* * *

"Pull this hat down over your eyes," Olivia said.

"What good will that do?"

Olivia walked over to a cabinet and pulled out a pair of wire-rimmed glasses. "Here, put these on. They were my father's." After doing as she suggested, he said, "This is no good. It's still me with a pair of glasses on."

"Don't shave for a few days. If you pull a hat down over your eyes, wear the glasses and have a stubby beard, it should at least fool anyone who sees you from a distance. If you see someone we know once you enter the brothel, you will be safe. What are they going to do, go home and tell their wife they saw you in a brothel?"

After putting on the glasses and a fedora, he looked in the bedroom mirror. "I think with a little facial hair, this might work."

NORTH AFRICA
TUNIS

The heat was intense, yet the sun was barely over the landscape. Gabrielle made her way down the pier, seeking out the *Libertà*. She wore a modest white dress and no makeup, yet with rare exception, the crew members of the docked vessels studied her as she passed. Fishing boats made their way out to the Mediterranean. Visible on the horizon were the tiny masts of a dozen others.

She passed several boats until she arrived at the final one. A heavy-set older man waved, and in French shouted, "Are you, Gabrielle?"

She approached. "*Oui.*"

"I am Jacopo. Let me help you onboard."

He took her suitcase and handbag, then offered his arm and guided her into the boat. There were two additional crew members. They gawked at her, grinned, then one of them mumbled—*puttana.* In Italian, it meant prostitute. She sneered at him.

At the command of the captain, the men leaped from the boat and untied the mooring lines before jumping back in. The captain fired up the engine, opened the throttle, and they pulled away from the pier.

"Go down below. A beautiful woman will attract patrol boats."

They had not been at sea long before Gabrielle's stomach churned from the swells that rolled under the hull. She lay down in one of the four bunks, choosing the one whose filth she found least repulsive. With her head resting on her handbag, and her suitcase on the deck next to her, she kept her eyes on the stairwell, hoping the three men on deck would remain there. She quickly fell asleep.

She awoke to the sound of the hatch closing at the top of the stairwell. One of the Italian deck hands twisted the handle to lock it. She sat up and scooted to the rear of the bunk until her back was pressed against the bulkhead. As he made his way toward her, he undid his belt buckle and pulled his trousers down. Wearing no undergarments, he exposed himself fully to her. Gabriele reached into her bag, removed a Ruby pistol and pointed it at him. With an icy stare, he slowly bent down, pulled up his pants, buckled his belt, and returned to the main deck.

Gabrielle soon followed, clutching her handbag. She stared

at the Italian who had entered the cabin, then at the other.

The captain said. "Don't worry about them, they mean no harm."

Gabrielle pointed at the groin of the Italian who had entered her cabin below. She held up her hand, pinching her fingers so they were nearly touching. "*Pene piccolo*," she said in Italian, informing the young man he had a small penis.

He angrily lunged toward her. The other Italian laughed, then stepped in front of him to block his momentum.

After they arrived at Sicily, she turned to the bow of the boat to see the Bay of Palermo. There were German and Italian ships that lay sunken in the shallow water, victims of British air raids. The attacks had damaged several buildings along the waterfront. Fallen walls exposed interiors of rooms that once housed families and small shops. The diesel fumes paired with the motion under her feet made her ill again. She wanted to get on dry land.

The engine chugged. With the shoreline more visible, she saw military boats at the docks. Isolated on the opposite side of the bay, smaller fishing boats and schooners bobbed in the water, tied to the pier.

"So why are you here?" The captain asked.

Gabrielle ignored him, sensing the question wasn't just small talk. Double agents sold information not just to the highest bidder, but to anyone willing to pay.

"Look," the captain said. "I know who paid me to bring you here. They pay me to bring certain people to Sicily all the time. Sometimes in broad daylight like today, other times in the dark of night, and they swim ashore. Why they come here is of no interest to me."

"So why ask me?"

"Because the others I have brought weren't beautiful women."

* * *

Except for two businessmen, the patrons milling on the sidewalk were German and Italian soldiers. Several were stumbling about, careful not to spill the contents of the wine bottles they were swigging. The cat calls began the moment they saw Gabrielle. The smell of alcohol was intense, as she strode past them, slapping their hands away before she entered the brothel. The half dozen patrons in the lobby were less obnoxious.

From a rear room, a girl entered the lobby with a customer. His arm was around her waist. She rubbed his shoulders and kissed him before he turned for the door.

In broken Italian, Gabrielle said, "I need to see Lucia. I need a job."

The girl recognized Gabrielle's accent, and said, "You are French, *non?*"

"*Oui. I am French.*"

"*Bonjour,* my name is Hortense Vernier. What part of France are you from?"

"Rouen. *And you?*"

Hortense replied, "Me. I was born in Cherbourg, but have spent much of my life in Paris. I have only been here a year."

"I am Gabrielle Fontaine."

"Follow me, I will introduce you to Lucia."

They made their way down a hall. Cigarette smoke, the smell of booze, and a hint of incense intercepted them as they made the journey to the back office. A few of the doors were open, and Gabrielle looked in to see customers in various stages of undress. Some putting on clothes, others removing them. From behind the doors that were closed, she heard grunts, groans, and panting.

After they entered the back office, Hortense said, "Lucia, this young lady is Miss Fontaine. She would like to see you. She is looking for work."

Lucia looked at her, and in Italian, said, "*Oh mio, sei bellissima.* Come, have a seat. You will bring in many customers."

"I hope you will pay me well for bringing them in."

"Where are you from?" Lucia asked.

"Rouen."

"Your Italian sounds good enough. Do you speak German?"

"I know a few words when I hear them, but I can't have a conversation. I know English."

"English won't do you any good in Sicily, although your French will work wonderfully for a few of our German clients." Lucia looked at Hortense. "One in particular comes to mind, wouldn't you say, Hortense? You wouldn't mind sharing General Richter with Miss Fontaine, would you?"

"Of course not. I need a break from him."

"You may start tonight," Lucia said.

"I would prefer to start tomorrow. I still need to find a place to stay."

Hortense spoke up. "You may stay with me."

* * *

It was late afternoon when they arrived at Hortense's apartment. It was above a corner market they could access by an external wooden stairway. Upon entering, Gabrielle watched Hortense toss her jacket on a sofa before entering the kitchen.

"Would you like a glass of wine?" Hortense asked.

"I was hoping you would offer."

As she handed the glass to Gabrielle, Hortense asked, "How did you end up in Sicily?"

"I came here to escape bad people. They wanted to hurt me."

"In our line of work, we can't escape them. How old were you when you started whoring? What is your story?"

"I was fourteen and living in Rouen. During a blustery winter, a man by the name of Kilian invited me into his home. He was an old Irishman. Because of his gray hair everyone assumed he was my grandfather. I shared his bed, but I didn't care. He was kind to me, and for the first time in my life I felt loved. We were together for three years. One day I came home from the market to find Kilian dead on the floor. His pension disbursements kept coming to the apartment, so I would falsify his signature on the payments to survive. Eventually, the payments stopped. To support myself, I invited men to the apartment, and they paid me to satisfy their urges. Once the landlord caught on, I was out on the street again. Within weeks, a stranger told me of the warm climate and endless flow of money from wealthy dignitaries in southern France, and for a cut of my earnings, he could get me there. The following morning, I boarded a train for Toulon. A year later, I was broke, and imprisoned in a little room on the second floor of a brothel. I overheard one of the guards say they were going to send me to Tunisia. One night, I slipped away. That's why I'm here in Sicily. I don't think they will find me here."

"Your story is like so many of the girls at Lucia's. At least the ones who aren't Sicilian."

"What is it like working in Palermo?"

"We have an advantage, you and I."

"What's that?"

"We are French. Most of our clients are German officers. They like French women. At least the ones we will see. There is a small group of them who hire us. Lucia has a stable of three French girls to service them, including me. You will be the fourth once you earn her trust."

"I find that word offensive."

"What word?"

"'Stable.' It makes us sound like workhorses."

"To those who run brothels, we are. But that's not who you and I are, Gabrielle. We are thoroughbreds."

"Does that make you feel better?"

"A little."

"Do you ever think about your future, Hortense?"

"Just tomorrow."

"Don't you have hopes and dreams."

"You mean like being swept off my feet by a rich customer? We all have that dream. Yet here we are."

"I didn't see any officers at Lucia's place."

"There are some, but not many. Mainly, we go to them."

"Is that what I will be doing, traveling to them?"

"Eventually. Lucia will keep you at her place for a while. Once you prove your worth, she will send you out on dates. I have a feeling, the way you look, that day will come soon. It will be good for you. Most of the German officers pretend to be gentlemen. They take us to fine restaurants and the opera."

"The opera?" Gabriele said. "I have always wanted to go to the opera."

* * *

"I'm here to see Gabrielle," Manuel said to the hostess.

"There is someone with her. We have other girls who are available."

"I'm rather fond of Gabrielle."

After taking his money, she said, "Make yourself comfortable."

A German soldier emerged in the hallway, followed by a beautiful, dark-skinned girl in her twenties.

The hostess spoke to her, then nodded toward Manuel.

Gabrielle took his hand. "*Buongiorno, signore,*" she said as she led him to a back room, her slender hips swaying from side to side. When they arrived, she closed the door and laid her robe in a chair, revealing a short silk nightgown. "What would you like?"

Manuel removed his hat and glasses. "You look familiar. Have you ever been to Venice?"

She sat down on the bed and retrieved a cigarette from the nightstand. "I have been, but I was a small child. You must have me mistaken for someone else."

"I was also there as a child. Perhaps we met at that time."

She nodded toward a wooden chair in the corner. "Have a seat."

Manuel positioned the chair next to her before sitting. He leaned forward, keeping his voice just above a whisper. "My name is Manuel Roseman. I am the proprietor of the Roseman Cameo Shop on Piazza Fonderia. It is just a few blocks from here in the primary shopping district near the waterfront and is the only cameo shop in that part of the city. I was told you were sent here by others and that we are supposed to work together. I was told that perhaps you might have information that should be shared with our mutual friends."

She lit the cigarette, never removing her eyes from him. "I just arrived. I have nothing to report."

"I understand. But when you do have information, you know where to find me. If I'm not available, my wife Olivia will be in the store. She will relay the information to me."

"I don't like having too many people involved."

"You can trust Olivia."

"How many people are in your network?"

Manuel opened his mouth to reply, then caught himself. "You know I can't tell you that."

"Of course. I just want to know how many people know I am here."

"You can trust those who do."

After an uncomfortable silence, he nervously stood, returned the seat to the corner, and turned toward the door.

"Don't leave," she said. "How much time did you pay for?"

"Thirty minutes."

"If you leave too soon, it will look suspicious."

* * *

The evening air was chilly. As instructed, the four women sat inside a café. Gabrielle was beside Hortense. The other two girls sat across from them. Hortense was a few years older than Gabrielle. The other two girls were younger, perhaps in their late teens.

"Where do you think they will take us this evening?" One of the younger girls said.

"Maybe another party," the other said. "All the food and champagne were wonderful."

Hortense offered each of them a cigarette. Only Gabrielle accepted.

She took a puff, then looked through the plate-glass window. Across the street, an elderly couple held hands as they approached a bus stop. When they arrived, they sat on a bench and he wrapped his arm around her, and she kissed his cheek.

Gabrielle's heart ached. Loneliness overcame her as she looked down and closed her eyes.

"I think that's our car," Hortense said.

Gabrielle looked up to see headlights turn the corner and approach the café. The Mercedes staff car stopped in front of them. The driver, a low-ranking German officer, got out and entered the cafe. All eyes were on him as he entered. He scanned the room before noticing the four women at the window. He advanced toward them. "Ladies," he said, while making a hand gesture toward the door.

On the sidewalk, he opened the door to the back seat. They climbed in. His attentiveness toward the young girls and Hortense was fleeting, preferring to focus his courteousness on Gabrielle, the last to climb in.

During their journey, the conversation between the other girls had become white noise. Focused, Gabrielle knew she had a job to do, and that was to become the mistress of Generalmajor Richter. Would she meet him tonight?

The headlights shone on an angel in the center of a sizeable roundabout. As their car got closer, Gabrielle noticed it was on top of an inactive fountain.

They turned right, drove around it, then halted in front of a two-story stucco building. It was the only stand-alone structure on the intersection. Attached to the other buildings that encircled the fountain were residences and storefronts. The driver parked the car at the front entrance which comprised two dark wooden doors. They appeared twice as tall as Gabrielle. There were two first story windows facing the street. The second floor comprised three more windows, with a wrought-iron balcony in the center, just above Gabrielle's head. French doors allowed access to the balcony.

The driver opened the door to the house, and they entered a large foyer with a stairway off to the right side. At the top of the stairs, a younger German officer with blonde hair looked down.

"*Bonjour*, welcome ladies," the Hauptmann said.

As he made his way down the stairs, Gabrielle noticed he was paying extra attention to her. He approached Hortense, kissed her hand, then did the same with the other two girls. He positioned himself in front of Gabrielle. "You were the one Lucia was telling me about—the new one. You just arrived from France."

"*Oui*. It is a pleasure to meet you. I am Gabrielle."

He held her hands, looked into her eyes, and kissed both cheeks.

"Come, follow me."

Not releasing her hand, he led Gabrielle to the back of the house, the other women trailing behind. Gabrielle heard them whispering but couldn't understand what they said.

The room they entered had a large Persian rug on the floor, with sofas on either side. A fireplace was on the opposite side of the room. Next to the fireplace was a high-backed leather chair. He led Gabrielle to the chair and directed Hortense and the other two women to the sofa.

"Please excuse me," he said. "I will let the others know you have arrived. We will only be a moment."

When he was in the adjacent room, Hortense whispered to Gabrielle, "He likes you."

"Who was he?"

"That was Hauptman Schroder."

"Are they all handsome like him?"

Hortense and the other girls laughed. Regaining their composure as the door opened. Schroder stood to attention as four officers entered. Three were similar—late forties to early fifties with graying hair. They were thick around the middle. The exception was the fourth officer—the highest-ranking. He was tall and thin, and the first to step forward. "Good evening, ladies. It is so good to see you again."

"Good evening, Generalmajor Richter." The other three said in unison. Gabrielle remained silent.

He approached Gabrielle's chair. "You are the new one. Lucia said you were breathtaking. Her assessment was correct. Where are you from?"

"Rouen."

"Where in Rouen have you lived?"

"Many places. Most recently, on Rue Saint-Gervais."

"Ah yes. I know it well. That is near Mont Saint-Aigné."

"I beg your pardon, generalmajor. But you are mistaken. Rue Saint-Gervais is nowhere near Mont Saint-Aigné."

"I must be confused. It has been several years since I was in Rouen. My memory has failed me."

Hauptmann Schroder said, "Dinner is ready, generalmajor. Would you like to be seated now, or after cocktails?"

He turned to the other three officers. "Gentlemen, shall we eat?" He turned to Gabrielle and extended an arm to her. "Will you join me, Gabrielle?"

"I would be delighted."

* * *

The morning sun shone through the window. Gabrielle stared at the ceiling. Generalmajor Richter lay on his side. He faced away from her. His snoring was intense, and his morning breath permeated the room.

She considered waking him but thought better of it, concerned that he might be frisky. Glancing around his bedroom, she looked for anything that might be of value, noticing his attaché case resting in a corner chair. She shook him gently, yet he remained asleep. After pulling the covers back, she tiptoed across the room, making it halfway across before Richter rolled onto his back.

She picked her clothes up off the floor.

"Where do you think you are going?" Richter stretched his arms over his head.

"I was cold. I was just getting dressed."

"Don't bother. Come back to bed. I don't need to leave for another hour."

PALERMO SICILY

The destruction in the harbor made him question if they were winning the war, as Mussolini's propagandists had been telling the Italian people.

The address Primo Capitano Bonetti gave Vito was in the center of the city. Unlike the destruction near the waterfront, this part of Palermo was intact, and the streets were busy with pedestrians and military vehicles. Vito approached a fountain with an angel as its centerpiece. It was in the middle of a roundabout. He slowed to a crawl, keeping his balance by dragging his boots on the pavement. He stopped and let the bike idle as he pulled a piece of paper from his coat pocket to double check the address.

He glanced up at a second-floor balcony. There was a German officer smoking a cigarette. He was older, perhaps in his fifties, tall and slim, with a touch of gray. His white shirt was unbuttoned to his waist, and his suspenders dangled at his sides as though he had just slipped his pants on to smoke his cigarette.

A woman appeared behind the officer. Vito's heart raced. She was flawless. Her features were dark—perhaps Italian—but more likely middle eastern. She wore a skimpy silk undergarment. Even from a distance, her bright red lipstick was apparent. She stepped forward and wrapped her arms around the German. He turned and kissed her, then led her back into the room.

Vito watched the door close behind them.

You lucky kraut bastard.

CHAPTER 7

"Follow me, Children. Walk single file and stay close together," Isabella Leone shouted as she led the group of nine children up a hill. They ranged in age from six to twelve. Except for a few thin clouds, the sky was blue. The wind had picked up, and it was blowing Isabella's long black hair in her face. She stopped, removed a yellow scarf from her neck, and used it to tie her hair back.

A chubby boy in the back yelled, "Miss Leone, this hill is steep. Can we rest?"

Two girls behind Isabella giggled. She stopped and turned to them. "Shh... Don't make fun of Peppe. Don't make fun of anyone. Do you understand me?"

"Yes, Miss Leone."

Isabella shouted, "We are almost there, Peppe. Just a little longer. When we get to the Abbey, Father Russo and the nuns will have lunch ready."

Isabella Leone had spent her life in the mountains of Sicily. Now eighteen, she volunteered three days per week at The

Abbey of Santa Maria, where she had attended school when she was a little girl.

Following the ascent up the hill, they traveled a short distance and entered the open gates of the abbey.

Isabella said. "Did you enjoy visiting the waterfall?"

"Yes, Miss Leone," they all shouted. "Thank you for taking us."

"I smell the food," Peppe shouted, as he ran toward the kitchen.

The girls giggled again. This time, Isabella couldn't help but grin herself. She shook her head, wondering why Peppe lost no weight even though food shortages in Sicily had begun shortly after the Germans arrived.

Appearing from his office, Fr. Russo met Isabella at the courtyard. "Will you join us for lunch, Isabella?"

"I must get home. Papa and I are getting an early start for Palermo in the morning."

"When you are in Palermo, could you pick up a few supplies for me?"

"Of course."

"Wait here, please, Isabella. I will get my list and some money."

"We only want the list, father. Papa won't take money from the orphanage. You know that."

"I do know that. He has never taken my money, but I never want to assume the supplies you bring me are a gift."

While she waited for Father Russo, Isabella leaned against her pickup truck.

She watched the wind blow dust across the open courtyard. She heard children in the distance. They were raucously making their way to a small classroom off the kitchen where they ate their meals. Her heart was lonely. Isabella was only six when her mother died, and since then, her life had been consumed with working Bellissimo Valle with her father Lorenzo, her grandfather Bruno, and her brother Aldo, who was her closest friend before he died in the fighting in Ethiopia. Her only escape was her time at the Abbey. She loved the children, and Father Russo and the nuns adored her.

"Here you are, Isabella," Father Russo handed her his list of items he needed replenished. "I'm sorry it is so long, but with the war, the number of children we have taken in has increased as fathers get sent away to fight, and mothers are struggling to manage on their own."

"That's fine, father. As my papa always says, God has blessed the Leone family, and it is our duty to help wherever we are needed."

Isabella climbed into the truck and started the engine. It sputtered at first, then rumbled to life.

Father Russo said, "Tell your papa and grandpapa how grateful we are. I have told them many times, had it not been for the Leone family, this orphanage would have vanished years ago."

* * *

It was directly overhead. The unmistakable sound of an airplane engine. Isabella looked up to see a single fighter with a British roundel painted on its side. Black smoke was pouring from its engine, and it was descending fast. She sped up, her eyes alternating between the plane and the road. The road she was on was narrow and bumpy, causing the truck to jostle. In the sky above, a parachute descended. She followed it, making a mental calculation where it would land.

Further down the road, dust trailed behind a Wehrmacht troop carrier as it sped down a narrow path, running parallel with Isabella. When the two lanes merged, Isabella slowed to give the truck room to enter in front of her. The debris from the tires bounced off her windshield. A soldier sitting in the back made eye contact with her before the truck drove over a crest, then dipped low. Within two kilometers, the troop carrier turned left, climbed a steep hill, then turned into the woods before coming to a stop behind another Wehrmacht truck. Isabella continued her journey for another quarter kilometer before pulling over. With caution in every step, she slipped into the woods. She heard voices. They were German. Another voice shouting in English, but with a German accent. She peeked through the shrubbery to see a British airman on his knees. Blood poured from his nose and mouth. Isabella gasped, then covered her mouth and ducked behind a bush. She looked again to see the airmen take one more rifle butt to the head and another to his abdomen. He fell forward, appearing to be unconscious. She retched, vomiting from the sight of the brutality. With one final glance, she saw them tossing the airman into the first truck. She ran to her vehicle and sped away.

CALTANISSETTA
ITALIAN 213ᵗʰ COASTAL DIVISION

Vito said, "You sent for me, *Primo Capitano* Bonetti?"

Bonetti reached into his drawer and pulled out an envelope. "Take these documents to battalion commander Casio in San Giuseppe. Wait for him to sign them, then you will take them to German Generalmajor Richter in Palermo. You must deliver them to him personally. You are not to hand the envelope to anyone else. Only Generalmajor Richter. Is that understood?"

"Yes, sir."

"It's getting late. Leave first thing in the morning. I expect you back tomorrow afternoon."

"But sir., Tomorrow is Saturday. Would it be okay if I stayed an extra day to attend Mass on Sunday? There are many beautiful churches in Palermo. I admire them as I travel through the center of town. I haven't been to Mass since arriving in Sicily."

After lighting a cigarette, Bonetti removed it from his mouth. "You, Bianchi? You are telling me you go to Mass. I'm supposed to believe that?"

"Sir, it is men like me who really need to attend Mass. I am a sinner."

Bonetti shook his head. "Okay, Bianchi. The other messengers are here to cover your ass. Stay in Palermo and cleanse your soul, or whatever you plan on doing. But I need you back here early Monday morning."

"Yes, sir. Thank you, sir."

* * *

The stop in San Giuseppe had taken longer than he had hoped. *Generale di Divisione* Casio was inspecting anti-aircraft guns and didn't arrive until lunchtime. Once Casio signed the documents, Vito made his way to Palermo. He located the German HQ and Generalmajor Richter's office.

Vito entered the foyer. In Italian, he said, "I'm here to see Generalmajor Richter. I need to deliver this document to him personally."

The two Wehrmacht soldiers behind the desk looked at each other. One went into the back office. An *Oberstleutnant* appeared and addressed Vito in Italian. "What do you need, Caporale?"

"I was instructed to hand deliver this document to Generalmajor Richter."

The officer reached his hand out. "I'll give it to him."

"I'm sorry but I was told I must hand it to him personally."

"He is not here."

"When will he be returning?"

"Who is the document from?"

"It was signed by *Generale di Divisione* Casio in San Giuseppe."

With no further comment to Vito, the officer returned to the back office.

Vito remained in the entranceway. On the wall, hung a photo of Adolf Hitler. Vito's stomach turned. He questioned who he hated more for dragging Italy into war—Hitler or Mussolini.

The *Oberstleutnant* returned. "You are to take the envelope to Generalmajor Richter at his residence. It is seven blocks from here on Via Cantore. It is in a roundabout. There is an angel fountain in the middle."

* * *

When Vito turned the corner, he recognized the balcony. It was the same balcony where he had seen the girl. He put the bike on its kickstand and approached the front door—his eyes glancing up at the second-floor wrought-iron railing.

He knocked. After waiting, he knocked again. The door was opened by a pretty girl, but not the one who had been on the balcony the other day.

"You have a document?" she asked in Italian.

He held it up yet said nothing.

"Enter," she said, before making her way up the stairs.

The stairway was on the right.

To his left was a small sitting room with two chairs and a short sofa.

Above his head he heard heavy boots heading to the landing of the stairwell. Richter made his way down the steps. Like his previous sighting, his pants were on, yet his tunic was off, exposing a white shirt. His suspenders hung to his side. At the bottom of the stairs, he snatched the envelope from Vito's hand and made his way into the sitting room. He sat, pulled a pair of reading glasses from his shirt pocket, and ripped open the envelope. The document appeared to be lengthy. Vito waited for instructions.

As Richter read, movement at the top of the stairs caught Vito's attention. It was her. The exotic girl from the balcony. She wore a short red nightgown that appeared to have nothing underneath it but her. Her brown legs and feet were bare. She was magnificent. After bringing a cigarette to her mouth, she blew out the smoke, smiled at him, then turned and withdrew into a room.

NEW YORK CITY

As Nino rode the bus home from work, he took several deep breaths, grateful to soon be in the comfort of his home and away from the stresses of his day.

Jack Dugan had put Nino in charge of the welding shop, a skill he had no experience with. This caused resentment among the older yard workers who questioned and resented having to work under the supervision of someone so young and inexperienced. Their sarcasm and verbal taunts toward Nino were relentless, yet he held his head high and counted his blessings, happy that he was able to support his family with a wage that was higher than that of many New Yorkers. There was also tension among his men because since the war had broken out, and white workers were sent overseas to fight, black workers were hired to replace them. Five of the forty-two men who worked under Nino were minorities. Although this was common throughout the shipyard, most of the foreman gave the minorities the hardest, dirtiest, and most dangerous jobs, while shielding the white workers from those tasks whenever possible. However, Nino insisted on an equitable system of rotating his workers in and out of those assignments. On more than one occasion Nino had been confronted by a group of white workers in an attempt to intimidate him into changing this policy, yet Nino held his ground.

The bus stopped two blocks from Nino's apartment, and when he exited, Angelo stood before him wearing the uniform of a sergeant in the U.S. Army Air Corps. Nino embraced him. "It is good to see you, Angelo. I wasn't expecting you."

"I just left your apartment. Hannah said you get off the bus every evening about this same time. I figured I would greet my little brother."

"You look sharp in that uniform. How was training?"

"It was brutal. The heat in Florida makes New York summers seem frigid."

They turned and made their way back to Nino's apartment. Nino said, "How long are you home?"

"I have to catch a train in two days. I'm headed to Norfolk,

Virginia. From there, my squadron will board a ship to someplace."

"Where is someplace?"

"They won't tell us. But rumor has it we are going to west Africa to train with the RAF."

PALERMO SICILY

Vito stood across the street from the fountain and watched the balcony. Then his eyes dropped to the front door.

He rubbed the back of his neck and looked around, then crossed the street, stopped, studied his surroundings, then knocked. There was no answer, so he knocked again.

"He's not there," the voice of an elderly woman shouted. He turned around but saw no one.

"Up here."

Across the street, Vito saw an old woman sweeping her second-floor balcony.

"The German general. He left this morning."

Vito crossed the street and looked up at her.

She said, "He arrives on Thursday evening. Then leaves on Sunday morning. He just left an hour ago. The house will be vacant until Thursday afternoon when his mistresses arrive before him."

Vito said, "Do you know the names of his mistresses. In particular, the dark-skinned one. She looks Arab. Do you know anything about her?"

"What is to know? She is a whore. When she is not here, she is at the brothel near the waterfront."

The old woman stopped sweeping and studied Vito. "You

weren't looking for the general, were you? You were looking for one of his women."

"No, no, of course not. I was looking for the general. I am a messenger. Someone told me he had a message to take to field headquarters. The person who told this to me must be mistaken. Thank you for your time. I am sorry to have bothered you."

As Vito turned toward his motorcycle, the woman on the balcony shouted. "Young man."

Vito turned around.

"Let me warn you. I am a good judge of character. You seem like a good boy. Be careful with her. I sense she is trouble."

* * *

"The dark-skinned one. That's who I would like to see," Vito said.

"You need to be more specific. We have three dark-skinned girls."

"The one that looks Arab."

"That narrows it down to two."

"The one that spends the weekends with the German general."

Lucia raised her eyebrows. "How do you know that?"

"I have been to his house on military business. I saw her there."

"Her name is Gabrielle," Lucia said.

"Then I want to spend my time with Gabrielle."

"I don't think you can afford her. You only have two stripes on your uniform. Two stripes doesn't pay you enough for Gabrielle. I'll set you up with one of our other girls."

Vito removed a wad of bills from his tunic and tossed them on the counter. "I can afford her."

"She is French. Do you speak French?"

"My mother was French. Why are you trying to talk me out of my time with her?"

"It will be another twenty minutes before she is available."

"I'll wait."

* * *

Vito saw an Italian officer emerge from the back hallway and leave by the front door.

Lucia said, "She is the second room on the right."

Without responding, Vito entered the hallway.

As he approached the door, his heart raced. He had always been confident around women. Why did this one rattle him?

When Vito entered, she was lying under the covers smoking a cigarette. She had folded her nightgown neatly and laid it in a chair.

In French, he said, "My name is Vito Bianchi, and you are even more beautiful up close."

Gabrielle said, "You were the one at the bottom of the stairs at General Richter's apartment."

"*Oui.*"

"How did you find me?"

He shrugged. "From the moment I first saw you, I knew I must see you again."

"You didn't answer my question. How did you find me?"

"Why does it matter?"

She took a drag of her cigarette, then crushed it into the ashtray on the nightstand. "Your time is limited; do you want to spend it talking?"

He sat on the bed, took her hand and kissed it. "You are one of God's greatest creations. You are magnificent."

She tilted her head back and laughed. "You are a charmer, aren't you?"

He leaned down and kissed her neck.

She pulled the covers back to expose her nude body. "You might want to take your clothes off."

"You are lovely. I have never seen anyone so exquisite," Vito said as he unbuttoned his tunic and threw it on the floor. "Will you go to dinner with me sometime?"

"I don't date customers."

He paused, reached down, and picked up his tunic from the floor and put it back on. "Then I will not be your customer." As he buttoned it, he asked, "Will you go to dinner with me now?"

Smiling, she said, "I don't know if I should be flattered that you want to take me to dinner or insulted that I'm lying here nude and you can resist me."

"Oh, my lovely, do not be insulted. Your nude form is truly glorious. It is taking everything I have to keep from touching you. But to me, you are not a transaction. You, my darling, are someone who I could spend a lifetime worshiping."

She shook her head, then said, "When do you want to take me to dinner?"

"When can you go?"

"Tonight."

"Where do you live? I want to pick you up."

"I don't let customers know where I live."

"I'm not a customer, remember?"

"I don't know you. You must earn your way into my apartment. There is a restaurant at the corner of *Via Albanese* and *Via Cavi*. It is called *Cucina delle nonne*. I will see you at 1900 hours."

* * *

Vito arrived early. Next to Gabrielle's place setting, he placed a bouquet of flowers. He took several deep breaths. He was sweating as he stared at the front door. It was 1910 hours.

What if she doesn't show up?

The waiter approached. May I bring you something before your companion arrives?

"Bring a bottle of red wine."

He drank the first glass, then the second.

More time passed. The bottle was nearly empty. Vito looked at his watch. It was 1950 hours.

"Would you like to order food, *signore?*" The waiter asked.

"No, thank you. Just bring me my check."

* * *

Gabrielle sat in the center of her bed. The room was dark, and Vito turned on a lamp. When he approached her, she sat back against the wall.

"I'm sorry I stood you up. Please don't be mad."

He sat next to her. "I thought something had happened to you. I have done nothing but think about you since we were together. Where were you?"

"I changed my mind about having dinner with you."

"Why?"

"I don't know. I just had a bad feeling."

"A bad feeling? Did you think I would hurt you?"

"Not physically."

"How?"

"Vito, girls like me don't..."

"Don't what?"

"We don't fall in love. When we do, we get our hearts broken."

"It was just a dinner. Nothing more."

"Maybe to you."

"Forgive me, but I'm confused."

"Just go, Vito. I'll tell Lucia to give you your money back."

"I don't want my money back. I want to spend time with you away from here."

"Why are you trying so hard?"

"Because you are worth it."

"I won't always be worth it to you."

"You won't always do this."

"You mean be a whore?"

"I have never looked at you that way. When I see you, I see a beautiful woman who deserves to be loved."

"When do you have to go back?"

"Tonight."

"How much time did you pay for?"

"Thirty minutes."

"Close the door and come here."

1943

CHAPTER 8

W ashington D.C. was a city immersed in egotistical personalities, many of whom resented William Donovan for his close relationship with FDR. Donovan was an influential hard charger and had built a career with charisma and a forceful personality. Some had questioned why he had unlimited access to the Oval Office. The few who knew what Donovan did for the president never questioned their close relationship.

"You wanted to see me, Mr. President?"

"Please have a seat."

Roosevelt removed his cigarette holder from an ashtray, placed it in his mouth, then wheeled his chair from around his desk, before resting it near Donovan's chair.

"Bill, the clock is ticking, and I need you to act fast. My visit with Churchill in Casablanca resolved many questions in Europe. Foremost, what is our next step now that it appears we will be victorious in North Africa? My first choice was a massive invasion in western Europe. Although I initially protested an invasion from the south, that is in fact what we have agreed to do. As we have discussed, the Russians are becoming increasingly impatient waiting for a counterforce to relieve their fight in eastern Europe. Churchill believes that if we invade from the south, Hitler will have no choice but to redirect forces from the east and drive them south to protect their underbelly."

"Are we looking at southern France, Mr. President?"

"No, Bill—Sicily. That's where you come in. Unfortunately, out of the potential choices for an invasion, Sicily is the one where we have the least intelligence. Our contacts there are limited and unreliable. We need to know force strength, landscape, location of radar sites and airfields. We also need to know the mood of the civilian population and the morale of the troops, both German and Italian."

"How soon do you need this information?"

"Now."

"What is our timeline for invasion?"

"This summer."

"It's February, Mr. President. So, you need this information in the next three months."

"No, we need it much sooner than that. Eisenhower has requested it to help plan the invasion."

Donovan said, "My first instinct is to locate U.S. citizens who have family in Sicily. There are many first- and second-generation Sicilians, particularly in New York. Many of them came here to escape Mussolini's fascism. Perhaps we have resources more readily available than we think."

"I like that, Bill. That is why you have the job you have. The question is, how do we decide who to contact? How can we determine which Italians in this country despise Mussolini and

Hitler enough to help us obtain this intelligence?"

"Mr. President, does the name Cesare Mori ring a bell to you?"

"It sounds familiar."

"During the 1920s and 1930s, Mussolini sent Mori from Rome to Sicily to drive out the mafia. He used extreme and often brutal tactics to accomplish the task. With a rare exception, he was successful. To this day, there are members of Sicilian crime families incarcerated on various islands around Sicily. However, many members of those families escaped and came to America."

"And they simply transferred their crime activities to our soil."

"That is correct, Mr. President. However, some of them undoubtedly still have connections in Sicily. Connections who would rather cut Mussolini's throat than fight for him."

Roosevelt drew on his cigarette and gazed off into space while pondering the suggestion from Donovan. "Under the circumstances, I'm not opposed to implementing this strategy. However, it is a strategy that must never be made public, even after the war. We must never let a single member of Congress know of this plan. If my political opponents caught wind of the fact that we were using the New York City mafia to help us win the war, they would bury me with it."

"I believe I can do this with a small, trustworthy team. I will immediately have them dig deep and locate likely candidates."

"Once you find these 'likely candidates,' what is the next step?"

"Train them. Then send them to Sicily."

PALERMO SICILY

"It is wonderful to see you, Vito. It's been thirteen days."

"I'm sorry, my darling. It's not that I haven't been thinking of you. All of my runs have been to the eastern side of the island. I had to be in Porticello late last evening, so now I'm here."

"Did you pay just to see me?"

"Of course. Lucia won't let me see you for free."

"Let's leave."

"Will she just let you go?"

"Lucia doesn't own me. There are many girls here to make her money today. Besides, I was with Richter the last three days. He always wears me out. I need a break."

Vito looked away. She regretted blurting out the statement so casually. It occurred to her he didn't view the other men she slept with as merely transactions.

"I'm sorry, Vito. I shouldn't have—"

"It's okay. Let's go have fun, my darling. I don't need to be back until the morning."

Throughout Palermo, bells rang. Citizens bustled in the streets, making their way to the various churches peppered throughout the center of town.

As they walked, Gabrielle asked, "Do you believe in God, Vito?"

"Si, of course. Do you?"

"I'd like to. But I think that if there is a God, I'm mad at him for allowing so much evil to exist in the world. How do you explain that?"

"I can't. I'm not God."

"Do you pray?"

"Not very often."

"Then you don't actually believe in God, do you?"

"Why do you say that?"

"Because if you truly believed in God with your whole heart, would you not always be talking to God?"

"I'm freeing him up to help others. He has already blessed me. Take you, for example. Here I am spending my Sunday with his most magnificent creation. It would be rather selfish of me to drop to my knees and beg for more, don't you think?"

"You don't believe that?"

"Oh, but I do."

Vito reached for Gabrielle's hand. She pulled hers away.

"Why won't you let me hold your hand?"

"Because I don't want you to."

"Why?"

She stopped and looked up at him. "I don't want to get too close to anyone."

"You don't want to love someone?"

"Of course, I do."

"You don't want to love me. Is that it?"

"You treat me nice. You don't treat me like..."

"Like what?"

She glanced down to maintain her composure, then looked back up at him. A tear rolled down her cheek. "You don't treat me like a whore and I'm afraid that's all I am. That is all I have ever been. One day soon you will realize that, and you will be gone. I just think I am better off being who I am rather than pretending I can be something else."

Vito pulled her close. "Are we going to have this conversation every time we're together? I've already told you I don't see you like that. You are a beautiful young woman who I want to spend time with."

"Why?" She pushed him away, turned her back, and walked away.

"Where are you going?"

"I'm going home. Do you want to come with me?"

TUNISIA

The metal hut was stifling hot, and the restless crew of the B-25 wanted to get on with it. His palms were sweating, and his throat dry. It would be his first mission, and Sergeant Angelo DiVincenzo was eager to employ his countless hours of training. He had been added at the last minute as a second waist gunner.

The captain said, "Aerial reconnaissance has reported a new radar installation near Mussomeli. Our job will be to find it and eliminate it."

"How many will be with us?" The copilot asked.

"Three more B-25s."

"No escorts?"

"Not this run. The good news is that the deadliest of the anti-aircraft placements are fixed along the coast. Mussomeli is near the center of the island. We may hit a few mobile anti-aircraft units, but our biggest challenge will be the Luftwaffe and the Italian Royal Air Force."

The bombardier said, "Do we have aerial photographs, so I know what I'm looking for?"

Major Rawlings handed the photos to him. "We are wheels up in two hours, gentlemen. I'll see you on the flight line."

The Island of Sicily

The blasts echoed off the side of the mountain. Isabella stopped the truck at the side of the road and ran to the top of a hill. Across a valley, a mobile antiaircraft gun fired into the sky. She looked up to see a single twin-engine aircraft. Behind it trailed two fighter planes.

* * *

"I can't find the target. Are we in the right spot?" the bombardier asked.

"It's supposed to be down there," Major Rawlings said.

The tail gunner said, "Our ass is hot. Two fighters closing in."

Ack-ack from ground fire below exploded around them.

Angelo took hold of the starboard side waist gun. He saw nothing.

The copilot said, "It's time to scrub the mission. They've either moved it, or those photos they gave us are from somewhere else because there is no radar down there."

"It has to be," Major Rawlings said. "Just one more pass."

After spotting one of the German ME-109s fighters, Angelo opened fire. Round after round of fifty-caliber machine gun tracers passed in front of the target. He adjusted his point of origin two degrees. Moments later, a puff of smoke escaped the engine of the fighter plane, followed by thick black smoke.

"I hit one!" Angelo shouted.

"I have the other in my sights," the tail gunner said.

He heard thud-thud-thud as shrapnel from another round of ack-ack penetrated the fuselage. Angelo turned to see a sizeable opening on the port side. The other waist gunner lay on the deck. It had blown his face off.

"The left engine is on fire," shouted the pilot. "We are going down. Everybody out. Now!"

The plane banked to the left. The hole in the port side was large enough that Angelo could see that the wing surface around the engine was ablaze. He stumbled, then dropped to his knees before slamming against what the explosion left of the fuselage. He felt lightheaded. As he reached for something to pull himself up, he noticed his right leg was awash in blood. The area from his upper thigh to his boot looked like it had been through a meat grinder. Overcome with a mental fog, his thinking and reactions slowed. Inches from Angelo's face, the tail gunner was screaming at him while lifting him to his feet. Angelo watched the tail gunner's lips move but couldn't make out what he was saying. To keep his wits about him, Angelo took several deep breaths. With the plane now flying on its side, the tail gunner grabbed hold of Angelo's parachute release and shoved him through the large hole.

While spinning like a top, Angelo felt his body jerk. His chute took hold of the air, and he looked up to see a white mushroom above his head. On the horizon, a fiery blaze that was once his plane was taking a nosedive. He saw three more parachutes, which meant that only four of the six crew members had escaped. Looking down, he saw that an open area surrounded by greenery waited to catch him. His eyes closed and blackness overcame him.

* * *

The road climbed and fell sharply, and Isabella found herself airborne more than once. She guessed where the chute would come down, and made her way there, eventually leaving the road and driving over a grassy area before cutting through the woods. She had lost sight of the falling airman, but continued to her original destination. Slowing her speed, she slalomed around trees before arriving in an open area encircled by shrubbery.

He was lying face down, his chute fluttered meters away. She made her way to him and knelt. His lower extremities, particularly his right leg, were covered in blood.

Realizing that soldiers would soon arrive to capture him, she considered her options. She rolled him on his back and disconnected his harness, then removed the handgun from its shoulder holster, which was embossed with the letters, U.S. She climbed into the truck, placed the weapon under the seat, then reversed slowly until the tailgate was only a few feet from the downed airman.

Angelo wasn't a large man, but Isabella was small in stature herself. She bent down. She flipped her hair over her shoulder and onto her back. She put her hands under Angelo's shoulders and tried to hoist him into the truck. She stopped to rest. Angelo eased his head from side to side before opening his eyes and looking at her.

"Can you stand?" she asked in Italian, not expecting an American to comprehend the statement.

"*Dove Sono?*" Angelo asked, enquiring as to his whereabouts.

"You speak Italian?"

"Si." Angelo said, forcing himself to remain cognizant, although he was woozy.

"You must stand. I can't lift you. Please hurry. If they find you, they will beat you."

Angelo reached up for Isabella and wrapped his arm around

her shoulder. She lifted with both legs. He could only use his left.

"Lie in the back of the truck. I'll cover you."

She dragged the parachute into the woods and attempted to bury it under dried leaves, but most of it remained exposed.

After getting into the truck cab, she traveled deeper into the forest and stopped before leaping out.

Glancing into the truck bed, she said, "Lie still."

She looked for any loose vegetation she could find—leaves, twigs, and branches, mainly. She tried to cover him completely, but she heard vehicles approaching.

"We must go. Be still," she said to Angelo before getting into the truck.

She made her way down the same unmarked path she had entered the woods through, driving slowly and keeping an ear out for the vehicles. She heard them again and stopped. The sound of the military machines grew louder. She stopped behind a dense tree line. They drove by—four troop carriers in all. When she could no longer hear them, she put the truck in gear.

* * *

Bellissima Valle comprised one hundred and twenty-four acres and was in the center of one of the most luscious valleys in Sicily. The growing season wouldn't start for eight more weeks, and most of their field hands were off until spring. Isabella's father, Lorenzo, was in Catania on business, and her grandfather, Bruno, would be preparing dinner in the main house at this hour.

The citrus trees were bare this time of year, which concerned her, because when they were full, they blocked the view of the various outbuildings they had scattered throughout their orchards. They used them to shelter tractors, harvesting tools, and bushel baskets.

Isabella knew of a barn toward the back of their property that was located at the edge of a wooded area. A narrow road cut through the woods behind the barn. She believed this to be the safest place to hide the downed American airman.

She arrived at the little barn, which contained an ox wagon they hadn't used in years. Next to the wagon was an open area, large enough to pull the truck into.

After closing the barn door, she climbed a ladder to the hayloft, which was stacked high with wooden bushel baskets. There was a small path leaving her little room to the front, where she opened a hatch, allowing both air and light to enter.

* * *

Angelo opened his eyes and removed the debris the girl had placed over his face.

He heard a noise from the hayloft and glanced up to see a girl climbing down a ladder. She wore a gray, short sleeve, knee-length dress. She appeared to be young, late teens—perhaps younger. But he hoped not.

She made her way down the ladder and hopped in the back of the truck with him. "You are awake."

Dirt smeared her face.

"Where am I?" Angelo asked.

"On my family's citrus farm."

"Is this Sicily?"

"Si, your plane was shot down."

"What about my other crew members? Do you know anything of them?"

"They landed far away from you," she said as she removed the debris from his mangled leg.

"How many did you see?"

"I need to go to the house and get some fresh water and bandages to clean your wound."

"How many of my crew members did you see come down?"

"You were the closest one, so I came after you. I am unaware of their fate, or how many there were."

"What will you do with me?"

She paused before answering. "I don't know."

"Why are you helping me?"

"Because if I don't, they will find you and beat you mercilessly."

"How do you know that?"

"I've watched them. He was a British airman. I doubt he lived through it."

Isabella leaped from the truck and cleared away a small section under the loft. She took the leaves from the rear of the vehicle and made a bed. She lowered the tailgate. "I will help you get out, but you need to move on your own."

Angelo sat up and made his way toward Isabella who waited at the tailgate. He scooted to the edge and put his arm around her neck before sliding off the edge—landing on his left leg, leaving his injured right suspended. She guided him to the makeshift bed where he sat in the leaves.

"I'm going to the house. I'll bring you food, water to drink, and water and bandages to clean your leg."

Angelo stared up at her. It struck him how someone so young could be in control of this uninvited and difficult situation.

"What's your name," he asked.

"Isabella Leone."

"You are brave."

She shrugged. "Maybe, I don't know."

As she brushed the leaves from her dress, she asked, "How is it that your Italian is so good?"

"My father is Sicilian. He moved to America many years ago. My grandfather still lives here somewhere."

"What is your name?"

"Angelo—Angelo DiVincenzo."

Isabella froze. "Did you say DiVincenzo?"

"Si."

"Is your grandfather Alfonso DiVincenzo?"

"Si, do you know him?"

* * *

The barn door creaked open. Angelo reached for his Colt 1911, only to find the holster empty. Lying motionless, he felt relieved when Isabella turned the corner.

She set a bucket of water down, then threw a basket of bread and a few bandages on the ground next to him. "Mend yourself."

"Why are you angry? What did I do?"

She crossed her arms and stared back at him.

Angelo squinted his eyes and tilted his head to the side. "What's happening?"

Isabella said, "Why did it have to be you I saved?"

"I don't claim to be the smartest guy, but I'm confused. What has happened? When you found me, you were a sweet girl who risked her life to save mine. Now you look like you could kill me yourself. Will you tell me what I did?"

"You did nothing. It's your grandfather. He is a murderer

125

and a tyrant. He has terrorized half the families on this island for decades, including mine."

"I know nothing of my grandfather other than his name. I have never met him. My father seldom spoke of him. If he has done something to you, your family, or the people of Sicily, I'm sorry, but that has nothing to do with me."

Isabella turned her nose up and stared into the hayloft as though something up there might inspire her words. She shook her head before dropping to her knees next to him, then placed the breadbasket on his chest. "Shut up and eat."

She reached for the water bucket and submerged a tin cup before handing it to him.

He emptied it with one swig. "Can I have more, please?"

She gave him more water before grabbing the bandages. "Don't drink all of it. I need some to clean your leg. "

He handed her the cup and lay down.

"I'm freezing," he said. "Do you have a blanket?"

"You are perspiring," Isabella placed the back of her hand on his forehead. "You have a fever."

She tore a bandage, dipped it into the bucket, and patted his forehead. She repeated the process several times. Angelo stared at her face. He wanted to tell her she was pretty but thought better of it.

"I brought you blankets. They are in the truck."

Angelo watched her walk away. She was tiny, almost childlike, and her skin tanned. Her actions, not her appearance, displayed her maturity.

She returned, opened one blanket, and laid two more next to him. After covering him with the first, she repeated the process with a second before kneeling beside him. "Is that better?"

"Si, thank you."

She reached into a pocket in her dress and pulled out a small bottle. "This is alcohol. I'll use it to clean your leg. It will sting." After she pulled the blanket back, exposing his shredded trousers and mangled leg, she grimaced.

"Is it that bad?" Angelo asked.

"I may need to get you to a doctor."

"And a doctor will turn me in. I think I would prefer to take my chances here."

From the same pocket as before, she removed a small set of scissors. Starting at his boot and working her way up, she cut what remained of his pant leg until she got to his upper thigh.

"I'm glad the shrapnel hit me where it did. A little higher up and I could never have any fun again."

She looked at him and held her stare. Her lips clenched. Angelo realized she was strictly business and didn't appreciate his comment.

He asked, "How old are you?"

"Why do you care?"

"Because you look so…"

"Young? Is that what you are trying to say? Do you think I'm a little girl?"

"No. I think you are…"

"You think I'm what? Spit it out." She patted his leg with a damp towel.

"I think you're beautiful."

She grinned, glanced at him, and shook her head.

"What kind of response is that?" he asked.

"You men are all the same."

"What does that mean?"

"It means you need me, so I'm beautiful. Once your leg heals and you can walk, I will go back to being a little girl."

"*Are you* a little girl?"

"I'm eighteen. How old are you?"

"I'm twenty-four."

She splashed a cloth with alcohol and applied it to his wound.

"You are an old man," she said with a grin.

"That hurt."

"What, the alcohol?"

"No. Calling me an old man."

He watched as the towels containing his blood piled up on the dirt floor next to her.

Isabella said, "There are many little pieces of metal in your leg. I really think you need a doctor."

He gripped her arm. "Please, no."

They locked eyes momentarily before she returned to work on his leg. "I'm not a doctor."

"You are doing fine. How do you know what to do?"

"I tend to our animals here—mainly our horses. My grandpapa taught me everything I know. He was a medic in the Great War. If your fever doesn't break, I may bring him here to you. I don't think he would turn you in. But I don't want to take the chance. He may turn you in because you are on our land, and he doesn't want to be accused of helping the enemy. There would be severe consequences."

"Other than your grandfather, who lives here with you?"

"Just my papa and grandpapa. My brother, Aldo was killed in North Africa."

"If your brother were alive, what would he think if he knew

you were helping the enemy? What about your papa and grandpapa? What would they do?"

"I don't know," she said. "But I don't view you as the enemy. I don't think my papa or grandpapa would either."

"I don't understand. I came here to bomb your country—to defeat you."

"Papa and grandpapa hate Mussolini. Many Italians do. They just won't say it publicly because there would be consequences."

"If anyone finds me, I'll tell them I broke into the barn and that you didn't know."

"And where did you get the food and bandages? Have you thought of that?"

"I stole them from someplace."

"You have it all figured out, don't you?"

"Can I have my gun back?"

"No."

"You just said you didn't view me as the enemy. Don't you trust me?"

"I can't be too cautious. You are an American. I'm Italian. Why should I trust you with a gun? Our countries are at war."

"I trust you, Isabella."

"You shouldn't. In the end, I may turn you in myself."

WASHINGTON D.C.
THE OFFICE OF WILLIAM DONOVAN

"Mr. Donovan, Randolph Hobbs is here to see you."

"Send him in, Miss Gruber."

"Mr. Donovan, I believe we have our candidate. Although I would consider him our second choice."

"Please explain."

"I had my connections at the FBI research first and second-generation Italian Americans who they considered to be members of organized crime, and who may also still have connections in Sicily. They presented me with a handful of subpar candidates. However, there was one who I had considered to be a pot of gold."

"Did they ask why you needed this information?"

"They know better, sir. This isn't the first time I have asked for their help. The ground rules have been well established."

"What do you give them in return?"

"Typically, cash or whiskey."

"Go on."

Hobbs lay a file on Donovan's desk and opened it to a photograph. "This man is Salvador DiVincenzo. In 1921 he moved to New York from Sicily to avoid a murder conviction. He was eighteen years old at the time and had no family here, only himself. Shortly after arriving, he mixed with the wrong crowd—other Sicilians. Most of them knew little English and couldn't find work. They quickly learned that they could survive by using strong-arm tactics extorting money. Apparently, he has a lot of charisma, and quickly climbed to the top of the various gangs that emerged. All the other thugs wound up working for him. He branched off into gambling, prostitution, and when prohibition went into effect, his business thrived from a network of illegal distilleries and speakeasies all over New York."

"I appreciate your research, Randolph, but look at this rap

sheet. He is clearly all about himself and is no patriot. He'll never help us. Besides, I'm thinking we need someone younger. Someone who can move on his feet."

"I'm getting to that, Mr. Donovan. This Salvador DiVincenzo has two sons. The first, his name is Angelo, I thought would be our man, but he was shot down recently during a bombing mission to Sicily. We currently list him as M.I.A, but I suspect a designation of K.I.A. will soon follow."

"And the other son?"

"He actually has a different last name. He uses his mother's maiden name—Servidei. I'm not certain why. My guess is to separate himself from his father, since they both live in the Bronx. The kid is squeaky clean. A few years ago, he went to Rome to become a priest. He never finished his education. Now he's married with a couple of kids. He works in the Navy Yard."

"So, other than his father, what is so special about this kid? What connections does this family have in Sicily that could work to our advantage?"

"That is the best part of all, Mr. Donovan. Salvador's father—Nino's grandfather is a man by the name of Alfonso DiVincenzo. He is the *Capo du Tutti Capi* of Sicily—the godfather. With many of the local people, he has more authority than Mussolini himself. He was one of the few mafioso who survived Cesare Mori's wrath. He is like a cockroach. Nobody, not even Mussolini, has been able to take him down."

Donovan added, "And nothing would make him happier than to see Mussolini defeated."

"And he probably has goons on his payroll scattered all throughout Sicily who can easily obtain the information we are looking for."

"This Servidei kid, does he speak Italian?" Donovan asked.

"I know his brother Angelo did. I'm assuming Nino does too. But we won't know until we talk to him."

Donovan leaned back in his chair yet remained silent.

Hobbs said, "It looks like the gears are turning, boss."

"Do you remember that Catholic priest I was telling you about?"

"Morlion? Yes, I remember."

"Get a hold of him. Tell him I need to see him."

"Yes, Mr. Donovan."

PALERMO

"You will need to stay in the bedroom when my staff arrives," General Richter said. "What we have to discuss is not for your ears."

Gabrielle stood in a knee length, white silk bathrobe. "You forget, I don't speak German. I would have no understanding of what you were saying."

"Just stay in here until I come get you. After our meeting, you can come out and mingle."

"I will bathe while you are at your meeting."

Gabrielle entered the bathroom and ran the steaming water into the tub. With her foot, she checked the temperature, withdrawing her foot and adding a touch of cold water. When the tub was full, she shut off the water.

She heard the bedroom door close. After confirming that Richter had joined the others, she returned to the bedchamber and pressed her ear to the bedroom door, where she heard the men speaking in German. Laughter erupted, then the clinking glasses as if they were toasting something.

Across the room, Richter's briefcase sat on a desk in the corner. She approached it and attempted to turn the clasps, discovering it to be locked. The trousers Richter wore earlier in the day were laying across the chair. She reached into the pocket. First the left, then the right, where she located his key ring. There were several small keys. She tried them one at a time before the fourth one opened the first latch, then the second. She opened the case, revealing several documents, none of which she could read. After removing them one by one, a map of Sicily appeared. Circled in ink were two locations north of Gela marked with red X's. He had also circled three southern beaches. One near Gela, another near Licata, and the last near Sciacca. An additional sheet revealed a diagram of a mechanical device. It was cylindrical, with three prongs protruding from the top.

She heard amplified voices. Richter said something to his officers, followed by more boisterous laughter.

She placed the papers back into the briefcase, returned the keys to the trousers and positioned them how they were before she rifled through the pockets. Gabrielle crossed the room, entered the lavatory, and carefully closed the door behind her. After hanging her robe on a hook attached to the door, she gently stepped into the tub.

BELLISSIMA VALLE

Angelo peeked through the slats of the barn. He could see movement, but it was too dark to know how many German soldiers were outside. There was laughter. One of the soldiers approached the shed until the toes of his boots were inches from the boards Angelo was staring through. Lying motionless, Angelo heard the urine spray against the side of the barn. A splash landed on his cheek. The leaves he lay in would rustle if he moved, so he remained still. The soldier buttoned his trousers and turned to rejoin his comrades as they made their way to a troop carrier idling on the road. The tailgate slammed, followed by the grinding of gears before the vehicle drove off.

Realizing that he too, felt the need to relieve himself, Angelo tried to stand, his exhaustion made it difficult. His fever had returned. His leg was throbbing. The pain was more intense than it had ever been. He made his way to the barn door and felt the cool breeze when he opened it. Hopping around to the same side as the German soldier, he unbuttoned his trousers. He didn't notice it until he had finished, but as he turned to make his way back into the barn, he saw a Mauser rifle leaning against the planks.

The German — he will return for it.

THE BRONX NEW YORK

Hannah sat next to Solomon's highchair. She wiped the face of the fourteen-month-old after he had reached for a handful of oatmeal in a futile attempt to feed himself. Lilia sat beside Nino.

"I hope Mama brings the paper with her this morning," Nino said. "I can't stop thinking of Angelo. I need to know what is going on in North Africa."

"You must trust in God. He will protect Angelo."

"For once, you have more faith than me. I don't have a good feeling."

"That's because you have no control over the war," Hannah said. "You're a take-charge person. When there is a problem, you get busy fixing it. With this war, you feel you're a bystander, and it's eating you up inside. You want to get involved."

"You know me well."

They heard footsteps coming up the stairs. Nino sat Lilia on the floor, stood, and opened the door to see Maria. She wrapped her arms around him and sobbed uncontrollably.

"Mama, what's wrong?"

Maria pulled away. She tried to speak but couldn't.

"Is it Angelo?" Nino asked.

Maria nodded her head yes, still unable to speak.

Nino led her to the table and pulled a chair out.

After sitting, she removed a handkerchief from her purse, touching it to her nose. "His plane has been shot down somewhere over the Mediterranean Sea."

Nino bent down and wrapped his arms around her. He looked at Hannah. Her tears flowed as she removed Solomon from his highchair, holding him tightly and kissing the side of his head.

BELLISSIMA VALLE

"I brought biscuits for you," Isabella said as she knelt next to Angelo.

She shook him, but he remained asleep. His forehead was hot to the touch. Again, she shook him, this time with a sense of urgency. "Wake up, Angelo."

She leaped to her feet, climbed into the truck, and sped to the house.

Isabella was grateful that her papa was in the fields working when she located Bruno in the house. The journey back to Angelo was tense. Bruno was behind the steering wheel.

"Isabella, you had no business hiding an American airman without telling us. Do you know what would happen to all of us if he were found on our property?"

"I'm sorry, grandpapa, but I couldn't bear the thought of what would have happened to him if they caught him."

When they arrived, Bruno pulled the blanket back and gazed at Angelo's leg. "We need to get him to the house and break his fever. This shrapnel must come out."

"Did I wait too long to get you?"

"As I told you, you should have never brought him here in the first place, but you did, so we have an obligation to save him."

Bruno, a large, burly man, lifted Angelo in his arms as though he were an injured pony. "Bring the blankets, Isabella."

As he left the barn to place him in the truck, Isabella snatched the blankets from Angelo's makeshift bed. With her feet, she stirred the leaves to remove the indentation left by Angelo's body. Her foot hit something. She reached into the leaves and found the Mauser.

Where did he get this?

She placed it behind a stack of crates.

"Isabella, what is taking so long?" Her grandfather shouted from outside of the barn.

"I'm coming."

Climbing into the bed of the truck with Angelo, she covered him with the blankets.

From the other side of the tree line, they heard a vehicle approaching.

"Someone is coming, Isabella. We must go."

Isabella lay next to Angelo. Bruno drove off, cutting between the trees of the orchard and climbing a small incline. Isabella raised her head and peeked back at the barn. She watched as a German *Kübelwagen* came to a stop next to it.

* * *

Lorenzo Leone pumped water from the well at the side of his house and washed his face. Though not concerned, he questioned where his father and daughter were. He looked up at the truck speeding from the orchard to see Bruno behind the wheel. He met him at the courtyard.

"What is going on here?" he asked as he saw Isabella in the back. Bruno climbed in the truck bed with her.

Bruno said. "Isabella found this American airman. He's injured. I need to mend his leg. It is swollen from shrapnel."

"Why did you bring him here? Are you both crazy? Do you know what would happen if they caught us with him?"

Bruno said. "Help me get him in the house."

"Did you hear me?" Lorenzo said. "They will arrest us if they find him here."

As they scooted his body to the edge of the truck bed, Angelo's eyes opened momentarily, but soon closed again. Lorenzo grabbed Angelo's legs, and Bruno cradled his upper body. They took him through the front door and laid him on the kitchen table.

Bruno said, "Isabella, get me several buckets of water, alcohol, towels, and blankets. While you do that, I'll get my surgical kit."

They scrambled from the room, yet Lorenzo remained and looked down at the injured American. He thought of his son Aldo.

When Isabella and Bruno returned, Lorenzo turned toward the door. Before storming out of the house, he said, "I don't like this. If he survives, we are turning him over to the authorities."

Isabella hovered over the face of the unconscious Angelo, patting his forehead with a damp cloth. She watched Bruno wrap his leg with bandages. "Will he survive, grandpapa?"

"I don't know. I've removed the larger pieces, but I'm afraid there may be smaller fragments I'm unaware of. All we can do is keep him comfortable and try to drive his fever down."

The kitchen door flung open. Lorenzo shouted, "A German vehicle is approaching. There are two soldiers in it. We need to get him upstairs. We'll take him to Aldo's room. Papa, grab his legs."

Lorenzo positioned his hands under Angelo's arms and lifted. They guided him up the stairs while Isabella trailed behind. They placed him in Aldo's bed and covered him with a blanket.

When they came down, bloodstains were visible on the table.

Lorenzo said, "Isabella, clean that up. We'll step out and greet the soldiers outside."

They were met in the courtyard by a German *Oberfeldwebel* and an Italian *Capitano* acting as his interpreter.

"How may we help you?" Lorenzo asked.

"Gentlemen," the Italian said. "My name is Capitano Giovani Pudda. I am with the Italian 10th Motorized Division. Gesturing toward the German, "This is Oberfeldwebel Dettmer. We are sorry to trouble you, but a group of German soldiers stopped on your property last evening to relieve themselves, and unfortunately, one of them left his Mauser behind. He is being detained by his command until we retrieve the weapon.

He believes he left it leaning against one of your barns near the woods. We searched the perimeter of the structure but could not locate it. Is it possible you may be holding it for us? If so, the soldier who left it would be most grateful if you would return it."

"We know nothing of a weapon," Lorenzo said. "However, if we locate such a firearm, we will most certainly return it to you. How can we contact you?"

"We are stationed on the property of Mr. Alfonso DiVincenzo. Are you familiar with his compound?"

"Everyone on the island is," Bruno said.

After a brief discussion between Pudda and Oberfeldwebel Dettmer, Pudda said to Lorenzo, "Our journey today has been rather dusty. Would you mind if we came in for some cool water?"

Lorenzo looked at Bruno, then back at Pudda. "No, of course not. Please come in."

Isabella had finished setting the table for lunch when Pudda and Dettmer followed Lorenzo and Bruno into the kitchen. The place settings were on top of a white tablecloth she used to cover the bloodstains.

Lorenzo approached the faucet, filled two glasses, and handed them to their guests.

"Thank you for your hospitality. This water is refreshing," Pudda said.

While Pudda made small talk with Lorenzo and Bruno, Dettmer paced the room. He sipped his water while glancing at family photos and looking out of the back door. He then turned and asked Pudda a question.

Pudda then addressed Lorenzo. "Mr. Leone, we recently

shot down an American bomber. We believe we have recovered all the crew members but one. We found his parachute near here, and there were bloodstains and tire tracks near the same location. When we were searching the barn on the far end of your property, we also located blood mixed in among some leaves on the dirt floor."

Bruno spoke up. "The blood was left over from a hog I recently slaughtered. We have fresh meat available if you would like to join us for lunch."

"We appreciate the offer; however, we need to continue our search."

"Perhaps next time," Lorenzo said.

"Perhaps."

After an uncomfortable silence, Pudda added, "There is one more thing. When we pulled up to the barn, a pickup like the one parked outside was pulling away. Would you mind if we were to search your property?"

Lorenzo said, "Search wherever you wish. We have barns and sheds scattered all throughout our land. Or maybe he is in the woods."

"We were thinking more along the lines of your home."

Lorenzo stepped toward Pudda and loomed over the shorter man. "Are you suggesting we might be harboring the enemy?"

"I'm not suggesting anything. Why are you so defensive?"

"Capitano, the body of my son is currently resting somewhere in North Africa. He gave his life in battle defending the very Italian soil we stand on. I suggest you and your German friend leave my home."

Pudda translated the conversation to Dettmer, who upon

hearing the interpretation stared coldly at Lorenzo and spoke in German to Pudda.

Pudda in turn addressed Lorenzo. "Oberfeldwebel Dettmer expresses his condolences for the loss of your son and because Germany and Italy are allies, *for now*, we will respect your wishes and leave your property."

CHAPTER 9

"I need your help. And we must act fast." William Donovan said as he offered Father Morlion the seat across from his desk.

"And what do you need my help with?"

"I can't give you details, other than to say I need to recruit a man. Not just any man, but a specific man. His name is Nino Servidei. He is a devout Catholic. In 1938 he traveled to Rome to become a priest. While there, he met a woman and gave up the priesthood to marry her. They are currently living in the Bronx with their two children."

"What am I to tell Mr. Servidei when I meet him?"

"That's the tricky part. In theory, you and I have never met. Yet I need you to arrange a meeting between him and me."

"With all respect, have you considered contacting him yourself?"

"I have. However, I considered the fact that because you are a priest and are on board with our cause, you may be more influential."

"I will do what I can, but he is going to ask me what we

need him for. What should I tell him?"

"I can't tell you that. I can't even tell *him* that. Not until he has been fully assessed and trained, can we brief him."

"When do you want me to leave?"

"I would like you to catch the train to New York tomorrow."

"Do you have an address?"

"Yes."

"Once I find him, I'll wait for the right opportunity to approach him."

"Don't wait too long. We need him now."

"I'll be on the morning train."

"There is one more thing, Father Morlion."

"Yes."

"His brother was shot down during a bombing run. He may have been killed."

THE BRONX NEW YORK
THE CHURCH OF OUR LADY OF MERCY

An array of candles illuminated the altar. Nino had just lit one for Angelo.

He knelt and prayed for his brother's soul. His faith was deep, and his talks with God were penetrating. Until he met Hannah, Nino had led a life of solitude, yet he seldom felt lonely, for he always felt God's presence.

He crossed himself and rose to his feet. When he turned, a priest stood behind him. A priest Nino had never seen before.

"Good evening, father."

"Good evening, Nino."

"I'm sorry, father. I have a rather good memory. I don't

believe we have ever met. How do you know my name?"

"I make it a point to know important people."

"You clearly have me mistaken for a different Nino."

"You are Nino Servidei, correct?

"Yes."

"Do you have a moment to chat?"

Nino hesitated, tilted his head, and studied the priest. "Where would you like to talk?"

He watched Father Morlion scan the church. Except for two others at the altar and a woman in the second pew, the church was empty.

He pointed. "How about the back corner? It is quiet there."

They made their way to the back pew and moved to the end. There was a wide marble column that blocked them from the view of anyone entering the church.

"Nino, my name is Father Felix Morlion. I am looking for people to help me—Catholics in particular. Catholics with a strong faith who are bilingual and have been to Europe."

Nino crossed his arms and remained silent.

Father Morlion said, "I understand your skepticism. Unfortunately, I can't tell you the specifics right now. My purpose today is simply to plant a seed and give you something to think about."

"What do you want me to think about?"

"The world is evil, Nino."

"It can be, yes."

"When you were in Italy, what did you see?"

"I don't understand."

"How were people being treated? Specifically, Jews. How were Jews being treated?"

"They were being oppressed. Many of their rights had been removed."

"And that was in Italy. Italy is an ally of Germany. How do you think Jews have been treated in other parts of Europe? Poland and Belgium for example."

"I've heard rumors."

"What have you heard?"

"That they are being taken away and are not returning."

"Those rumors are true. But it is even worse than that. Jews are being murdered. In Eastern Europe, the Nazis have marched into villages, rounded up the Jewish population and slaughtered them. Men, women and children have been forced into the woods, stripped naked and machine gunned simply because they are Jews."

"How do you know this?"

"I have contacts all over Europe. Catholic priests and nuns in these villages have witnessed what I just told you. They have made their way to other parts of Europe—England, Spain and Portugal. They have made their sightings known."

"I don't understand. What you claim is sickening, but what does this have to do with me?"

"The American government is looking for people. Brave Catholics who can travel to Europe and help the cause."

"What cause?"

"The war effort."

"Why Catholics and why me?"

"I can't get into details. I don't even have all the specifics. But from the little I know, there is a precise mission that is critical to the war effort. A mission that, if successful, could save thousands of lives."

THE BRONX NEW YORK
NINO AND HANNAH'S APARTMENT

He liked to count the cars, telling himself he wasn't going back in until he reached one hundred. When traffic was light, Nino would be out on the fire escape for hours. Other times, Hannah would join him. Many of their deepest conversations took place there.

Nino heard the window slide open and turned to see Hannah's smiling face. She sat on an old crate he used as a bench, nuzzled next to him, then wrapped them both in a large blanket. "Why do you insist on sitting out here in the cold?"

"I don't know. Sometimes I think it is because I feel guilty about being too comfortable while others are sacrificing."

"How does freezing help a single soldier?"

"It doesn't. Are our little ones asleep?"

"Finally. While I was bathing Solomon, Lilia asked me why I climb on top of you at night and make funny noises."

"What did you tell her?"

"I told her now that you are working again, we need to find an apartment with a second bedroom."

They laughed.

"You have been spending a lot of time out here, Nino. Why are you so distant?"

"My brother's plane was lost somewhere over the Mediterranean. He is most likely dead, but we will never know."

She squeezed his arm. "I know that, Nino. You are hurting, and I understand. But while I've done my best to support you, you have pushed yourself away. After dinner, Lilia wanted you to play with her and you just kept reading the newspaper. That isn't like you."

Nino looked away. A moment of silence lingered. He then turned to her. "I have been talking to someone."

Hannah grinned and moved her face close to him. "What is her name?"

Nino laughed and kissed her nose. "You know I would never be unfaithful to you."

"Yes, I do know that, and I am so grateful to be married to a husband I can trust."

He put his arm around her, and they kissed passionately before separating.

"I worship you, Hannah. You, Lilia and Solomon are my entire world."

"We know that. You are a wonderful husband and father, but where is this conversation leading? Who is this person you have been talking to?"

"His name is Father Felix Morlion. He is a Catholic priest and is somehow affiliated with the War Department. A few weeks ago, I was at the church praying. After I finished, Father Morlion was standing behind me. He introduced himself and asked if we could talk."

"Is he an Army chaplain?"

"I don't believe so."

"What did he want?"

"We have met three times. He said the War Department has something they would like me to do for them. They say I am the only one who can do it."

Hannah's eyebrows went up. "That is peculiar, Nino. What is this 'something' that only you can do?"

"I don't know. They won't tell me. Father Morlion wants me to speak to someone else."

"Who is this someone else?"

"He wouldn't tell me that either."

"Are you going to talk to this other person?"

"I feel I must."

Hannah looked away, initially silent. She returned her gaze to Nino. "Will they ask you to go away? To be in the war somehow?"

"I don't know, sweetheart."

"This scares me, Nino. It scares me because I know how you are. I know you've been racked with guilt for not joining the army like Angelo did. But there are other ways to serve the country. Your job at the Navy Yard is critical to the war effort, and raising a strong family is serving your country."

Nino sneered. "As we sit, there are men in foxholes and on battleships all over the world who have families at home. Why should I be different? You know I adore you and those two little angels in there. I would do anything for them. Every father fighting in this war misses his children desperately." Nino got a lump in his throat. "What you don't understand, Hannah, is that is why they are fighting. They are fighting to protect their families. They are fighting to protect the world from evil. You saw what was happening in Italy. You saw what happened to you simply because of your Jewish heritage. Father Morlion has told me it is much worse now."

Hannah looked down at the street below, taking in his words. He looked at her.

"Hannah, imagine yourself living in Europe right now. In France, in Belgium, in Poland or Austria. Father Morlion has told me that his connections are reporting entire families of Jews locked in cattle cars and shipped away to work camps. He said that he has received reports from eastern Europe of entire villages being taken into the woods, stripped and mowed down with machine guns. I can't get those images out of my head. What if that were you, Hannah? What if that were Lilia and Solomon? I can't go to sleep in a warm bed every night knowing that is happening when I might be able to do something about it."

Tears rolled down Hannah's cheeks. "I know the way you are, Nino. The reason I'm so passionately in love with you is because you have such a caring heart. If you see someone hurting, you help them. You've always been that way."

Nino pulled a handkerchief from his pocket and handed it to Hannah. She wiped her face and blew her nose.

Hannah said, "Go talk to this man. Whoever he is, go talk to him and see what he has to say."

They embraced. "I can't lose you, Nino. Whatever they want you to do, just go do it, be careful, and come home to me."

THE BRONX NEW YORK
436 EAST 149TH STREET
OPERA HOUSE HOTEL

Nino followed Father Morlion into the hotel room of William Donovan.

"Thank you for agreeing to meet with me, Mr. Servidei. I know this has been a difficult time for your family. You have my condolences over your missing brother."

"Can you provide me with any details?"

"He was a side gunner in a B-25. They were on a bombing mission to Sicily and never returned to North Africa. They were separated from the other planes and no radio transmission was ever received. They may have gone down over the Mediterranean or on the island of Sicily itself. We have no way of knowing."

Nino bowed his head. He swallowed hard to fight back his tears. "When we were growing up, Angelo would torment me mercilessly. I would get so mad I wanted to hurt him. But whenever I was in a jam, he always came to my rescue."

Nino grinned and added, "When I was leaving for Rome to study to become a priest, he slipped me some money so I could buy a prostitute when I got to Italy. He wanted to make certain I had sex at least once before becoming a priest."

"Sounds like a loyal big brother," Donovan said with a chuckle.

Nino asked, "How may I help you, Mr. Donovan?"

"I can't get into specifics now. At this stage I just need to know what your level of interest is in collaborating with us."

"I have been intrigued by my meetings with father Morlion. I am looking for a way to help with the war effort. Father Morlion has indicated you have some ideas."

Leaning back in his chair, Donovan said, "Mr. Servidei, we have something in the works that I can't share with you at this time. There is a possibility it may not happen at all. If that is the case, your services may not be needed. However, if it takes place, we will need your help. In order for you to help us, you will need to be well trained."

"I don't understand any of this."

"You're not supposed to. At least not yet. What I am

proposing is that you become part of our organization. You will be paid. All we ask is that you go through our training so that in the event we need your services you will be well prepared."

"What type of training are you referring to?"

"I can't get into that either."

"So, you're telling me you want me to quit a job I just recently got, join an organization I know nothing about, so I can go on a mission that may never happen. Do I have all of this correct?"

William Donovan leaned forward in his chair. "I know I'm asking you to move forward with blind faith, but I can tell you this: There is a precise mission that is critical to the war effort. If you agree to help us and are successful, your efforts could save thousands of American lives."

* * *

Nino entered his apartment to see Hannah was at the table trimming the length of her hair. "Don't cut off too much, my lovely."

"I have to cut off at least four inches."

"Why four inches?"

"That's what the war department needs."

"Why does the War Department need your hair?"

"I was talking to Mildred down the hall, and she said they use light colored hair in optical devises for bombers. I'm just doing my part for the war effort. Don't worry, it will grow back."

Nino peeked into the bedroom to see Lilia sleeping in their bed, and baby Solomon in his crib. He then poured himself a cup of coffee. "We all need to do more for the war effort."

"Your hair is too dark and too short."

Nino remained silent.

"That was a joke, Nino. What is wrong with you? You have something on your mind. Did something happen at work?"

"I didn't go to work today."

"Where did you…?"

She paused. "You met with them, didn't you?"

Nino watched her, analyzing her mood, yet remained silent.

"What do they want?"

"For now, they just want to train me."

"Train you for what?"

"I don't know exactly."

"They will give you more information, won't they?"

"They can't."

Hannah put the scissors down and crossed her arms. "You told them you would do it, didn't you?"

"They wanted me to leave tomorrow. I told them I needed more time to say goodbye to my family."

Hannah's lip quivered. "When do you go?"

"Next Thursday. I'm going to a training camp somewhere in Virginia."

THE ISLAND OF SICILY

The sun was setting over the western mountain peak when Vito returned the Moto Guzzi to the motor pool. "It is a finely tuned machine, *mi Amico*. You have done a masterful job of maintaining it."

"That's good, Caporale, because I wake up every day thinking of how to improve your life."

"And it shows in your fine work."

"That was sarcasm."

"Either way, you are a master mechanic, and I am grateful you were the one who built the engine."

As the mechanic shook his head, Vito heard screaming from the other side of camp. "What was that?" Vito asked. "It sounds like someone is being tortured."

"They are. Three American airmen. The SS is interrogating them."

"Did they find them all?"

"They believe the plane they were in had six crew members. Two went down with the plane, then those three. So, there is one more out there somewhere."

"Do they know where?"

"If they knew where, they would have him by now, wouldn't they?"

"Maybe he died in the crash."

"There were no bodies. But they'll find him. The patrols will be out until they do. When that happens, he'll suffer the same fate."

Vito turned toward the center of camp as he heard more screams mixed intermittently with what sounded like the pounding of flesh. "It sounds like they are killing them."

"What do you care? They were probably on their way to bomb Palermo. They are getting what they deserve."

CHAPTER 10

"Is she sleeping?"

"Out cold."

"And Solomon?"

"He's asleep too," Hannah said with a grin, while she slipped her nightgown off and slid into bed next to Nino. He removed his boxers, tossed them to the floor and rolled over and snuggled with his wife.

"We only have two more nights together before I leave."

"You'll be back."

"There is nothing more wonderful than feeling your skin next to mine."

Hannah threw her leg over Nino and straddled him. "I know something that feels better."

Nino ran his hands over her body. "You are perfection, my lovely."

She leaned down and kissed his mouth. Their tongues intertwined. They moved in rhythm before Lilia stirred in her bed.

Hannah whispered to Nino, "Shh ... lie still."

Nino lay motionless; his arms wrapped around Hannah.

Lilia continued to stir. Hannah giggled.

"What's so funny?" Nino whispered.

"If we ever want more children, we will need to find an apartment with a second bedroom."

"I think she's quiet now," Nino said before kissing Hannah's neck.

"I have to pee-pee, Mama," Lilia said. "Will you take me?"

Hannah laughed as she rolled off her husband. "I'm sorry, Nino. Let me take her and I'll be right back."

Hannah threw her nightgown over her head and turned on the light. "Come on, sweetheart."

Nino lay in bed, looking up at the ceiling.

Although frustrated with his pent-up desire, he smiled, grateful for his family.

Dear God, you have blessed me far more than I deserve.

He heard the front door open. Lilia ran into the room and leaped into bed with Nino. Hannah trailed behind her. "You need to go to your own bed, Lilia."

"I want to sleep with you and papa."

Hannah picked Lilia up and laid her on her mattress. "Not tonight, sweetheart. You need to sleep in your own bed."

"Please, Mama."

Hannah tucked her in. "No, Lilia,"

She turned off the light and cuddled next to Nino, then whispered, "She'll be asleep soon. Then we can have our playtime."

She kissed his lips and caressed his chest. "Just wait a little longer."

They held each other, waiting for Lilia to doze off.

Hannah sat up and removed her nightgown, then laid back

down. Nino positioned himself on top of her. He kissed her lips before moving to her neck. Hannah kissed the top of his head as he progressed down her body.

Solomon stirred in his crib. Nino froze. Solomon screamed.

Lilia said, "Mama, Solomon wants you."

Nino rolled to his side of the bed, and Hannah laughed before saying to Nino, "I'll ask Mildred if she will babysit tomorrow night."

PRINCE WILLIAM COUNTY VIRGINIA
CHOPAWAMSIC RECREATIONAL DEMONSTRATION AREA

The ride from the train station was quiet. The road was narrow, and the headlights lit up the branches of the trees that hugged the dirt road. Nino tried to start a conversation with his driver, but once they got in the car, the Staff Sergeant was tight-lipped and stone-faced.

The vehicle stopped in front of a nondescript, one-story wooden building.

"This is where you get out," the driver said.

His instructions were to bring nothing but the clothes on his back.

Except for a light in an office at the far end of the hallway, the building was dark.

"Hello," Nino shouted.

"Servidei, get your ass in here," a gruff voice shouted.

Nino entered a small office where a uniformed officer said, "Why are you just getting here?"

"Today is Sunday, and I went to Mass with my family this morning. I took the last train from New York."

"You're kidding me."

"No, sir."

"Damn, you really are a devoted Catholic. They warned me about you. Anyway, there won't be any of that shit while you are here. We don't have time for it. That's why you're here on a Sunday, so we can get an early start in the morning.

"I'm Colonel Crawley. You have a lot to learn and not a lot of time to learn it. I don't know where the hell they are sending you, but whatever your mission is, it is special. This is the first time they have ever asked me to ram one guy through so fast. Our typical training period is nine weeks, and there are twelve at a time. My orders are to have you ready in five weeks. You will be in barracks thirteen. It's about a quarter mile east of here. You have the entire barracks to yourself."

The colonel reached behind him and removed a box from a credenza.

"Everything you need is in here. Uniform, toothbrush, and soap. We usually shave your head, but for some reason you're different. I was instructed to just get you in and out and on your way. I'll see you at the grinder tomorrow morning at 0430 hours."

"What's the grinder?"

"Sergeant Kendrick will wake you at 0400 and escort you there. Bring your balls with you, you'll need 'em."

* * *

Nino opened his eyes and moaned as he rolled out of bed. His limbs lay heavy, and his muscles felt as though elephants had trampled over him. For the past month, he had survived on four hours of sleep per night. He estimated that his morning runs totaled one hundred and twenty miles and he had swum dozens of laps in a pool, some of which were in complete darkness. They had trained him how to operate several wireless devices, both voice and Morse code. They had also trained him to maintain and fire multiple types of weapons; some whose origins were German and Italian. His intent was to never use them.

Dressed in his green battle uniform, Nino did as Crawley instructed him and ran to a small discreet building on the opposite side of camp. Upon entering the building, Nino removed his cap and used it to wipe the perspiration dripping down his face.

"In here," shouted the voice of Crawley from a room down the hall.

When he entered, Nino snapped to attention.

To his surprise, William Donovan and another officer Nino had never seen before were with Crawley. They were near a table that had sand piled on it.

"Approach, Servidei," Crawley said.

As he made his way forward, his eyes locked onto the surface of the table and there before him were the first clues to his mission. A model of the island of Sicily lay exposed. There were cities, towns, roads and a handful of pins of varying colors.

"Good morning, Agent Servidei," William Donovan said.

"Good morning, Mr. Donovan."

Turning to the other officer, Donovan said, "This is Major Grayson. He is here to brief you on your mission."

Grayson said, "Agent Servidei, before we begin, I need to make something clear. The information I am about to present to you is not to be shared with anyone. Not your wife, not your priest, not your mistress, nobody. Is that clear?"

"Yes, sir."

Major Grayson picked up a wooden pointer and touched the end to a small town on top of a low mountain range. "Agent Servidei, do you know the significance of this town?"

"No, sir."

"This is the town of Ficuzza. Does that mean anything to you?"

"That's where my father grew up. My grandfather lives there."

Grayson pulled the pointer back. "We need you to pay your grandfather a visit and persuade him to help us."

"Help us with what?"

Donovan spoke up. "We need information, and we need it now."

"Information, sir?"

Donovan nodded to Grayson, who then spoke up. "We need intelligence to know how prepared the Germans and Italians are to defend Sicily. We need to know where they have key defenses, what their troop strengths are, and what their morale is, particularly of the Italian soldiers."

William Donovan said, "Your grandfather is the most powerful civilian in Sicily. He has connections. More importantly, he has men who work for him who are loyal, and they too have connections. They travel the island and see things."

"You are making assumptions," Nino said.

"Maybe," Donovan said. "But we feel confident our assumptions are accurate based on logic."

"With all due respect, what you are asking is a long shot at best. I have no more influence over my grandfather than any of you do. I have only met him during one brief encounter and during that encounter I insulted him. Now you want me to find him and ask him to help my country gather intelligence that will defeat his. What if his loyalties are to Italy? He could have me arrested and I could be shot as a spy."

Donovan said, "We don't believe that will happen. Agent Servidei, you are an educated man. Based on your family background, I'm sure you know the history between Mussolini and the Sicilian mafia."

"I do."

"Your grandfather will have no loyalty to Mussolini. He wants him out of power more than we do. That alone will motivate him to help us. As for you and your relationship with your grandfather, that is something you will need to overcome."

"And if I refuse to do this—what happens?"

"To you—nothing. You go back to your cozy life with your beautiful family in the Bronx. But to the American and British soldiers who need this information, they may get slaughtered."

Nino turned away from the men in the room. He felt ill. He rubbed the back of his neck. That last comment was a blow, and Donovan knew it. Nino sensed that Donovan had that arrow in his quiver, waiting for an opportunity to shoot it through his heart.

"Are you okay, Agent Servidei?" Grayson asked.

Nino turned to face them. "I'm fine. What is your time frame to get started?"

"We want you in England next week. From there, you will travel to Sicily by submarine."

"Submarine?"

"The sub will surface off the coast in the dark of night and you will paddle to the beach in a rubber raft."

"What am I supposed to do once I arrive on the island? How do I get to my grandfather?"

"We don't have that answer. You will need to be creative once you are on dry land."

"And what happens when word gets out to the German and Italian armies that a stranger with an American accent is roaming around Sicily?"

"You will have papers and what we believe is the perfect cover."

"Which is?"

"Four years ago, you went to Italy to become a priest. You will arrive in Sicily as a recent graduate of the *Pontificio Collegio Etiopico*. You lived in Rome and are familiar with the layout of the college. If someone asks you a question in an attempt to trip you up, you will have all the answers."

"So, I'll roam the island of Sicily under the pretense that I'm a priest?"

"You won't just be 'roaming' the island. Our mutual friend Father Morlion has a contact in Sicily who will help you."

"Are you certain of that?"

Donovan said, "Agent, let me be clear about something. In war, there are always uncertainties. You will have uncertainties when you arrive in Sicily. The purpose of your mission is to eliminate uncertainties for others. Father Morlion's contact is Father Russo. He runs an orphanage on top of the Sicani mountain range. It is isolated from any major towns and will provide you with a safe haven."

"How will I communicate with you?"

"Father Russo has a wireless," Grayson said.

Donovan added, "And he isn't working alone. He has a small group of partisans in his network who have already been providing us with limited intelligence, but they can't cover the entire island."

"I'll need more information about how this is all going to work."

"You'll receive all of the information you need," Donovan said. "But nothing more."

"Once I have done what you have asked, how will I get home?"

Grayson said, "We have several contingency plans to extract you from Sicily. The one we choose will depend on various factors. You will need to remain flexible and trust that we will bring you home when the time is appropriate."

THE ISLAND OF SICILY
THE SICANI MOUNTAIN RANGE
THE ABBEY OF SANTA MARIA

The roar of an engine caused Father Russo to glance at the entrance of the Abbey gate. It was Lorenzo's flatbed truck. With squeaking brakes, it came to a halt.

Leaping from the vehicle, Lorenzo said, "How are your rations holding out?"

"We are running out of staples like flour, and salt. We have added four more children this week. Their fathers have been drafted and their mothers have sent them here because they can't feed them."

"I am heading to Palermo on Thursday. I will return on Saturday with more supplies."

"We need grain too."

"Do you need anything else?"

"We need another milk cow. Elsa can't keep up with the demand."

"I'm afraid I can't help you, father. I'm a citrus farmer. I need the only one I have."

"I know. The war hasn't helped. The Germans and Italian troops have moved in and they too need to be fed. There are shortages of everything."

They heard the sound of another engine and turned to watch Manuel Roseman enter the gate in his four-door Fiat.

After he approached, Lorenzo asked, "How was the drive up from Palermo, Manuel?"

"Aggravating. There are military vehicles everywhere."

"Come into my office, gentlemen."

Father Russo sat behind his desk. Lorenzo and Manuel sat in the two chairs across from him.

Father Russo said, "I have received a coded letter from my contact in America. I don't have details, but someone will soon arrive who will need our assistance."

"Assistance with what?" Lorenzo asked.

"We will find that out when they get here."

PALERMO

The cameos in the display cases were stunning. Some were blue, others had an ashen tint, yet most were white. Gabrielle assumed the woman behind the counter waiting on a customer was Olivia—Manuel's wife. She glanced at more cameos, then looked toward the back office for any sign of Manuel.

The register rang. Olivia handed the customer a small box and watched her leave.

Gabrielle approached the counter. "Are you Olivia?"

"I am."

Gabrielle turned her head toward the door, then scanned the store a second time. "My name is Gabrielle Fontaine. Your husband told me to contact you if I had information."

Gabrielle's heart raced as Olivia studied her. Her stare was icy cold, and Gabrielle wondered if coming here was a good idea. Olivia made her way to the door and locked it. Returning, she said, "It's nothing personal, but I don't like you being here. It's risky."

"Do you want me to leave?"

Olivia exhaled. "You are here now. What information do you have?"

"Do you have a pad of paper and pen?"

Olivia retreated to the back office, then returned with pen and paper. She lay them on the counter.

Gabrielle quickly sketched a map of Sicily, putting an x at the general locations where she remembered seeing them on Richter's document. She then circled the southern beaches near Gela, Licata and Sciacca. Turning the paper over, she sketched the cylindrical mechanism she had seen on Richter's document, careful to draw the three protruding stems as accurately as possible. The door rattled. Olivia looked over Gabrielle's shoulder, and Gabrielle turned to see a German officer attempting to enter the store.

Gabrielle said, "I've seen him before. He was at an event I recently attended."

She slid the sketch across the counter to Olivia. "Hide this."

Olivia returned to the office. The German rattled the door a second time, then a third, before pressing his face to the glass and cupping his hands over his eyes to block the sun. Olivia returned, reached into a display case, removed a cameo, and handed it to Gabrielle.

After unlocking the door, Olivia said to the officer, "I'm sorry, sir, but the door was locked because I was preparing to close after this young lady completed her purchase."

The officer ignored Olivia and entered the store. He approached Gabrielle. "I watched you enter the store. I believe you are a friend of General Richter's. We met recently."

"Yes, I believe we did."

"What are you purchasing?"

She handed him the cameo Olivia had given her.

"It's lovely," he said with a smirk. "General Richter must pay you well if you can afford such a piece."

Gabrielle said nothing, then turned to Olivia. "Perhaps the major is correct. I'm afraid I can't afford this. However, it is lovely. Thank you for showing it to me."

The major asked, "When is the general due back in town?"

Gabrielle advanced around him and turned the doorknob. "You work for him. You should know."

"Perhaps we could spend some time together before he returns?"

"I don't believe that would be appropriate."

CHAPTER 11

THE BRONX NEW YORK

He leaned forward in his seat, awaiting the bus coming to a stop. One more turn. Then there it was. Nothing more than a rundown old building to most who passed it. To Nino, it was his sanctuary. It held all that was precious in his world.

Squealing brakes—a jostle.

Nino seized his bag, rose to his feet and was on the sidewalk in an instant before sprinting across the street.

He ran through the front door of his building and up the stairs. At his own apartment door, written in finger paint, a sign hung. It displayed three handprints. A large one from Hannah, a smaller one from Lilia, and a tiny one from Solomon. In both English and Italian, it read, *Welcome home Papa. We missed you.*

Before he could insert his key, the door opened. Hannah held Solomon.

Lilia yelled, "Papa!" as she ran to him and wrapped her arms around his leg.

He picked her up and kissed her cheek. "I missed you so."

"I missed you too, Papa."

Stepping forward, he hugged Hannah and kissed little

Solomon, who patted his papa's face. "How is our baby boy?"

"He is well."

"I missed you, Hannah."

"We all missed you terribly."

Nino noticed a refrigerator against the wall. "Where did that come from?"

"Grandpapa bought it," Lilia said.

Nino looked at Hannah.

She raised her eyebrows and nodded. "It's electric."

Nino removed Solomon from Hannah's arms and held him tight, then approached the appliance. He opened the door to see it packed with meat and dairy products. "It must have cost a fortune."

"I told your mama how I had to run to the market every day to buy fresh food. She must have told Salvador, and this arrived a few days later."

Lilia ran into the bedroom, then returned with a large, quilted blanket. She tripped over the corner as she approached Nino.

He said, "That is a little big for your bed, isn't it?"

"I told grandmama I have been cold at night, so she got it for me."

"We all got one," Hannah said.

"Why were you cold?"

"The coal furnace went out for a few days. It works now. Mr. Foley just fixed it."

"You were without heat?"

"We are fine now."

"Hannah, I'm sorry. Why didn't you tell me?"

"Tell you how? In a letter in the middle of your training?

You would have left and come home. I couldn't have that."

Nino said, "At least, Foley fixed it quickly. He must be the worst landlord in New York. It usually takes him forever."

"He was a little slow to respond at first. Then your father got involved, and Foley fixed it the next day."

"I don't know that I like the way my papa is forcing himself into our lives."

"He isn't forcing anything. You need to give him a chance. He will never admit it, but he is trying to make up for how he treated you. You want nothing to do with him, so he is making amends by caring for your family."

"I don't need Salvador DiVincenzo's help to take care of my family."

"Don't be so defensive. It's no reflection on you. You should be grateful he confronted Foley. We wouldn't have heat otherwise."

* * *

Nino watched Hannah light the candles. "It has been a long time since we have been alone together—just you and me."

She looked at him with a playful grin. "I have been planning this for weeks."

"It is nice of Mildred to watch Lilia and Solomon."

"Your Mama offered to watch them, but I don't want Solomon and Lilia that far away. I feel better knowing they are down the hall."

Hannah blew out the match, returned to the stove, and stirred a pot of stew.

Nino said, "I remember when I first saw you."

"I love this story."

"I had never seen anyone more beautiful in all of my life."

"And."

"My heart filled with emotions that up until that moment, I had tried to avoid."

"I've never heard this twist. What emotions were you trying to avoid?"

"Lust. I was going to Rome to become a priest. I had trained my mind to force out lustful thoughts. Then I saw you and all of that discipline left me in an instant."

"Oh, really. That is the first time you admitted you felt lustful toward me that morning."

"I think it was the black lace stockings I noticed when you sat on your steamer trunk. I remember wondering what else you had on under that waistcoat and skirt."

She turned off the stove, placed the pot to the side, and approached Nino. After sitting on his lap, she wrapped her arms around him, and they kissed. Just a peck at first, then their lips pressed together—their tongues caressing. She withdrew yet remained in his lap and looked into his eyes.

"Are you hungry?"

"I am."

"Would you like stew?"

"That's not what I am hungry for."

Her head leaned back and she laughed. "Well, I'll make you a promise. Let me feed you, then if you are a good boy and clean your plate, you won't have to wonder what I have on under this dress."

Hours later, Nino adjusted the covers and rolled on top of Hannah. "Are you ready to play some more?"

"Just one more time until morning. You are wearing me out."

"I might be gone a while. We need to store up."

"I don't think it works like that."

He kissed her neck, then moved to her lips. He caressed her silky skin, starting first at her face, then working his hand down her body.

After their third love making session of the evening, they lay nuzzled under the covers and Nino felt sleep approach. Hannah kissed his face, then lay with her head on his chest.

"I'm scared, Nino."

"Everything will be fine."

"Where are you going?"

"We have discussed this. I can't tell you."

"Why? Do you think I'm a spy?"

"Maybe you are."

"Be serious. I have a right to know."

"I don't even know all of the details. Sharing where I am going could put lives at risk."

Hannah got a lump in her throat as she fought back tears. "That includes your life, doesn't it?"

Nino remained silent.

She pulled the covers back and climbed out of bed and put on her nightgown before entering the kitchen.

He too dressed and followed her. She was sitting at the table weeping. He stood behind Hannah and wrapped her in his arms.

"It will be fine. I promise."

"Lilia and I will pray for you, Nino."

He sat next to her. "There was a time when you didn't believe in God."

"That was before."

"Before what?"

"Before He sent one of his angels to be my husband."

The following morning, Hannah placed two fried eggs on Nino's plate. "You leave in two days. Before you go, I want you to speak to your father."

"Why is that so important to you?"

"It's not for my benefit, it is for yours."

"You and Mama talk to him all the time. Isn't that enough?"

"You are stubborn."

"Why have you gotten so chummy with him?"

"He isn't the same man who kicked you out of his home. You should see him with Lilia and Solomon. He adores them."

"He is a murdering thug. I could never figure out why someone as sweet as my Mama could stay with him. Yet, after all these years, she remains loyal to him. Now my wife and children have fallen under his charms. I don't understand it."

"He has changed, Nino."

"Oh, really? Does he still have a stable of women that make money for him? Does he still extort local businesses and force them to pay him protection money? Does he still distribute opium? That's right. I bet you didn't know about that one. After prohibition ended, he replaced his illegal distilleries with opium distribution. I learned that from Angelo. I'll tell you this, Hannah, if it were not for you and my Mama being so close and she adores our kids, I would forbid you from taking them to that apartment."

"I can't argue with anything you have said. I know your father has an evil streak. But he is good to the kids—and me. I also know he wants to make amends with you. You need to hear what he has to say."

A stillness lingered in the room as Nino looked away from her.

Hannah rose from her chair and sat in his lap. She kissed his neck and whispered in his ear. "If you promise to talk to your father before you leave, I'll promise to play with you one more time this morning before I go get Lilia and Solomon."

THE BRONX NEW YORK
LUIGI'S RESTAURANT

On the sidewalk outside of Luigi's, Nino wished they would have chosen some place other than a restaurant. His stomach was tight, and he had no appetite, feeling as if he would throw up on the sidewalk. Upon entering the maître d' asked, "Do you have a reservation?"

"I'm here to see Salvador DiVincenzo."

"You must be Nino."

"I am."

"Follow me, please."

Nino trailed behind the man as they made their way to a back room. The maître d' approached, stopped at a red curtain, and pulled it back for Nino to enter. Once on the other side, two large brutes escorted him to another room. The door was open, and Nino entered. Before him, smoking a cigar and sitting at a lone table, was his father.

Salvador pointed to the seat across from him. "Have a seat, Nino."

Nino stood motionless before stepping forward and pulling the chair out. After sitting, his eyes locked on his father's. Nino, with his back to the door, sensed a bodyguard still in the room.

Salvador said, "Thank you for agreeing to see me, Nino."

Nino unfolded his napkin and placed it on his lap. "Why is one of your men standing at the door. Do you not trust me?"

Without speaking, Salvador gestured to DeFazio to leave the room. Nino heard the door close behind him.

"Do you feel safer now?"

Nino was stoic.

"Are you going to speak to me this evening, or are we going to sit in uncomfortable silence?"

"I'm here because Hannah persuaded me to come. I would have preferred to stay home."

"You married a persuasive woman. I know firsthand. I like that one—Hannah, I respect her. You did good when you gave up the priesthood for her. She is special."

"On that, we agree."

"I sense this is going to be a difficult evening."

"We should make it short."

"Nino, I'm not the same man who sent you packing eight years ago."

"Oh?"

"I have a little less pride now. I'm humbler, your Mama says."

"What caused that?"

Salvador shrugged. "With age comes wisdom."

"You do look older. You've gained weight too."

Salvador laughed. "Yes, I have. You look good, Nino. You look like an athlete."

"It's the training…"

Nino caught himself, remembering such discussions were off limits.

"Hannah feeds me well."

"She said you got a new job with the government, and they are sending you away. Where are you going?"

"Away."

"Hannah said that when you were in Italy, you met my father—your grandpapa."

"Briefly."

"What did he say to you?"

"He said, 'What the hell do you want, kid?'"

Salvador let out a boisterous laugh. "That sounds like my Papa."

"He didn't know who I was."

"Did you tell him?"

"I did."

"What did he say?"

"He said nothing. I looked him in the eye and told him I found both you and him repulsive. Then I turned and walked away."

"I wish I could have seen that."

"Did Hannah tell you her first husband was murdered?"

"No."

"It happened in Sicily by one of Grandpapa's men. Grandpapa knew about it ahead of time and allowed it to happen."

"And you ended up with Hannah. So, you should be grateful."

Nino rose and turned toward the door.

Salvador raised his voice. "I was out of line with that statement. If you wish to go, I will not stop you. But I have things to say. I think you should hear them. Please return to your seat."

After hesitating, Nino sat down.

"Nino, for the past eight years, I tried to convince everyone, including myself, you were of no concern to me. I was a prideful man."

"Was?"

"You are correct. I still am."

"But back then, when you told the police that I was involved in that druggist's murder—"

"Mr. Giovanni was his name. He was a kind and wonderful man. He was my friend when few in the neighborhood would be because they were afraid to be associated with the son of Salvador DiVincenzo."

Salvador took a drag from his cigar. "May I continue?"

Nino nodded.

"When you told the police I was involved in... your friends' death—"

"You mean murder."

"God damn it, Nino, let me finish, will you? Do you think this is easy?"

Nino leaned back in his chair and crossed his arms.

Salvador said, "When you talked to the police, it was like a punch in the gut. You see, where I grew up family doesn't rat on family."

Nino opened his mouth; Salvador raised his hand. Nino silenced himself.

"Then you changed your last name to your mother's maiden name—Servidei. Her father was a drunk by the way."

"Unlike you, he never murdered anyone."

"I'm not here to discuss that. Anyway, I felt betrayed."

"I don't care how you felt."

Salvador shook his head. "This is frustrating."

"Go on," Nino said.

"What I'm trying to tell you is that I was wrong. I should have never sent you away to that boy's home. You were just a kid. I screwed up and have been regretting it all these years."

Nino looked at his father, who stared down at the table with his shoulders slumped. The man he had always feared sat humbled before him. For the first time, Nino looked upon him with pity.

"Why are you telling me this?"

"Because you deserve to hear it."

Salvador looked at his son, wanting a response, yet only receiving Nino's glare of contempt.

"Look Nino, for a long time I have been thinking about a few things. You know, getting things straight in my head."

"What things?"

"Things that are actually important, like family. Then, Hannah showed up to bust my balls about how I treated you. She's got a lot of spunk—that one."

"She does."

"When Angelo's plane went down. It hit me hard. Then Hannah started bringing the kids over to visit your Mama. It has reminded me of when you and Angelo were small and I…"

"You what?"

"I wanted to try to… you know, fix things."

Salvador glanced to the side, unable to look Nino in the eye. "Look, son—"

"I'm not your son. Remember, you told me that the day you kicked me out at the age of fourteen."

"Nino, you may never like me again, not that you ever did.

If that is the case, then that is how it is. I have nobody to blame but myself. But I wanted you to know all of this before you went away to wherever you are going. But also, I want you to know that your... He paused to regain his composure. "Your family is special. Your family is really special, Nino. Hannah and your kids. I care for them. Maria adores them. And I want you to know that when you are away, no matter what happens, we will take care of them. They will never need anything. We will see to that."

"You have my appreciation."

"There's one more thing, Nino. What I am about to say is long overdue..."

He hesitated. "I'm proud of you. I have always been proud of you."

Nino sat back in his chair and looked up at the ceiling, uncertain what to say.

The waiter knocked on the door, then entered. "Mr. DiVincenzo, can I bring you your usual bourbon?"

Salvador looked at Nino. "Do you want a bourbon?"

"I'll take a scotch on ice and make it a double. I think I'll need it."

Salvador added, "And bring us a couple of big ass steaks and two baked potatoes.

Pointing to Nino, cigar in hand. "Is that okay with you? Do you want a steak?"

Nino nodded in agreement.

The waiter turned to leave, and Salvador shouted, "And a big bowl of pasta. We'll share it."

"Yes, sir, Mr. DiVincenzo. I'll put your order in."

"Ya gotta have Luigi's pasta, Nino. There ain't nothin like it in the city. I don't know what he puts in his sauce, but it's the best."

"Thank you for telling me."

"About what, Luigi's sauce?"

"No, about telling me you are proud of me."

Salvador brought a match to a fresh cigar and inhaled several times. Nino watched the orange glare at the tip.

"Your mama did a good job with you. I ain't got nothin to do with how you turned out. Hannah even told me that the day she chewed my ass. How did she say it again? It was something like—she didn't know how you turned out to be so good with a papa so bad—or something like that. I ain't got the words right, but you understand."

The first hint of a grin appeared on Nino's face.

The waiter brought in their drinks and set them before the two men. After he left, Nino said, "What was it like growing up in Sicily? What was grandmama like?"

"I don't remember much about her. I was young when she died. Papa kept her pictures around, but didn't talk about her much. After that, he had a series of women before I came to America." Salvador laughed. "I think there were even a couple who weren't on his payroll."

"Tell me about grandpapa."

"What do you want to know?"

"Was he a good father?'

Salvador chuckled and sat up in his chair. "Where the hell do you think I got my parenting skills?"

Nino smiled back at him. "Did you work for him?"

"Why are you so interested in your grandpapa?"

Nino shrugged. "If we are going to get reacquainted, I'd

kind of like to know about your childhood."

"Yes, I worked for him."

"What did you do?"

"From the time I was a small boy, I traveled throughout Sicily with papa learning the business firsthand. I watched him acquire land and extort money through fear and intimidation."

"You say that with pride."

"I *am* proud, Nino. My father made me tough, and I have what I have today because of what he taught me."

"When is the last time you heard from him?"

"There is a business associate of papa's who has family here in New York. He comes here every few years. He always brings a letter from papa. I send one back. That's how we communicate. He was last here two years ago."

"Do you think grandpapa is loyal to Mussolini?"

Salvador tilted his head to the side and raised his eyebrows. He studied Nino. "That is an interesting question. Why do you ask?"

"I lived in Italy for three years. Their politics intrigue me."

"Alfonso DiVincenzo is only loyal to Alfonso DiVincenzo. If it helps him to be loyal to Italy, he will be loyal to Italy. If it helps him to *not* be loyal to Italy, he will not be loyal to Italy."

"I see you learned your selfishness from him too."

With a grin, Salvador said, "We are alike in many ways."

"Where do you guess his loyalties are now?"

"I don't have to guess. He despises Mussolini. Many of his men have been imprisoned by him. Mussolini has not been good for papa's business."

There was a knock at the door.

"Come in." Salvador shouted.

Two waiters brought in their food and lay it on the table, leaving a little open space. "Can we get you anything else, Mr. DiVincenzo?"

"Do you need anything, Nino?"

"No, thank you."

"That will be all," Salvador said.

The door closed, and it was just Nino and Salvador.

Salvador reached for a dinner roll. "Your mama is taking this thing with Angelo hard. If something happened to you, it would kill her. I don't think she could take it."

"I'm not going anywhere dangerous."

"What will you be doing in Sicily?"

"Sicily? I'm not going to Sicily. I'm not even leaving America."

"Bull shit. Don't insult my intelligence. You may be interested in Italian politics, but you don't give a shit about my childhood. You came here looking for information."

"You are wrong. You're making assumptions."

"I don't know what the hell they have you doing, but if it involves your grandpapa, be careful."

PALERMO

The wine bottle clinked the side of Gabrielle's glass as General Richter filled it for the third time. In addition to wealthy civilians, German and Italian officers occupied tables throughout the room.

"You look stunning, Gabrielle. Even more so than usual."

Although nauseated by him, she said, "You are always so kind. This restaurant is wonderful."

"Only the best for you, *mon amour.*"

As the waiter brought their food, one of Richter's officers approached. He leaned down, whispered something to Richter, who slammed his fist on the table. The other patrons looked on at the agitated general.

With his voice raised, in German he said something else to the officer, who turned and at a brisk pace departed.

"What is it?" Gabrielle asked.

He looked at her, then at the other patrons before whispering to her, "This afternoon, air strikes took out two of my ammunition depots. There is a partisan cell somewhere on this island. I am certain if it. I need to get to the bottom of who is reporting our locations."

BELLISSIMA VALLE

Angelo hopped across the room until he arrived at the door of the bedroom. He listened for any sign of movement, but all was quiet. He made his way to the stairs, where he jumped from step to step on his left leg, holding his right leg in the air. At the bottom, the kitchen was vacant.

Where is everyone?

He made his way to the rear of the house.

"Where do you think you are going?"

Angelo turned to see Isabella, who had just entered the kitchen from the front courtyard.

"I'm looking for the toilet."

"We've discussed this. You aren't to be down here. We never know who will show up."

"I'm not using that bucket again."

"You must."

"But it is humiliating to watch you tend to my bucket. I'm not doing that anymore now that I can walk."

"You aren't walking, you are hopping. Come here and let me help you to the water closet. It is down the hallway."

"I'll find it. You aren't helping me with this anymore." Angelo said.

He made his way down the hallway.

When he returned, Isabella gave him a crutch. "Grandpapa made this for you."

He placed it under his arm. "It fits perfectly."

"Now, get upstairs." Isabella said.

"Can I use the bathtub that was in the water closet? I must smell awful."

"Don't you like my sponge baths?"

"There's certain places only I can clean. They need attention."

"Go on, but hurry. I'll get you a towel."

THE BRONX NEW YORK
NINO AND HANNAH'S APARTMENT

Lilia ran in from the kitchen. "Papa, will you play with me?"

He picked her up.

"What do you want to play?"

"Will you help me with the puzzle Grandmama gave me?"

Hannah said, "Papa has to get ready, Lilia. He must go on a trip."

"Why are you crying, Mama? Are you sad?"

Nino squeezed Lilia tight. "How about I help you get started with your puzzle? You and mama can finish it, and when I get back, I can look at the beautiful puzzle you put together."

She squirmed, wanting him to put her down. "Come with me, papa."

"I'll be there in a minute, Lilia." He looked at Hannah. "Her English is getting better."

"She is a smart little girl."

"Too smart sometimes."

"She takes after her Papa."

He embraced Hannah. "Everything will be fine. I promise." She looked down. He kissed the top of her head. "Please don't worry."

He released her and approached the crib where Solomon was stirring. Nino looked down at him. Solomon looked up at Nino and grinned, reaching up. He picked up his son and gently nuzzled Solomon's cheek next to his.

An hour later, Nino said, "The bus will be here any minute. I need to go downstairs. There is no point in delaying the inevitable."

He picked Lilia up.

She said, "What is happening, Papa?"

"I have to go away for a bit to help some people. But I'll be back."

"When?"

"Soon, Lilia. I'll be back soon."

He set her down and took Solomon from Hannah's arms. "So long for now, my big boy." He kissed his forehead, then returned him to Hannah. "I love you, Hannah. You are my everything."

"I love you too, Nino."

They kissed deeply.

"I have a bus to catch." Nino grabbed his knapsack, entered the hallway, and sprinted down the stairs.

CHAPTER 12

I t was bitterly cold outside and although it blocked the wind, the little shack they had Nino wait in had no heat. He found several blankets folded in the corner and wrapped one around himself.

The outer door opened, and in walked three crewmen. They approached and shook Nino's hand. "I'm Captain Taylor. This is my copilot, Captain Kardos, and my Navigator First Lieutenant Bailey. We will fly you to Scotland."

Captain Bailey said, "I don't know who you are, Mr. Servidei, but you must be pretty goddamn important. They cut off this northern flight path in November. We lost two planes in one week. The assumption was icing on the wings. Whatever they have planned for you, they believe it is worth risking all four of our lives to get you there straightaway."

Nino asked. "How long will it take?"

Taylor said, "Two days. From here we go to Newfoundland, then to Greenland, where we will spend the night, refuel and get some grub. From Greenland we head to Iceland to pick up cargo before the final skip to Roseneath Scotland."

Kardos said, "If you don't mind me asking, what the hell is in Roseneath that is so important, Mr. Servidei?"

"I'm hoping for some very fine Scottish whisky," Nino said.

Captain Taylor said, "Let's get the hell out of here."

PALERMO

"Where have you been?" General Richter asked.

Gabrielle crossed the room and picked up her cigarette case from the nightstand. "I was in the sitting room. We are always in bed. Sometimes I need to get up and stretch my legs."

"Soon you will have plenty of room to roam."

"What does that mean?"

"I spoke to Lucia. You will be mine full time now. You are going to come live with me at the DiVincenzo compound."

ABOVE THE NORTH ATLANTIC

Their flight through northeast Canada had been turbulent. Nino spent much of the journey lying prone in the back cargo hold to keep from being ill. It didn't work. Fortunately, they had left him with a bucket.

Other than the bumpy ride, the trip to Greenland had been uneventful. The food during their stay there had been exceptional. Nino had fresh fish for both dinner and breakfast. Before leaving the island nation, they had loaded several crates of medical supplies into the cargo hold with Nino. They would have one last stop in Iceland before arriving in Scotland.

The modified Douglas B-18 Bolo had once been a medium bomber. It had been converted to a transport plane because of its inability to carry a sufficient bomb payload.

The front of the aircraft comprised two levels, the upper, where the cockpit was located, with the navigator behind the cockpit, and the bottom level, which still had an observation shield for a nose gunner.

During this leg of their journey, Nino had crawled to the lower level and lay on his belly so he could see the ocean below. There wasn't a cloud in the sky, and the morning view was magnificent. In the distance, the faint image of sun rising from the southeast created a silhouette of Iceland.

The sea below looked rough, and he imagined it was cold enough that if a man ever found himself in it, he would be dead instantly.

Although the view from the nose was breathtaking, he soon found himself bitterly cold as he lay face down in the small compartment.

Before leaving New York, they had issued him a set of thick coveralls, a bomber jacket, boots and gloves. Even with the added protection, his fingers and toes were numb. He slowly backed out of the tiny compartment, wondering how a nose gunner could stand it for long periods of time.

His seat in the aft cargo hold comprised a row of metal bars which supported canvas cushioning. He considered taking a nap. But his adrenalin was pumping, realizing that in only a matter of days, he would be back in Sicily.

He lay down on the deck and closed his eyes.

The sound of an alarm woke him. The plane was vibrating, and the nose angled down, as if they were approaching the runway. He heard the crew yelling instructions at one another, but he couldn't make out what they were saying. Looking out a small side window, he saw they were still above water, but toward the front of the aircraft was land — Iceland, he presumed.

The dark ocean below was rapidly approaching, but the ground was within reach if they could hold their altitude. He heard the landing gear come down. He returned to his seat, fastened his waistbelt, and bowed his head, asking for God's mercy.

With the alarm still sounding, the plane touched down, jerking hard, before getting airborne again, followed by another bounce before touching down again. With a deafening ripping sound, the nose buried itself deep into the snow. The momentum threw Nino forward with a sharp jerk, his seatbelt shifting to his ribs. With the nose of the plane buried deep in the snow, the tail of the plane rose, and momentarily stood on its nose before flipping over and landing upside down, bouncing once, then twice before settling. Nino hung suspended upside-down in his waistbelt. He screamed in agony, believing his right-side rib cage had just broken.

With both his head and feet dangling toward the top of the now overturned aircraft, and the seatbelt wrapped around his ribcage, he struggled to free himself. While suspended in midair, he looked toward the cockpit. There was no movement or voices. After guiding his hand along the length of the belt, he found the release mechanism and pulled. He dropped like a sack of potatoes. His head was the first to hit the top of the fuselage. He turned over on his back and clutched his side. The ordeal had knocked the wind out of him, and he was attempting to recover when the smell of oil overcame him. He glanced out of the window to see the black substance dripping from one engine.

Toward the front of the plane, traces of black smoke lingered. "Is everyone okay?" Nino yelled without hearing a response. He crawled forward. Blood from the pilot and copilot doused the instrument panel. Bailey, the unconscious navigator, hung suspended upside down. Nino rose, wobbled, then fell forward, landing on his face. He had a sense that the plane was spinning. He rose to his knees, struggling to stand. His head rang and his ribs throbbed. After getting to his feet, he stumbled forward until he was below the dangling navigator. Nino positioned himself under the man to absorb Bailey's weight when he released the harness. He undid the first clip, then the second. As the navigator fell, Nino guided him to the deck, where he observed his bruised face and bleeding nose.

The smoke from the cockpit, along with the dripping oil, concerned him. Nino crouched and made his way forward. Upon arriving, he checked for a pulse from both the pilot and copilot. He felt nothing, but he was no medical professional and doubted his ability to ascertain the status of their health. He examined them one at a time while yelling their names as loud as he could—Kardos first, then Taylor. He slapped them hard, hoping to stun them into consciousness. There was no response. Nino glanced down at his own jacket, startled at how much of their blood now covered him.

As Nino made his way back to Bailey, he noticed two BCF fire extinguishers behind Kardos' seat. He unfastened the first one, pointed it at the instrument panel, and dowsed the source of the smoke until the cylinder was empty. He then repeated the process with the second BCF Extinguisher.

Concerned about a potential fire, he considered dragging

Bailey outside, but it was bitter cold, and exposure to the elements appeared riskier than a fire that might never ignite. As a compromise, he dragged Bailey near the hatch to allow for a rapid extraction if needed. Bailey was only slightly larger than Nino, but Nino's injuries to his head and ribs made the ordeal of pulling Bailey to the door challenging. After arriving at the hatch, Nino turned the handle, but the door wouldn't open. He turned it again, this time ramming his shoulder against it. After his fourth attempt, a gust of wind entered the cabin and Nino stumbled out of the plane and onto the ice.

Growing up in New York, Nino had experienced cold, but nothing like the arctic chill that hit his face like a block of crushed ice. His body shivered. He tucked his head into his jacket, closed the door behind him, then took several steps away from the sanctuary of the fuselage. He turned around to inspect the downed plane. The port side wing had broken near the tip, the starboard side wasn't visible from his position.

Nino sluggishly rotated in a complete circle, staring at the outer rim of the shallow gorge the plane had settled in. To find his bearings, he made two steps west toward the direction they had come from but thought better of it after the cold air ripped through his clothes as if he were shirtless. Returning to the plane, the pressure of the wind made the door difficult to open. He pulled several times with no luck. He leaned against the fuselage. Then bent over and vomited. The throbbing in his head was unbearable. He sat down, resting his back against the aircraft. He wanted to sleep, but realized if he did, he would freeze to death.

Visions of Hannah, Lilia, and Solomon filled his head. He stood, grasped the handle, and placed his foot on the outer surface before pulling one last time. The door flew open, and Bailey tumbled out, his momentum forcing him at Nino. They both fell into the snow.

Nino on his back, with Bailey on top of him, said, "You're alive!"

"It looks like the same can't be said for Taylor and Kardos," Bailey said.

"They took the brunt of the impact."

"Have you seen any airplanes?" Bailey asked. "I heard Kardos send a distress signal as we were going down, but I didn't hear Keflavik respond."

"They were expecting us, weren't they?" Nino asked.

"We should have arrived by now. They will send a search party soon," Bailey said. "And they better make it quick. This time of year, the little bit of sun we now see only lasts a few hours."

THE DiVINCENZO COMPOUND

After a quarter kilometer gallop, Alfonso slowed Hercules to a trot. Riding the black stallion among the German and Italian troops gave his wounded ego a lift. Through intimidation, coercion, and violence, he had spent his life amassing power. In his mind, and in the eyes of many, he was the King of Sicily. But the arrival of Generalmajor Richter and his forces brought Salvador to his knees and forced him to relinquish his prized property to the very fascist philosophy that had tried to bring him down twenty years earlier. On the back of Hercules, he felt like royalty again. As the massive black stallion slowed to a walk, it carried Alfonso down a hillside, passing military tents and vehicles. The soldiers took notice.

The sight of Richter's staff car approaching down the driveway caught his attention. It came to rest at the front of the house. Richter and *Maggiore* Brambilla exited. Richter held the door, and a young woman got out of the back of the vehicle.

Now he is bringing his whores into my home.

* * *

"I have business to attend to in Gela," General Richter said to Gabrielle as they entered his bedroom. "You may put your clothes in that wardrobe. I will return this evening."

With a forced smile, Gabrielle said, "I'll be waiting."

After he left the room, she walked out onto the back patio. Questioning how her life had come to this, she felt the urge to weep. She thought of Vito, longing for his embrace, wondering if she would ever see him again.

She looked up to see an older man on a black horse riding toward the stables. Visions of a handsome man on a black stallion coming to her rescue frequently entered her mind. She grinned, realizing that in her dreams, none of the men ever looked like the old fat man currently in view.

She made her way to the barn, arriving as Alfonso dismounted. She rubbed Hercules's nose.

"Would you like to ride him?" Alfonso asked.

She grinned and shook her head. "No," she said, while continuing to rub the horse.

Alfonso led Hercules into the barn, and Gabrielle followed.

Handing the reins to Pierre, Alfonso said, "Wash him down, will you, Pierre? I rode him hard today."

"Si, Mr. DiVincenzo."

"This lovely young lady is Richter's *concubina*."

He looked at her. "I don't know your name."

In broken Italian, she said. "I am Gabrielle Fontaine."

"It is wonderful to have a beautiful woman on my property," Alfonso said. "You are welcome here. However, General Richter can rot in hell."

He then motioned to Pierre. "Gabrielle, Pierre here is my house manager. He is French. I am guessing by your accent that you, too, are French. Am I correct?"

"I am French, *Oui.*"

Addressing Pierre, Alfonso said, "If she needs anything, provide it for her."

"*Si,* Mr. DiVincenzo, I will make her comfortable."

Gabrielle watched as Alfonso tipped his fedora, then exited the barn.

She then addressed Pierre. "*Enchanté,* what part of France are you from?"

"I am from Normandy—Cherbourg."

She looked at the weathered face of the thin man, guessing he was in his forties. "How did you end up here?"

"Many years ago, when I was just twenty-one, I took a job on a steamer. We stopped in Palermo. I drank too much and fell asleep in an alley. When I woke and went to the docks, my ship had departed without me. I roamed the streets for weeks, begging for money and food. Mr. DiVincenzo's late mistress, Flora, was in town shopping. She was a wonderful woman and has since passed. She took me to lunch, then brought me here." Pierre laughed. "We walked in the front door and she told Mr. DiVincenzo that she had hired me to manage the house. He didn't even question it. As ornery as Mr. DiVincenzo can be, she had him wrapped around her finger."

"What is Mr. DiVincenzo like? He seems pleasant."

"To those of us who work for him, he is okay. For those who cross him, I pray. He is not a man who likes to be challenged. He wants what he wants and will do just about anything to get it. He has humbled in recent years though. The death of Flora last year softened him a bit. He has taken it hard."

"What happened to her?"

"The doctors aren't certain. She had always been a big woman, at least as long as I knew her. Suddenly she lost weight and became terribly ill. Mr. DiVincenzo took her to several doctors in Rome. They couldn't help her, and she passed on."

Pierre picked up a bucket and a soft brush and led Hercules to a hand pump behind the stables. Gabrielle followed. She watched Pierre pump the handle of the well, filling the bucket. She said, "You know why I'm here, don't you?"

There was an uncomfortable silence before Pierre asked, "Do you work for Madame Lucia?"

"Please don't think less of me, but yes, I am under her employ."

"I do not judge you, *mademoiselle*."

He dipped the brush in the water and scrubbed the back of Hercules. "Mr. DiVincenzo used to own Madame Lucia's place. He sold it to her."

"How long ago was that?"

"Many years ago, after he met Flora. She would have none of that. That brothel was one of his most profitable endeavors. Yet he loved her so much that he gave it up for her. That's when he sold to Madame Lucia."

Gabrielle said, "In its own odd way, it sounds rather

romantic for a man to give up a profitable business just to keep from losing a woman."

"She changed him in many ways. He can still be mean and ruthless, but not like he once was. Please don't repeat this, but he has ordered the murder of dozens of men over the years."

Gabrielle's heart raced. "Murders?"

"Too many to count. I guess it is possible that he still orders executions, but he doesn't discuss it like he once did."

"Should I fear him?"

Pierre laughed. "No, of course not. I know Mr. DiVincenzo very well. I can tell he likes you. He is no threat to you. However..."

He stopped speaking.

"However, what?" Gabrielle asked.

"That man who brought you here—General Richter. He needs to be careful."

KEFLAVIK ICELAND

Nino woke confused. He attempted to sit up, but his hospital bed was spinning. He leaned over the side to vomit on the floor, but nothing came out. A nurse ran over and handed him a bedpan. He spat into it, then lay back down.

"Where am I?" he asked.

"You are in a military hospital in Keflavik, Iceland."

"I remember something about an upside-down airplane. It was miserably cold. Was I dreaming that, or did it actually happen?"

"It happened."

"How did I get here? I remember nothing. I just remember the cold and thinking I would freeze to death."

"Ask someone else about the details. All I know is that you were in a plane crash."

"I think I broke my ribs."

She touched his left side.

"It's this side," he said, while pointing to his right side.

She probed him gently.

"Ouch!"

"Does it hurt anyplace else?"

"My head is spinning, too. I'm nauseous. These lights are bright. They're making my head hurt."

"Here, take these," she said while handing him aspirin, then placed a dark towel over his eyes.

A doctor attending to a patient in the next bed overheard the conversation.

"I need to check your pupils, Mr. Servidei," he said as he lifted the towel and flashed a light in his eyes. "Based on what you just told the nurse, it sounds like you have a severe concussion. You are going to be here a week—two, perhaps."

"That's not possible. I need to be somewhere."

"You aren't going anywhere until you are better. Wherever you need to be, it can wait."

"You don't understand. I need to be somewhere."

"I'm sure it can wait," the doctor said, before walking away.

Nino said to the nurse, "What about the other guy—Bailey was his name."

"Captain Bailey is fine. He is recovering from surgery."

"Surgery, what happened to him?"

"You ask a lot of questions, Mr. Servidei. You need to just lie down and rest. The more you rest, the sooner you will recover and be on your way."

"And the pilot and the copilot. Did they make it? They were hurt badly."

"Just rest, Mr. Servidei. Your job is simply to rest."

* * *

Nino slipped his feet into his slippers and pulled the belt of his robe tighter.

"What do you think you're doing?" shouted a nurse from across the room.

"I feel fine, nurse Edison. I've been in bed for three days. Can't I please just stretch my legs."

"You can walk to the end of the hall and return. But that's it."

"Thank you. I promise to be a good boy while I'm gone."

As Nino turned to leave his room, his doctor entered. "Mr. Servidei, you must have powerful friends in Washington, D.C., because, despite my concerns, your flight to Scotland leaves tomorrow afternoon."

CHAPTER 13

Hannah lay Solomon in the bed Nino had slept in as a boy. She kissed his forehead. Her heart felt warm seeing her precious son lying where her husband had once slept. She knelt and bowed her head, hovering over Solomon.

Please be with Nino, dear God. Wrap him in your arms and protect him. Bring him home to us.

She wiped a tear from her cheek.

Lilia ran into the room. "Come look at the lightning, Mama."

"Lightening?" Hannah asked.

Salvador entered Nino's bedroom. "Sleet is bouncing off my office window. You can't take Lilia and Solomon out in this. Spend the night here?"

"I don't know about that." Hannah said.

Maria stood at the door. "Wouldn't you like to sleep in your papa's room, Lilia?"

"Can we, Mama? I want to sleep in Papa's bed."

Hannah laughed. "I guess I'm outnumbered."

"So, we can stay?" Lilia said.

"Yes, we can stay."

Salvador said, "I'll have DeFazio drive you home in the morning."

After they ate dinner, Lilia and Solomon fell asleep in Nino's bed. Hannah helped Maria with the dishes.

"I think I might be pregnant again," Hannah said.

"So soon? You just had Solomon."

Hannah laughed. "That apparently doesn't matter."

"You seem concerned. Are you not happy?"

"I'm scared, Maria. I don't…"

She regained her composure. "I don't have a good feeling about Nino. He has been gone for so long, and I haven't heard from him."

"You knew that would be the case. Have faith." Maria embraced Hannah. "He'll survive. You know how Nino is."

Salvador entered the kitchen. "What the hell is going on?"

Maria looked at Salvador. "Hannah thinks she might be pregnant."

"Is that good or bad? Why is she upset?"

Maria said, "Salvador, I'll talk to you about this later. Will you leave us alone, please?"

He turned to leave the kitchen, then paused. "Hannah, you need to get a telephone at that place of yours. It ain't good to be pregnant with no telephone."

Hannah wiped the tears from her eyes. "The neighbor down the hall has one. She said I could use it whenever I wanted."

BELLISSIMA VALLE

Isabella sat on the edge of the bed and gently removed Angelo's bandages. "Your wound is improving."

Angelo propped himself up on his elbows. "I'm grateful."

She wiped his leg with a damp cloth.

Angelo said, "Your papa and grandpapa still haven't asked me my last name. If they do, what should I tell them?"

"Make something up. Anything other than DiVincenzo. They will surely turn you in if they know Alfonso DiVincenzo is your grandfather."

"I'll think of something."

"Think of something soon. It's only a matter of time before they'll ask you."

He lay back on the bed.

Isabella asked, "Did you get along with your papa?"

"Only because I feared him. He likes to be feared."

Isabella remained silent as she dipped the cloth into the water, wrung it out, then reached for a set of clean bandages. Angelo watched her wrap his leg. She started at his ankle, then worked her way to his upper thigh.

After she applied the final dressing, Angelo said, "I can never repay you for what you've done for me."

"I'm not asking you to."

She looked at him and grinned. "Why do you keep staring at me?"

"I don't think I should tell you."

"What does that mean?"

"I think you're beautiful. Every time you enter the room my heart races."

She leaned forward and kissed his cheek. "I think you are handsome."

With a soft caress, Angelo placed his hand on her face before he pulled her closer. They kissed.

She climbed into bed with him. "I liked that. You can kiss me more if you wish. But nothing more. Only kissing."

The Bronx New York
Nino and Hannah's Apartment

With her arms cradling Lilia, Hannah laid in bed and stared at Solomon's crib. He was stirring with the sunrise and would soon want his breakfast.

Hannah heard men speaking from the street below. She rose from the bed, cautious not to wake Lilia. Her bedroom window gave her an unobstructed view of the street. The voices were of three workmen standing next to a truck. One man pointed in Hannah's direction while speaking to the others. He then turned and approached the entrance of her building. Hannah replaced her nightgown with a dress, then entered the kitchen to make breakfast. Moments later, there was a knock at the door. She opened it to find the workman on the other side.

He glanced at a clipboard. "Is this the Servidei residence?"

"It is," she replied.

"I have a work order to install a telephone in this apartment."

Hannah shook her head and smiled. *Salvador!*

Roseneath Naval Base
Roseneath, Scotland

Nino arrived at Roseneath House after sunset. His journey from Keflavik, Iceland to Mill of Camsail, Scotland was on board a British Lancaster.

The effects of his concussion still lingered, and other than the air crew, nausea and a headache had been his only companion.

He entered the building and noticed a U.S. Navy Lieutenant and an enlisted man asleep in two corner chairs. Nino scanned the room yet saw no one other than the sleeping sailors. He approached them and cleared his throat. They stirred before leisurely rising to their feet.

The Lieutenant said, "May I assume you are Mr. Servidei?"

"I am."

"Good evening Mr. Servidei. I am Lieutenant Donaldson, the liaison officer of the *S.S. Barb.* We are sorry to hear about your ordeal in Iceland, yet glad you survived the crash."

"Others weren't so lucky," Nino said.

"That's what we heard."

Donaldson turned to the second-class petty officer standing beside him. "Go bring the car to the front."

"Yes, sir."

Donaldson turned to Nino. "Whatever your mission is, it must be highly important to hold a crew of sixty submariners up for four days."

"I'm sorry about that."

"No need to apologize. The motivation of my statement was respect, not resentment. You must be an especially important man."

As they exited Roseneath House, Donaldson said, "The *S.S. Barb* is only minutes from here. When we arrive, I will introduce you to Captain Ferguson. He will brief you on the role we will play in your mission."

* * *

After handing his lone bag to a crew member, Nino made his way down the conning tower. The captain met him on the bridge.

"Mr. Servidei, my name is Captain Raymond Ferguson. I am the commanding officer of the *SS Barb*."

"It is a pleasure, Captain."

"We will get underway momentarily. Until then, Senior Chief Harth will take you below and show you your sleeping quarters. Have you ever been on a sub before, Mr. Servidei?"

"No, sir. This is my first time."

"I hope you aren't expecting much in terms of privacy. As you can imagine, space is limited."

"I will be fine with whatever accommodations you have available."

"Once we are through the Irish Sea, and out of Saint George's Channel, I will be available to meet with you. At that time, we will discuss the plan to get you onto the island of Sicily."

Once underway, Captain Ferguson and Nino met again. "Mr. Servidei, I would like you to meet my executive officer, Mr. Ordway, and you have met my Command Senior Chief, Mr. Harth."

The captain continued. "Our orders are to insert you onto the island of Sicily in six days, during the dark of the moon. Upon completion of this briefing, Senior Chief Harth will run through your gear. I know they trained you at Chopawamsic, so it should only be a review. Having said that, we may already have a problem. With their defeat in North Africa, our enemy has increased their patrols along the southern coast of Sicily. If when we arrive in the Med your insertion point appears tumultuous, we may need to adjust our plan. But, as of now, our original objective is intact."

"Adjust our plan how, Captain?

"We won't know until we arrive at our destination. But I can assure you, we will do our best to put you in the best viable position for success."

PALERMO

The Borage herb was hearty and easily survived the Sicilian winters. Its Bright blue petals formed a star, which made it distinctive, even from a distance. On his way to Gabrielle's apartment, Vito found a patch of it growing wild outside Palermo. He stopped and picked enough to make a bouquet.

Arriving early, he knocked on her door. It was quiet. Richter's routine would have him away from Palermo during the week, and today was typically her off day from being at Lucia's.

He knocked again.

Hortense opened the door just a crack. "May I help you?"

"I'm looking for Gabrielle. We have a date."

"You must be Vito."

"I am."

"Come in."

Vito inspected the apartment, looking for any sign of Gabrielle.

"Vito, I'm sorry, but things have changed. General Richter approached Lucia about keeping Gabrielle with him all the time. She will now be with him during the week, too. Not just the weekend."

"Why didn't she refuse?"

"She tried, but she didn't have a choice. Richter gets what he wants."

"Why didn't she just walk out of the brothel?"

"And do what, Vito? Become a schoolteacher or something?

You don't understand what our life is like. We have no other options, so we have sex for money."

"Where does he live during the week?"

"Somewhere in the mountains. She is at the estate of someone by the name of DiVincenzo."

"Where in the mountains?"

"I don't know. You'll have to ask around."

Vito paced the apartment, then handed the bouquet to Hortense. "I will find her."

* * *

"Where is Lucia?" Vito asked a scantily clad woman sitting behind the counter of the brothel. He had seen her there before when he visited Gabrielle. She appeared twice the age of most of the girls.

"She isn't here," the woman said.

"I'll wait."

"She hasn't been here all day and probably won't be here until late in the evening."

Considering his options, Vito turned to face the door. He wanted to wait for her but was due back at camp by sundown. So far, he had never missed an assignment or a roll call. If he did, he might lose his messenger duties, which would mean no freedom and no Gabrielle.

He turned back to the woman behind the counter. "I'm looking for the estate of someone by the name of DiVincenzo. Do you know him?"

She laughed. "Know him? I used to work for him. He once owned this place."

"Where does he live?"

"Just outside of Ficuzza. I haven't been there in a few years, but if I remember it was south of the town. You can't miss it. Look for a thick forest of tall trees."

As Vito sped through the hills of Sicily, he planned what he would say when he reached the compound. He slowed when he arrived at the main road, passing a multitude of parked military vehicles on either side of DiVincenzo's driveway. When he approached the house, he slowed, stopped, then revved the motor while looking around for any sign of Richter's staff car. He entered the courtyard to find no other vehicles.

His heart raced when he knocked on the door. He heard stirring, but there was no initial answer.

Pierre opened the door. "May I help you?"

"I am looking for a girl. Her name is Gabrielle Fontaine."

"Did the general send you?"

"He wants me to give her a message."

"You can give it to me, and I will pass it to her."

"I was told to give it to her personally."

Alfonso entered the room and stood behind Pierre. "I told Richter and Brambilla no foot soldiers. Get the hell out of here."

"I have message for Gabrielle from general Richter."

"Give it to me."

Realizing his initial plan wasn't working, he tried a different approach. "Are you Mr. Alfonso DiVincenzo?"

"Why are you asking?"

"*Signore*, my name is Caporale Vito Bianchi. I am a close friend of *Signorina* Gabrielle Fontaine. I am requesting that you allow me to see her."

Alfonso turned to Pierre and grinned, then turned back to Vito. "What kind of friend are you? Are you her lover? And by lover, I mean she doesn't charge you."

"Si, I am her lover in that way."

"Vito!" Gabrielle shouted from across the foyer.

All three men looked in her direction.

"Gabrielle," Vito said, as he approached her.

"How did you find me?"

"It was easy."

They embraced.

Alfonso said. "Carporale... what did you say your name was?"

"Bianchi."

"Right, Caporale Bianchi. How did you get here?"

"My motorcycle is out front."

"Take it around back in case you need a fast escape."

Alfonso addressed Pierre. "Call down to Enzo. Tell him that if he sees Richter's car approach, to let you know."

He then turned to Vito and Gabrielle. "You and Miss Fontaine are welcome to use General Richter's bed. You will be forewarned if Richter returns early."

* * *

Vito stroked Gabrielle's back as they lay naked under the covers. "I want to take you away from here."

"What does that mean?"

"I don't want you doing this anymore."

"It's not that easy, Vito."

"I will send you back to Milan. My father is a well-respected doctor. I come from money. My family will protect you until the war is over and I can return."

"You are talking crazy."

"What if I were to marry you?"

Gabrielle laughed. "Vito, you know nothing of me."

"I know enough to know I can't live without you."

Gabrielle sat up in bed. "You are serious, aren't you?"

Vito too sat up. "Of course, I am."

She rose to her feet and put on a robe, then lit a cigarette. "I'm not going to marry a man I know nothing of."

"But you will sleep with any man who slips you a few *lire*."

"The truth comes out, doesn't it? That's what you really think of me. I'll never marry you. Get out of here."

"Gabrielle, I'm sorry. I didn't mean that."

She screamed at him. "Get out now, I said. I don't want to ever see you again."

CHAPTER 14

The sun would set within the hour. Captain Ferguson twice rotated the periscope three hundred and sixty degrees to the right. The first time checking the surface of the Mediterranean Sea and the second time, scanning the sky above it. Addressing the officer of the deck, he said, "Mr. Ordway, we have multiple contacts. Take us to a depth of three hundred feet."

"Aye-aye, sir."

Nino watched the crew tend to their specific duties. Well trained and professional, the submariners were deliberate in their actions. The oil and diesel odors permeating throughout the vessel made him nauseous. Although sensitive to the touch, the pain radiating from his broken ribs had lessened since he boarded the submarine six days prior. He was grateful that he had recovered from his concussion.

Once submerged, the captain pulled the periscope down and approached Nino. "I don't report good news Mr. Servidei."

"What's the problem, captain?"

The captain stepped toward the chart table and laid his finger on the image of Sicily. "I know the objective was to get you to Gela. However, the area is thick with Italian patrol boats. It is no better near Sciacca. In recent weeks, the Italians have been harassing the British with depth charges. They lost a sub two weeks ago. The best I can do is drop you off in the west, near Marsala."

"But I need to reach the peak of the Sicani Mountain Range. Marsala must be one-hundred miles from there."

"I'm aware of that. But I won't risk my sub and my crew. We can scuttle the mission for now. It's your call. But it won't be getting any easier."

"What's the weather like?"

"It's raining, windy, and the water is choppy. The good news is that in a few hours, the cloud cover will block the moonlight, and it will be pitch black. You will have plenty of darkness as you approach the beach."

"How close can you get me to shore?"

"You will have some rowing to do."

Nino combed his hand through his thick black hair, took a deep breath and weighed his options. He thought of the words of William Donovan. 'Your mission is critical. The lives of thousands of men may hinge on your success, and we have little time.'

The captain said, "I need your decision now. You will only have a few hours of darkness to get ashore and bury your raft without being spotted. And I still need to get you to Marsala."

Nino reached into his jacket pocket and touched his mother's rosary. His thoughts were with his wife, Hannah, and his two small children. His mind drifted to his brother Angelo.

Dear God, be with me. Give me guidance, and whatever my fate, please protect my family. Speravi in te. *My trust is in you.*

Nino said, "I'm ready to go."

The captain turned to Mr. Ordway. "Steer a course to 37° 47' North and 12° 22' East. All ahead full. Get us to Marsala. Now!"

* * *

Captain Ferguson shook Nino's hand. "Good luck, Mr. Servidei."

"Thank you, for your hospitality, captain." Nino turned to climb the ladder of the conning tower. He looked topside to see Senior Chief Harth looking down.

"We are ready for you, Mr. Servidei," he shouted.

Nino took a deep breath, questioned what he had gotten himself into, and proceeded to ascend to the surface of the warship. He climbed hand over hand, foot over foot. The thick rubber suit they issued him restricted his movements. Underneath the rubber suit, he wore dark pants, a white shirt and a dark vest.

When he arrived topside, two additional crew members were with Senior Chief Harth. The sub sat idle at the surface of the Mediterranean Sea. There was a light drizzle, the wind was brisk, and small waves sloshed the side of the vessel.

"How are your ribs?" Harth asked.

Nino patted his side. "They get better every day. As of tomorrow, it will be two weeks since the plane crash."

"And the concussion?"

"The fog is clearing."

"And none too soon, aye, Mr. Servidei?"

They approached the raft, which was positioned on top of the submarine, just above the aft engine room. Mr. Harth pointed to each piece of gear in the little gray boat. "Besides your suitcase and your knapsack, I put a few extra food rations in the raft. It is a long way to the beach, and the current looks rough. By the time you hit the beach you will be starving."

With caution, Nino entered the raft. The two crew members held it steady while he sat down in the center.

Harth shook his hand. "Good luck, Mr. Servidei."

"Thank you, Senior Chief."

Fastened to each side of the raft was an oar. Nino reached for the handles. He watched the three crew members reenter the conning tower, Mr. Harth the last to climb in. With one hand on the hatch, Senior Chief Harth saluted Nino, who returned the gesture.

A sick feeling overcame him. Before meeting Hannah, he had spent much of his life in solitude, yet seldom felt alone because God was with him. But after watching the hatch close, he scanned the sea to the east to see the dark silhouette of Sicily. To his west, the eerie darkness of the Mediterranean Sea greeted him. Loneliness overcame him as it never had before.

Be with me, dear God. Let your will be done.

The sound of clanging metal erupted simultaneously with a vibration under the rubber raft. Behind him, the sound of churning water as the screws of the submarine turned, first a little, then with an increased urgency. The *U.S.S. Barb* moved forward, only slightly initially, then accelerating as it submerged beneath the surface, pulling Nino forward until his raft no longer contacted the top of the sub and he was floating. Only the conning tower of the *Barb* remained visible, then it too disappeared beneath the sea. He turned the raft around so his back was to Marsala, then pulled on the oars, once, then twice, then repeatedly, hoping the current would cooperate and get him to the beach before sunup.

* * *

With a rope from the raft tied around his waist, Nino waded through waist deep water. Waves knocked him off his feet, and the undertow dragged him back into the sea. Shivering, he leaned toward the beach to fight the tide. Step by step, he lunged forward until his momentum was greater than the current. After falling again, he dug into the wet sand. The continuous surge of frigid sea water refused to release its grasp. Losing the raft was less significant than the supplies within it. When the next wave came ashore, he used his forward momentum to drag the boat onward, pulling it to dry land before the outgoing current could seize it again.

Exhausted, Nino dropped to his knees before falling forward onto his face. He lay motionless for less than a minute, before sluggishly standing, realizing that he must keep moving.

There was enough moonlight to see a silhouette of tall grass at the base of a hill. With the rope to the raft still around his waist, he made his way inward. His objective was to bury the boat in the trees at the bottom of the hill.

After crossing through the grass, he entered the woods and sat inside the raft, where he opened the knapsack Senior Chief Harth had packed for him.

As they had reviewed, it contained a shovel, a knife, a second canteen of water, and some canned goods. Also staring up at him was a Colt M1911 pistol.

The canteen refreshed him. He had downed his other fresh water during his arduous journey ashore. The canned goods were very welcome.

He glanced at his watch; it was 0322 hours.

After removing the rubber suit, he grabbed the field shovel, searched for an open area away from the tree roots and went to work.

The hole was not deep, but sufficient. He deflated the raft and threw it in the pit. The rubber suit followed, then the empty cans from his food rations, along with the knife and anything else he no longer needed. He picked up the gun. The Colt model 1911 had been a constant companion during his training at Chopawamsic. The cold metal felt natural in his hand. During his firearm instruction, he had forced the image of the murdered policeman out of his mind, but today, the appearance of the man's face returned. Nino threw the gun into the hole with the other items.

He slipped the black priest cassock over his civilian clothes. It was ankle length, buttoned down the front from collar to knee. It wore like a robe.

Nino had tried it on during his training in Virginia. When he had seen himself in the mirror, he laughed at how Angelo would have made fun of him for wearing a dress. After buttoning the cassock, Nino slid the white roman collar through the small sleeve around his neck. For a final touch, he placed his mother's rosary around his collar. The likeness of the crucified Christ hung at his chest.

It was 0441 hours, and although the hill beside him obstructed the rising sun, the morning glow was evident on the reflection of the Mediterranean Sea.

Before closing the suitcase, he picked up his Bible and caressed it, then laid it on top of the few extra clothes he brought. After taking one last sip of water, he made his way up the hill.

The higher he climbed, the steeper the incline. Halfway up,

he slipped and gripped thick shrubbery with his left hand, while clinging to his suitcase with his right.

When Nino arrived at the top, he found a shanty house at the end of a dirt road. From the outside, it appeared to comprise two rooms. He imagined there was a time when the chipped and peeling paint was once vibrant. Several meters from the house he saw a barn. Beside the barn was an oxcart.

The sun was emerging, and Nino glanced at his watch to see it was nearly 0500 hours. Dirt clung to his cassock, and he bent over to brush it off.

Exhausted, he made his way to the barn, hoping to find a pile of hay to sleep on, if only for a moment. Upon arriving at the door, a voice shouted, "Get off of my property."

Nino turned toward the house to see an elderly woman brandishing a shotgun. She wore a white nightshirt, the hem of which dragged on the ground. She was tiny. When she approached, he could see that she was slightly bigger than the shotgun she was now pointing at his face.

"Please forgive me madam," Nino said. "I am a priest passing through. I was hoping to rest in your barn. Then I need to be on my way."

"What is a priest doing roaming around here? Where did you come from?"

"I am to report to my new assignment at the Abbey of Santa Maria. I am on my way to Marsala to catch a bus."

"You still didn't answer my question. Where did you come from?"

"Sciacca. A kind man offered to take me as far as he could, but he was almost out of fuel. So, I have been on foot since he sent me on my way."

"And this Abbey of… what did you call it again?"

"Santa Maria."

"Where is that?"

"Somewhere in the Sicani Mountain Range."

"What is that accent? Where are you from?"

"I am from Naples, but I studied in America for many years. That is why I sound as I do."

She lowered the shotgun. "My name is Mirna Fabio."

"I am Father Nino Servidei."

"Are you hungry, Father Servidei?" I was headed to the barn for eggs. Why don't you help me, and I'll make you breakfast? Then I will take you to Marsala. It is still rather far from here. Too far for a handsome priest to travel on foot."

* * *

With his suitcase in the back of the oxcart, Nino stared at the ass end of the old mule pulling them down the narrow, dusty road. The clomping of its hooves was rhythmic. Mirna seldom snapped the reins, preferring to offer 'Otto' words of encouragement as he struggled to pull them over an occasional incline. It crossed Nino's mind that had he chosen to walk to Marsala, he would be well beyond their current location.

"How old is Otto?" Nino asked.

Mirna chuckled, then lowered her voice so Otto wouldn't hear her. "He won't be around much longer. But neither will I. I'm hoping by the grace of God we somehow go on the same day. Do you think you could pull some strings for me, Father? We only have each other. I'm afraid that if I go first, poor Otto will starve in the barn with no one to feed him. He'll wonder where I am. It could take weeks for my body to be found."

"Are you a widow? Do you have children?" Nino asked.

"My husband died thirty years ago. I have a son. He lives in France. He teaches music in Paris and has offered to take me in, but this is my home, not Paris."

"What is Sicily like now that war has arrived? I hear the Americans and the British make regular bombing runs."

"I see their planes. We may see some this morning. I hear explosions too."

She pointed east. "There are two massive guns over that ridge. They fire into the air whenever planes fly down the coast."

"Have you ever seen one get shot down?"

"No, but I know they have. I've overheard the men in town discuss it. Apparently, there is a prison camp somewhere on the island where they keep downed British and American airmen."

Nino's heart raced with a sudden hope that Angelo might be one of the prisoners.

For the remainder of their journey, he asked Mirna questions, hesitant to answer any of hers for fear he may slip up and reveal information that contradicted his narrative.

When they arrived in Marsala, Nino said, "You have been very kind, Mirna. Thank you." He then kissed her on the cheek.

She, in turn, placed both of her hands on his face. Her nose inches from his. "Your mama raised a good boy; I can sense such things. You be safe on your journey and once you are settled in, please come back and see me."

"I will," Nino said before leaping from the oxcart, grabbing his bag and patting Otto on the nose. "Take your time getting home, Otto. You have a special passenger."

* * *

"You are here early, father. The first bus doesn't leave for an hour," the bus station attendant said as his keys rattled in the door. "Where are you heading?"

Nino was sitting with his back against the outer wall of the station. He had dozed off. After rubbing his eyes, he said. "I need to get to The Abbey of Santa Maria."

"Never heard of it."

"It is in the Sicani Mountain range."

"Where did you come from?"

Nino told him the same story he had shared with Mirna.

"I got a ride from a kind old lady. I told her I needed a bus stop, and she brought me here."

The bus stop attendant squinted his eyes. Nino sensed his curiosity.

"Whoever gave you a ride from Sciacca, didn't do you any favors. You would have been better off catching a bus from there."

"Maybe so, I'm uncertain. I have only been to Sicily once. That was two years ago, and I never left Palermo.

"Where are you from? That accent has a little Sicilian in it, but you sound more like an American."

"I am originally from Naples. I went away several years ago to study in America. I must have picked up the accent. For the past four years I've been studying in Rome at the *Pontifico Collegio Etiopico*—the Vatican. The Abbey of Santa Maria is my first assignment."

"Come inside, we'll look at a map and figure out the best bus to get you there."

Nino followed the attendant. A map of Sicily hung on the wall.

"The Sicani mountains are here, in the center of the island. It is vast, and most parts are desolate. Do you know what town this Abbey is near?"

"I only know of the Abbey."

The man went to his desk, opened a drawer, and pulled out a chart.

"Without knowing where this Abbey of..."

"Santa Maria."

"Si, the Abbey of Santa Maria. Without knowing exactly where it is, I do not know how to direct you. The best I can do is to get you to Poggioreale. It is at the western base of the mountain range. Once there, you could hire a car to take you to the Abbey. Do you know if this Abbey of Santa Maria has a telephone? Could you call them? Maybe they could pick you up."

"They have no telephone. I have already inquired."

"Well for now, I suggest you take the bus from here to Salemi. Once you get there, you can take another bus to Santa Ninfa, then another to Partanna. Your final transfer will be to Poggioreale."

Nino said, "It sounds like it could take hours."

"That's if you 're lucky and none of the busses break down or run out of fuel. Gasoline rations are getting stricter every week."

* * *

Instincts compelled him to roll to his side and cover his head when a series of booms woke him. He had fallen asleep in the rear seat of the bus. There was a second blast, followed by a third. Leaping to his feet and glancing out of the bus window, Nino saw three antiaircraft guns on the top of a hill firing in rapid succession. Camouflaged under green netting and vegetation, two more were hidden on an adjacent hill. He made a mental note that between the two emplacements trickled a minor stream.

Nino looked toward the front of the bus. The other passengers, few as they were, huddled on the floor between the seats. The driver accelerated down the narrow road. In between the blasts, Nino heard airplane engines. He looked up to see a half dozen planes flying low, each marked with the RAF roundel.

Nino fell to the floor next to an old man. "Where are we? What are we near?"

"We are halfway between Di Girolamo and Borgo Chitarra."

He mentally repeated the statement over and over, hoping he would remember the location of the anti-aircraft placements so he could report them.

* * *

The journey from Marsala to Partanna had been uneventful. Although the distance was not long, he had spent an hour at each of the previous bus terminals before his next departure. The layovers allowed him time to rest and think of his precious family. He had visions of Hannah and Lilia playing Piggly Wiggly, only to be interrupted by Solomon wanting their attention. It made him smile.

Nino climbed onto the final bus to Poggioreale. This one was smaller than his previous transfers, yet more passengers boarded, leaving few seats available. An Italian soldier sat next to Nino.

"Good afternoon, father."

"Good afternoon," Nino replied. "Where are you from?"

"I'm from here—Sicily. I was home visiting my family and just found out my wife is pregnant with our second child."

Nino's first instinct was to discuss his own children but caught himself.

"I'm sure fatherhood is a wonderful experience," Nino said.

"There's nothing like it. When I got home, my little girl— Emma is her name—she ran to me and wrapped her arms around my neck. She wouldn't let go. She is daddy's little girl."

"That's wonderful. I'm Father Nino Servidei, by the way."

"Alexander Giovani is my name," the man said as he nodded at Nino.

"What do you do? Are you a combat soldier?"

"I am part of an anti-aircraft unit."

"You have been busy in recent weeks."

"Now that the Americans have a stronghold in North Africa, their bombing runs have increased, as have the British."

"Have you been successful in shooting them down?" Nino asked.

"Some, but they have also found a few of our anti-aircraft positions. Three weeks ago, I lost four members of my unit— direct hits from American bombers."

"Do you move the guns around?"

"Some of our units are mobile. Mine is fixed and close to here. It's between Di Girolamo and Borgo Chitarra."

POGGIOREALE, SICILY

"I need to get to the Abbey of Santa Maria," Nino said to the bus station attendant.

The man pointed to a mountain top. "It's up there toward the highest peak."

Nino glanced out of the window of the little shack. "How do I get there?"

"You could walk, but I wouldn't advise it because it would take several hours. It will be nightfall before you arrive, and the nights get cold this time of year."

"No buses go there?" Nino asked.

"No need. Those who live at the abbey seldom leave. There are a few small villages and some farms up there, but those people have their own vehicles."

"So how do I get there?" Nino asked.

"If you have money, you can pay someone to take you."

"I have some money, but not much. I'm a priest after all."

"Let me make a phone call." The attendant said. "I'll be right back."

Nino paced the waiting room, then stared out of the window at the mountain in front of him. It had been a long day. He was hungry and exhausted.

The attendant returned. "Do you have forty *lire*?"

"I do."

"My brother will be here tomorrow morning. He'll take you. You are welcome to spend the night here in the bus station, padre."

THE ABBEY OF SANTA MARIA

Nino made his way through the gate. Children were playing tag in the courtyard. A young woman watched over them. He approached Isabella, and she turned. Nino sensed a look of curiosity. She studied his face.

"Good afternoon, *signora*. I am looking for Father Russo. Could you direct me to him?"

She hesitated, saying nothing at first. She tilted her head to the side as though hypnotized by the sight of him.

"Excuse me for being rude, father, but you look similar to someone I know."

"Is he handsome?"

She laughed.

"I'm sorry, miss. Please forgive me. Sometimes my attempts at humor cause me to say things that are inappropriate."

"I found it amusing." After a pause she added, "Your accent. Are you an American?"

I can't even fool a teenage girl.

"I attended school in America—my undergraduate studies. I guess I picked up a bit of an accent after four years."

She leaned forward and whispered, "We aren't used to having priests travel through here who look like you."

"How so?"

Isabella didn't answer as she turned. "Children, stay here and continue to play. I'm going to take father... I'm sorry, I didn't get your name."

"Father Servidei. My name is Father Nino Servidei."

Turning back to the children, she said. "I will return in a moment."

"Si, Miss Leone," the children said.

She said to Nino, "Father Russo is usually in his office this time of day. Please follow me."

They made their way through an arched entrance of a small courtyard, then into an open breezeway. An office door to the right was open. A heavy-set, balding priest sat at a desk.

"Father Russo, you have a visitor."

Isabella stepped aside and allowed Nino to enter the office.

Father Russo stood. "Good afternoon. I wasn't expecting any visitors."

Isabella said, "This is Father Nino Servidei. I will leave you two alone." Turning her gaze to Nino. "It was a pleasure to meet you."

"The pleasure is all mine."

Isabella returned to the children. Father Russo pointed to one of the two chairs in front of his desk. "Please have a seat."

Father Russo said, "I thought I knew every priest on the island, however you are a new face. How may I help you?"

"Father Russo, someone you know suggested I contact you."

"Oh. And who was that?"

"Father Morlion."

Father Russo raised his eyebrows. He studied Nino. "I have been a priest for many years. I have crossed paths with many colleagues. This father Morlion doesn't ring a bell to me."

Nino fidgeted in his chair. His stomach turned; he was concerned something wasn't right.

"He spoke fondly of you. He said to remind you of one of your favorite bible verses, Hebrews 13:6, *'and so we can say with confidence: With the Lord on my side, I fear nothing: what can human beings do to me?*

Father Russo stood and closed the door of the office. "I have been expecting you."

"I'm relieved to hear that. I wasn't certain what type of reception I would receive."

"We are on your side."

"May I ask you who '*we*' are?"

"There is a small group of us. Perhaps you will meet them."

"Do you trust them completely?"

"I do. They are good men."

"I need you to let it be known that I am a recent graduate of the *Pontificio Collegio Etiopico* and this is my first assignment. I will be your understudy. You will play the role of my mentor."

"That sounds reasonable."

"I will also need you to help me gather information. I need to know German and Italian force strength. Specifically, where their strongholds are."

"We have already begun that process. But we have received complaints we haven't covered enough of the island. During my wireless transmissions, they say they need to know what is along the southern coast. We are just a few men. It would take dozens to compile the information the Allies want."

"That is why I'm here. They have assigned me to recruit others."

"*Others*. Who are these others?"

"It is best you don't know. Nor will they know of you. It is for your protection and theirs. There will be two separate cells. You will report on Palermo and the mountains, as you have been doing. This other group will work the rest of the island, focusing on the southern coast."

"What is the significance of the southern coast?"

"I don't have that information, but we can speculate. Do you have a vehicle? I will need one."

"We have a small Renault Sedan. It is old, but it is free for you to use."

"Is it reliable?"

"Most of the time. Isabella's papa has offered to give us one of his trucks, but the Leone family is far too generous with the orphanage as it is, so I have declined."

"Does it have fuel?"

"Not much."

"Where can I get gas?"

"The Leones have fuel on their citrus farm. Farmers receive more fuel rations than everyone else."

"The wireless you mentioned. How often do you transmit? How concerned are you about detection?

"The Allies gave me a calendar with certain days of the month to transmit. They want communication to take place in an inconsistent pattern. Harder to trace, you see. They also want me to transmit from different locations, but that isn't possible. Hiding places to transmit on the mountain are few. The abbey is all I have."

"When is the next transmission?"

"Saturday evening. Three nights from now," Father Russo said. "Do you have specific information to send?"

Nino considered reporting the antiaircraft placement he passed on his journey up the mountain—Between Di Girolamo and Borgo Chitarra. He thought of the Italian soldier he sat next to on the bus—Alexander Giovani.

"When I got home, my little girl—Emma is her name—she ran to me and wrapped her arms around my neck. She wouldn't let go. She is daddy's little girl."

"Nothing specific," Nino said. "I just need to let them know I have arrived."

* * *

"These will be your quarters, Nino. You don't mind if I call you Nino, do you?" Father Russo said.

"Personally, no, but I think it is important that we maintain our professional courtesies, even when we are alone. It will reduce the chance of a slipup when we are around others."

"That is wise, Father Servidei. I will comply with your wish."

Nino inspected the small room. There was a fireplace in the corner that held only two logs. Pressed against the stucco wall was a wooden cot. The floor was dirt.

"It isn't much," Father Russo said. "But it's all we offer our male guests. The nun's quarters are a little more lavish. They have a wooden floor."

"This will be fine," Nino said.

"You may use my lavatory. It is down the hall from my office. Lorenzo Leone was kind enough to dig a well for us years ago, so we have working showers—cool water only. Or if you prefer, there is always the little lagoon where we have a lovely waterfall. Just exit the gate, turn left and follow the stream down the hill. However, be careful, sometime the nuns choose to bathe there. But you should be safe until summer. It's a bit chilly for them this time of year. Why don't you rest, Father Servidei? Dinner isn't for three hours. The dining hall is across the courtyard next to the kitchen. We eat with the children; I hope you don't mind."

Nino grinned. "Their laughter and little faces will be a blessing after my journey."

Father Russo gripped the iron handle of Nino's wooden door. "We serve dinner at 1800 hours."

Before the door closed, Nino said. "Father Russo, these other partisans—when can I meet them?"

"We are scheduled to meet two days from now—Friday evening. As I said, my next transmission is Saturday. We always meet the day before. They tell me what they have noticed."

"Has their information been valuable?"

"There have in fact been successful airstrikes because of their reports. Our Palermo contact has reported ship movements. The reports we have received back, express gratitude, but they emphasize the importance of the information along the southern coast. Hopefully, this other cell, as you referred to it, will be more helpful."

"That remains to be seen."

* * *

Lorenzo and Bruno entered Father Russo's office. Nino greeted them. Bruno shook Nino's hand and made cordial introductions. Lorenzo said nothing, crossed the room, and positioned a chair toward the center of the office.

Nino approached Lorenzo and looked down at the seated man. "Mr. Leone, it is my pleasure to meet you."

"Father Servidei, or whoever you are, I will tell you upfront. I have my doubts about you and your purpose here."

The discussion paused, and their heads turned when a car entered the courtyard. Dim headlights shone into the office window. Bruno peered through the curtain. "Manuel has arrived."

Nino returned his attention to Lorenzo. "Should I be concerned?"

"About what?"

"About where your loyalties lie."

Lorenzo rose. His face inches from Nino. "Let me make

something clear to you. I am here to rid Italy of Mussolini, not to kill Italian soldiers."

"I respect that and share your torment. I cherish life. Everyone's life, as I know Father Russo does."

"Nino!"

After hearing his name called, Nino turned toward the door. "Manuel!"

"It is me, my friend. I can't believe you are standing before me. I thought you were dead."

"Why would you think that?"

Manuel looked down before answering. "When papa took you, Hannah and Lilia to North Africa, he never made it back."

"What?"

"The wreckage of his boat was found. We think it was hit by a larger vessel. When a salvage crew found the *Cornelian*, the ship had caused it to disintegrate. Many small pieces were floating in the water."

Nino found a wooden chair and buried his face in his hands. Manuel approached, resting his palm on his shoulder.

Nino looked up at Manuel. "He died saving us."

"He died helping a family he cared about. He helped you make it safely out of Italy and would have no regrets."

Nino embraced Manuel again. "Hannah gave birth to a baby boy. We named him after your papa."

"You named him Solomon?"

"We did."

"How is Hannah?"

"She is fine and such a wonderful mother."

"And Lilia?"

Nino grinned. "She's a seven-year-old terror, but so precious. She is learning English."

"Olivia will be so glad to see you. Come for dinner."

"I will."

Manuel put his arm around Nino and turned toward the others in the room. "As you can see, I know him. He is married to my brother's widow. He is a fine man. We can trust him; I assure you of that."

"So, you are Jewish?" Lorenzo asked Nino.

"No." Nino replied. "I am a Catholic. But Hannah, my wife is Jewish."

Manuel said, "It is a long history. I'll explain it to you all later. But for now, we need to get the meeting started so we can get home."

Standing next to Father Russo's desk, Nino assessed the four men seated before him, concerned specifically with Lorenzo Leone, and how best to appease him.

"Gentlemen, my name is Nino Servidei. The American government has sent me, and we are seeking your help. It is imperative that you understand that my country does not view Italy as our enemy. We view Mussolini, fascism, and the Nazi war machine as our enemy. We would like you to view us as partners in ending their tyrannical rule and restoring your liberty."

"What would you like us to do?" Lorenzo asked.

"Not much more than what you have been doing. We just want to be part of it."

"So why are you here if our role doesn't change?"

"I have other duties on the island. I can't get into details, but there are others here on the island I need to contact. They will play a similar role as you."

"Who is this other group?"

"I can't share that for their protection and yours. If they don't know who you are and you don't know who they are, it limits releasing information during a potential interrogation."

"What about you," Lorenzo asked. "What if you get captured? Will you break?"

Nino remained silent, wanting to say he wouldn't, but that was a promise he knew he could never make with his knowledge of German interrogation techniques.

"I do not intend to be discovered."

Lorenzo asked, "But if you are, then what?"

Nino said, "We could all ask the same question of anyone in this room. We all know the risks. Anyone who isn't all in, we will understand if you want to remove yourself from the group."

Bruno spoke up. "Father Servidei, Lorenzo's son, my grandson, Aldo, was killed in North Africa fighting the British. I'm sure you can appreciate his hesitation."

"You have my condolences. The pain you are feeling is a pain I can't possibly know. Yet, that is the very reason we need your help. Our desire is to put an end to senseless death and suffering."

Lorenzo said, "I need your assurances that Italian soldiers won't be targeted."

"I can't make that promise. Sicily stands in the way of freedom for all of Europe. There are more Italians defending Sicily than there are Germans."

Lorenzo moved toward the door. "Then I am out."

Father Russo put his hand up. "Please wait, Lorenzo. There

is something I have been holding back from sharing. I think now is the time."

Lorenzo paused near the door, hat in hand. Father Russo stepped behind his desk, opened his top left drawer, and removed a stack of letters. He then reached into another drawer and tossed another stack on his desk, then another and another. When he had finished, dozens of letters lay on the surface of his desk. The mound was tall enough that a few slid onto the floor.

"I want all of you to know that I believe our task here is repulsive. Do you think that when I went to seminary, my intention was to order military air strikes on my fellow man— German or Italians? I too struggle with my conscience. At times, it is unbearable. Each day I enter the chapel and drop to my knees at the altar of our Lord, begging God for his mercy upon my soul."

A tear rolled down his cheek as he one by one, stared into the eyes of each man.

Father Russo continued. "These letters are from others, mostly clergy—some protestant—but mainly Catholic. There are letters from civilians too, sharing their accounts of watching their families murdered before their very eyes. There are two that have photos if you can stomach seeing them."

Father Russo reached forward and randomly retrieved a letter from the pile and read:

March 11th, 1941,
To all, who in the name of God cherish humanity.
My name is Fr. Wilhelm Jodl. I am of German descent. I moved to Poland from the Rhineland in 1928. My parish is in the Village of Lodz, Poland.

The story I am about to tell you is my own firsthand account.

Four months ago, the German army invaded our city of Lodz. Shortly after, the Waffen-SS arrived and forced the citizens into the streets and searched their property.

I watched as small children, including infants, were ripped from their parents' arms and placed in trucks. Three- and four-year-old babies screamed in fear as their little outstretched arms reached for their parents, who were being restrained by German soldiers. Parents dropped to their knees in terror as their children were driven away. Those who fought back, refusing to release their children, were beaten in the streets. I saw the faces of fathers and mothers covered in blood from the blows of rifle butts.

As time passed, two camps were built by slave laborers. After they completed the camps, the men who built them were loaded onto trucks and driven away.

Other trucks arrived at the two newly completed camps. On the trucks were children who appeared to be between the ages of six and sixteen. Girls were in one camp, and boys in the other.

It is rumored that medical experiments are being performed on these innocent children. From my home, I have heard the terror in their screams, the sound of which will haunt me endlessly until I take my final breath. I drop to my knees begging for God's mercy upon these innocent lives, and to give me rest from my guilt for doing nothing to save them.

This letter is an open cry to humanity to put an end to

what is happening in Poland. It is also a prayer to God to
please put an end to these atrocities.
   Father Wilhelm Jodl
   The Church of St. Joseph
   Lodz Poland

"There are over four dozen letters currently stacked on my desk. I'm sure there are endless numbers of clergy all throughout Europe who have received similar documents from partisan messengers. We need to get them to England. In the meantime, do you want me to read more of these letters to you, or would you prefer to read them yourself?"

Stillness lingered in the room as the men stared at the pile of documents.

"I keep these letters locked in my desk. If you ever have any doubts about whose side God is on, I will gladly give you the key so you can remind yourself of the evil we are fighting."

Father Russo approached Lorenzo. "Aldo was an exceptional young man with a good, caring heart. You have told me yourself, he wasn't fighting for Mussolini, but was a victim of Mussolini. As for the Italian soldier, whether or not they know it, they are on the wrong side of history. They are on the wrong side of humanity. The sooner this war ends, the sooner they can return home. May God's mercy embrace them and the innocent children of Europe."

Lorenzo turned to Nino. "Mr. Servidei, tell me what you need."

After the group dispersed, Father Russo escorted Nino into the chapel and they knelt behind the altar. Father Russo slid the door back and pulled out the wireless.

"I'm assuming you know how to use this," Father Russo said.

"I'm well-trained, father. I recently found myself freezing in Iceland and my teeth chattered in Morse Code."

Nino put the headphones on, powered the device and proceeded to contact the American submarine off the coast of Sicily. His message was, "Neptune, this is Redeemer. I am nesting safely."

* * *

"I have no tools if the motor doesn't start," Father Russo said.

Nino stared at the 1924 Renault Berline. It was a four-door sedan, with wood trim around the windows. "That's an interesting shade of green, Father."

"Isn't it though? Peppe, one of the children who lives here, says it looks like a green olive." Laughing, Fr. Russo said, "But everything reminds Peppe of food."

Nino laughed.

Father Russo said, "A man in Catania donated it."

"How often do you drive it?"

"Rarely. The Leones bring our supplies. Sometimes I'll take the school children who live in the village home if the weather is bad. On sunny days, I have been known to go for a joy ride. But not as much lately with the fuel shortages."

"If I arrive at the Leone farm, do you think they will supply me with gas?"

"If they have it."

"Other than the Leones, where can I get gas?"

"Palermo. But I always get mine from the Leones."

"When you travel, do people recognize it as belonging to the orphanage?"

"*Si.* It is very distinguishable. Is that a problem?"

"No, quite the contrary. If I'm seen on the road, I want people to know I am a priest from the orphanage. I'm hoping once the German and Italian patrols see me, they will leave me be, assuming I am just visiting the sick and elderly."

"Get in. Let's see if it starts," Father Russo said.

When Nino entered, it smelled of mold and mildew. With the turn of the ignition, the engine spit and sputtered before cutting off.

"Try it again," Father Russo said.

This time, it turned and rumbled to life. They both grinned and clapped their hands.

"You are ready to go, my boy."

Nino shut off the engine. "I'll be leaving in the morning."

BELLISSIMA VALLE

Springtime meant blooming citrus trees on the horizon as far as Nino could see. Over the crest of a hill, several acres of olive trees appeared. Intermingled amongst the orchards were side roads, sheds, and barns.

As he made his way into the valley, Nino turned onto a narrow road. A sign read *Bellissima Valle.*

* * *

Lorenzo and Bruno had ordered tractor parts and were on their way to Messina to pick them up from the latest ferryboat arrival. Isabella had taken a horse out into the field to inspect something, but Angelo was half asleep when she told him, and couldn't recall the details. Other than two field hands pulling a cart from the barn, the courtyard was deserted. Angelo carefully replaced the front curtain to its original position so they wouldn't see him.

Although still numb, his leg had healed nicely, and Bruno had made him a cane to replace the crutch.

"You must keep using it," Bruno would tell him. "The blood must flow through the smaller vessels, or it will never heal completely."

Angelo paced back and forth between the parlor and the kitchen, occasionally stopping to peek out the front for any sign of Isabella. He questioned his feelings for her. They continued to grow stronger, and their interactions puzzled him. She was flirty but distant at times. They had kissed on two occasions, yet she withdrew from his further advances. After several more laps around the kitchen, he returned to the front window. He smiled at the sight of Isabella galloping down the hill. He noticed a cloud of dust in the distance. He laughed out loud at the sight of the old green rattletrap making its way down the driveway. He retreated to his room.

* * *

When Nino entered the courtyard, two field hands were greasing the wheels of a cart.

He climbed out of the Renault and approached them. "I am Father Nino Servidei—from the orphanage."

"*Benvenuto*, I am Eduardo Butto, and this is my brother Pasquale. Isabella has told us about you."

"There isn't much to tell."

Pasquale chuckled, "Her papa and grandpapa tease her, claiming she has a crush—"

Eduardo elbowed Pasquale. "Don't listen to him. He doesn't know what he is talking about."

They turned at the sound of galloping hooves. Isabella arrived, pulled the reins back, and leaped from the towering stallion.

"How did you get up on him?" Nino asked.

"Please don't make fun of my small size, father."

"I wasn't making fun, Isabella. I'm impressed. You clearly have complete control of that massive beast."

Pasquale said, "That's how she is with all the men at *Bellissima Valle.*"

She smacked his arm. "You stop."

They erupted in laughter.

"As you can see, father, it isn't easy being the only girl here. They tease me without mercy."

"I'm sure it is only because they love you."

Isabella glanced over Nino's shoulder toward the house, confirming that Angelo wasn't visible. "Did you come to visit me?"

Pasquale snickered.

Nino said, "It is always wonderful to see you, Isabella, but I was hoping I could trouble you for fuel. I have errands to run on the island."

"Yes, of course. Follow me, to the rear of the barn. That's where we park the petrol truck."

Isabella slid the nozzle into the tank. "Where are you going today, father?"

"I would like to visit some of the other parishes to get acquainted with other priests. I would also like to familiarize myself with Sicily. I've only been here one other time. That was almost two years ago."

"Would you like me to be your tour guide? We can take one of our trucks. It would be more reliable than this thing Father Russo has loaned you."

"I would hate to trouble you."

"It's no trouble. I would like to drive you around."

"I can't ask that of you, Isabella, I'm sure you have much to do. And I don't know how long I will be gone."

"I'm a good driver. And I'm familiar with the roads."

"Maybe I will take you up on your offer one day soon."

"I would like that," Isabella said, as she replaced the nozzle to the back of the tanker truck.

THE DIVINCENZO COMPOUND

First it was two vehicles, *Kübelwagens*, driving in the opposite direction. They passed him on the narrow, unpaved road, forcing Nino's outer tires into the tall weeds. Once they passed, he turned the wheel hard to get the car back on the road.

At the crest of a hill, a convoy of troop carriers appeared, making no effort to avoid Nino, compelling him to again veer into the tall grass. With his tires spinning, he pressed the accelerator. After the vehicles were behind the Renault, he veered back onto the dirt road.

Within a few kilometers, he entered a canopy of trees. The sky was sunny, yet the thick forest offered a serene darkness.

His entrance into the woods revealed a display of military vehicles, both German and Italian. Some were on the move, most remained parked. There were troop carriers, wheeled artillery, *Kübelwagens* and tanks—French built—used by the Italians. Encircling them were field tents surrounded by soldiers working at maintaining the vehicles, yet others were relaxing. Those at the edge of the road appeared curious about the priest in the green Renault.

A sizable, single story white house enclosed within a matching wall came into view. Nino entered the open gate and parked in the courtyard. An Italian officer approached.

"May I help you, padre?"

"My name is Father Nino Servidei. I'm here to see Alfonso DiVincenzo."

The officer waved his hand at an older man in a white jacket who approached.

The officer said, "This man would like to see your boss."

Pierre looked at Nino with a raised eyebrow. "Is Mr. DiVincenzo expecting you?"

"No, he is not. My name is Father Nino Servidei. I would like to speak to him."

"Father, Mr. DiVincenzo sees no one without a scheduled engagement."

"Would you ask him if he will make an exception?"

"I will ask, but I already know what his answer will be."

"If you would be so kind. I'll wait," Nino said.

After the man entered the house, Nino turned to scan the property. The amount of activity was bewildering. He arrived on a mission to persuade his grandfather to help him defeat an enemy he had apparently embraced with enthusiasm. Nino's father's words rang in his ears.

"Alfonso DiVincenzo is only loyal to Alfonso DiVincenzo. If it helps him to be loyal to Italy, he will be loyal to Italy. If it helps him to not be loyal to Italy, he will not be loyal to Italy."

The officer said, "Are you his priest? This man DiVincenzo doesn't seem religious."

"Maybe he's not."

The officer laughed. "Are you here to lead him to God?"

"I will speak to anyone who will listen."

"Why this one? I've heard people in town refer to him as Satan himself."

Pierre returned. "I'm sorry, father. When I told Mr. DiVincenzo there was a priest here to see him, he laughed and told me to send you on your way."

Nino looked up at the trees and exhaled. "Could you tell him it is important and that I have some valuable information to share with him?"

"Padre, I'm sorry, but Mr. DiVincenzo has little patience. If I return to him, I will absorb his wrath, and I'm not willing to do that."

Nino sensed this was his only chance. If he failed today, there was no point in returning. "He has met me before. Perhaps you would be so kind as to remind him of our first encounter."

Pierre said, "No, I will not."

The officer said, "Give the padre a break. He came a long way to get here."

Pierre shook his head. Father, I gave him your name. He didn't remember you."

"Please return to him. Tell him I am the young man he met two years ago in Palermo. Tell him I'm the one who said that he and his son, the man living in New York, were both repulsive."

The officer chuckled. Pierre laughed.

"You want me to tell him that, father? And that's going to be what wins him over? Okay, padre. I'll tell him. I'm sure he will be amused."

After Pierre entered the house, the officer asked, "Did you really say that to him?"

"I did."

"What was his response?"

"I don't know. After I said it, I instantly turned and walked away."

The door to the house opened. Without coming completely out, Pierre yelled, "Father Servidei, he will see you."

Nino nodded to the officer, then made his way across the courtyard and followed Pierre into the house. There was a large foyer. They made their way to a side office and through a set of French doors. Except for a small fire in the fireplace and a desk lamp, the room was in darkness.

"That will be all, Pierre," Alfonso said.

Pierre left the room and closed the door behind him.

Nino watched embers float in the air as his grandfather rearranged fireplace logs with a metal poker. The room was warm, and perspiration moistened the collar of his cassock. He was experiencing the same anxiety he felt with his father at Luigi's Restaurant.

Still poking the logs, Alfonso said, "It's been almost two years since we met."

"Yes, it has."

"Are you really my grandson?"

"I am. My Name is Nino. My father is your son, Salvador."

"Why do you refer to yourself as Nino Servidei?"

"I legally changed my last name."

"Why? Are you ashamed to be a DiVincenzo?"

"It's a long story."

"During our first brief encounter you told me you found me repulsive. And if my memory serves me, you also said you find your father repulsive."

"You are correct, I did say that, grandfather."

"Now you are here for what purpose? Dressed like that, I'm assuming it is to save my soul. To protect me from my own repulsiveness."

"Repulsive is a word that I now regret."

Alfonso replaced the poker to its metal stand and pointed to a couple of chairs in the corner of the room and directed Nino to sit. "Never be afraid to speak your mind, grandson. It is a sign of courage."

"Maybe courage, but not wisdom."

Salvador shrugged. "So, why are you here?"

"It appears as though you are a patriot."

"A patriot? What do you mean?"

"Based on what I observed in your compound, you are clearly supporting the fascist war effort."

"Looks can be deceiving."

"Oh?"

"Do you think I invited all of this nonsense? Their vehicles are destroying my property."

"They are forcing this on you?"

Alfonso leaned forward. "I may very well be their biggest enemy. Even more so than the British and Americans. They are just too stupid to know it."

"You can't ask them to leave?"

Alfonso chuckled. "I have nine old men with shotguns and rifles who work for me. The Germans and Italian armies have machine guns and tanks. I had younger men before the war. They are all gone. Some are fighting the Russians; others are in North Africa. Hell, I just found out that one of them is stationed here on my property."

Nino asked, "What is your plan?"

"Plan for what?"

"To get rid of them."

"My plan is to wait and hope the British and Americans arrive to drive them out of here."

Nino sat back and grinned.

Alfonso raised his eyebrows. "Did I say something interesting?"

"Why do you think I am here?"

"I don't know. Twice, I've asked you to tell me, yet I still don't know."

Nino sat up straight. "The American government has sent me."

Salvador fixed his eyes on Nino. "Continue."

"They need information, and they were hoping you could help them get it."

"What kind of information?"

"Much of it is right here on your compound. They need to know where the Germans and Italians have positioned their troops, and in what strengths. They also want to know the morale of the soldiers, particularly the Italians."

"What are the Allies planning?"

"I don't have the details. I can only speculate."

"Do you think it is an invasion?"

Nino remained silent.

"Sicily, or the mainland?"

"They didn't send me to the mainland to get this information, did they?"

"You know what would happen to me if they caught us? You too, for that matter."

Nino shrugged. "They would execute us."

"Precisely."

"Does that bother you?" Nino asked.

"I've skirted death many times. But I am old. What about you? You are young."

"That's why we must succeed. Much is at stake, even my life."

"So, what now?"

"Do your men travel the island?"

"Daily."

"Are they ever questioned?"

"Frequently. But I have business interests everywhere. I have arranged for them to have documents."

"And where do you believe their loyalties lie—your men, I mean?"

"I don't know. Several of them have sons fighting. I can't trust them with this."

"Do you have any men whose loyalties to you are greater than to Italy?"

"Four—maybe five. They have been with me since they were young. They have stood by my side even through the darkest hours of Cesare Mori, and they have protected me. Even killed for me."

Although curious, Nino ignored the 'killed' statement. "We have little time. I will need to meet with these men—the four you trust."

"What do you need them to do?"

"I need them to scour the island and retrieve information. Some of it they may already have. Do you have a map of Sicily?"

Alphonso rose and crossed the room, opening a drawer of a large credenza. He pulled out several large rolls of paper and laid the first on a table in the room's corner. He turned on a floor lamp. "Will any of this work?"

Marked in ink, the first displayed various names of people. There were several in Palermo. Nino gasped. One name in the corner read 'Camilo Roseman,' Hannah's murdered husband. He studied the map and noticed dozens of names.

"Who are these people? What do these names represent?"

Salvador rolled up the map. "This one will do us no good. Let's use the others."

Nino watched him place the map with the names in the drawer. The experience was surreal. The man who authorized the murder of Hannah's first husband was before him, about to become his partner.

Alfonso opened another. "This isn't the one I want, either."

He rolled it up and returned it to the drawer. He unrolled the third. "Yes, this is it."

Roads and bridges were marked in detail.

Nino said, "This one will work perfectly. Do you have any photographs of the coastline?"

"A few, but they are old. Things change over time. They have built houses and hotels. Beaches erode and sand shifts."

"Do you travel the island much, grandfather?"

"Not like I once did. I prefer to stay home. Before these German and Italian bastards arrived, this forest was peaceful. It was my sanctuary."

"These four men of yours you speak of. May I meet them?"

"They are not here. I have them out... collecting funds."

Nino assumed he was referring to extortion activities. A business his own father was a master of.

"When will they return?"

"Most of my men meet every morning."

Nino said, "No others can be present. Just you, me, and these four men. No one else must know of our encounter."

"Return in three days—during mid-day. Most of the German and Italian officers are away at that time."

"I will return."

Pierre escorted Nino back to the entrance. A German officer emerged from a back bedroom. A beautiful girl trailed behind him. Nino locked eyes with her. He had seen her before. Her reaction indicated that she recognized him too. Then he remembered. It was in Algiers when he was escaping with Hannah and Lilia through North Africa. American agents had sent him to her to help smuggle documents.

* * *

After his meeting with his grandfather, Nino had contacted Neptune, and passed on the information he had gained from their discussion. They had passed on additional instructions and emphasized that time was of the essence, a reminder that had been drilled into his head since he first spoke with Donovan.

After entering the home, Alfonso greeted Nino and turned to Pierre. "Tell Enzo to notify us if he sees Richter's car approaching. When you leave, close the door behind you. We are not to be disturbed."

"Si, Mr. DiVincenzo."

Alfonso directed his four most trusted lieutenants to a round table in the center of the room. Nino joined them.

Alfonso said, "Gentlemen, this is Father Nino Servidei, the one I was telling you about. He is here to help return Sicily to us, and needs information, and he needs it quickly. Is this understood?"

"Si, Mr. DiVincenzo," they said in unison.

"Father Servidei," Alfonso said, "The floor is yours."

"Gentlemen, let me say first that it is imperative that what we discuss this evening doesn't leave this office. I would encourage you to not even discuss it amongst yourselves."

"My next question is this, are you okay with providing information that may get your fellow Italians killed?"

"The group looked at each other and laughed. The largest one, Giuseppe, looked at the others. How many Italians have we killed in our lifetime?"

Matteo shrugged. "Myself, I believe I have killed eight. Would that be your estimate, Mr. DiVincenzo?"

"At, least." Alfonso said.

"I've killed six," Giuseppe said.

Nino looked at his grandfather, who was lighting a cigar.

Alfonso stared back, "What? You are suddenly shocked. You came here to get intelligence, knowing that the information will get men killed, yet you look on us in judgement. Don't be so pious, father. You seek to have men killed for your reasons, and we seek to have men killed for ours. The point is, you want men killed, and we can help you kill them."

His grandfather's bluntness made Nino uneasy. Once again, he thought of the children of the young man he met on the bus. He looked at the thugs, who viewed the ending of another man's life as casually as his grandfather viewed extinguishing a cigar. He became nauseous, realizing that the man who killed Hannah's first husband may have planned his murder in this very room.

Addressing the group, Nino said, "I need to know where the largest concentrations of German and Italian troops are positioned, and what the heavy weapon strength is and where it is located—particularly tanks and large guns. Are there land mines or hidden bunkers? Are there mines in the water? Any information such as this is crucial."

The men looked at each other. "Is that all you need?" Giuseppe asked. "Hell, we can provide most of that to you right now. In a few days we will have more specifics."

Antonio leaned forward. "Open your eyes, Padre. Much of what you are looking for is right outside the doors of this very estate."

* * *

As the men met, Gabrielle approached Pierre. "That priest who went into Mr. DiVincenzo's office? Do you know his name?"

"His name is Father Nino Servidei. Why?"

"We have met. It was a couple of years ago. When they finish in there, may I speak with him?"

"I will let him know of your wish."

"I will be on the back patio."

* * *

As the men left the office, Pierre approached Nino. "Father, there is a young lady on the back patio that has requested your counsel."

Nino looked toward the rear of the house. "Do you know her name?"

"Gabrielle Fontaine. She is General Richter's paid mistress."

Nino met her on the patio. In English, Gabrielle said, "Do you remember me?"

"We met in Algiers."

She moved closer. "You are a priest now. But you were so in love with your wife. Did something change?"

Nino grabbed Gabrielle by the elbow and escorted her toward the stables. "I can't tell you why I am here. But you must promise not to tell anyone you know me or how we met. Please, I beg of you. You could get us both killed."

"Are you on some type of spy mission?"

"Please, Gabrielle. Don't ask me questions."

"Maybe you can help me. I need to get information to the Americans."

"I don't understand."

"Think about how we met in Algiers. The Americans sent you to me so you could get an envelope. You then smuggled that envelope somewhere for the Americans. Why do you think I am here whoring myself out to one of the highest-ranking German officers in Sicily?"

Nino looked over his left shoulder, then his right. "Do you have information now?"

"General Richter and I were drinking heavily the other night. I sensed something troubled him. When I asked him what it was, he hesitated at first, so I probed deeper. He told me that dozens of his fighter planes and torpedo boats were being transferred from Sicily to southern Greece. It agitated him, and he slammed his fist because he had been lobbying for the first Panzer Division to be transferred from France to Sicily for a potential invasion. He learned that they too will be transferred to Salonika and not Sicily. He referred to it as foolishness over some documents found on a dead British airman who washed up on the coast of Spain. Richter believes it is all too coincidental, and the Germans are falling for a trap, and that the Allies will attack Sicily or the southern boot of Italy."

Distracted, Gabrielle looked over Nino's shoulder. He followed her gaze and turned to see General Richter standing on the back patio, staring at them.

Nino returned to the house. As he strolled past the general, he nodded without speaking. The general raised his eyebrows.

Richter strode toward the stables and said to Gabrielle, "Why didn't you introduce me to your friend?"

"His name is Father Nino Servidei. He was here visiting Mr. DiVincenzo and was kind enough to offer me spiritual counsel."

"He didn't persuade you to find a new line of work, did he? You are far too talented at what you do now."

"That was in fact what he was trying to do. But don't worry, darling. I have no other talents. You won't be rid of me that easily."

THE BRONX NEW YORK

Tears rolled down Hannah's cheeks as she lay on the examining table. The doctor would enter the room in a few minutes to examine her. Yet she already knew the diagnosis. She had been pregnant four times in her life, and the only baby to make it to full term was Solomon. The pain now radiating through her lower back was both familiar and excruciating. She took comfort in knowing that Nino left for Sicily before knowing she was pregnant.

The doctor entered the room. "Has the pain decreased, Mrs. Servidei?"

"It's about the same."

He pressed the stethoscope to her abdomen. First on the left side, then the right. He then moved it to the top, then the bottom.

"I don't like that look on your face, doctor."

He looked at her and said nothing before applying the instrument to her stomach several more times.

"Mrs. Servidei, I'm sorry, but the last time you were here, the baby's heartbeat was strong. I'm not hearing anything today."

CHAPTER 15

THE ABBEY OF SANTA MARIA

The children listened to Father Russo give the blessing. Father Russo, Sister Anna, and Sister Catherine were at one end of the table. At the other end sat Nino and Isabella. Nine children sat between them.

"Only one potato, Peppe," Sister Catherine said. "Leave some for the others."

Isabella looked at Nino and giggled. "Peppe likes to eat."

Peppe was oblivious to the other children's smirking.

"Bless him," Nino said.

Isabella said, "How long are you assigned to the abbey for, Father?"

"I hope only a short time until I receive a permanent assignment."

"Do you not like it here?"

"It is wonderful. I love the children. Though, I am hoping for more duties, perhaps somewhere near Rome."

"You are ambitious, then."

Nino shook his head. "No, I just wish to be closer to home."

"Naples, was it?" Isabella asked while cutting into a turnip.

"Si, I am from Naples," Nino responded, hoping her

inquiries would not force him into more dishonesty.

"Tell me about your family. Do you have any brothers or sisters? Are your parents alive?"

"I have a brother. His name is Angelo. And yes, my parents are alive." Changing the subject, Nino asked, "What about you? Father Russo says, your family has been very generous to the orphanage. He says they 'wouldn't have survived without the generosity of the Leone family."

"We do what we can."

"It is kind of you to volunteer. The children adore you."

"They are wonderful."

Isabella leaned over to wipe a little girl's nose before asking Nino, "Why did you become a priest?"

"I believe God put me on this earth to help others. In my heart, I know that becoming a priest was the best way for me to serve my fellow man."

"You can help others without being a priest."

"As you and your family have proven."

"Do you not want a family?"

Nino thought of his first encounter with Hannah, who asked the same question. He laughed.

Isabella asked, "Why do you laugh at me?"

"I'm not laughing at you, Isabella. Your question is fair. I'm laughing because you aren't the first to ask about my desire for a family. There is someone very dear to me who also once asked that question."

"Is she pretty?"

He looked at her, smiled, leaned over, and whispered, "She's beautiful."

"I'm jealous."

"Of whom, God? He owns my heart. My loyalties are to him."

BELLISSIMA VALLE

Angelo sat at the breakfast table with Lorenzo and Bruno. Isabella placed a bowl of scrambled eggs between them before pulling out a chair and seating herself.

Lorenzo glanced at Angelo, "At least if you're here with us, you aren't dropping bombs on Italy."

Bruno laughed.

Isabella said, "Papa, stop that."

"He has a point," Angelo said.

"How is the leg?" Bruno asked.

"It feels better every day."

There was a period of silence in the room before Angelo said, "I'm grateful to all of you. I'm uncertain why you haven't turned me in, but I'm thankful you haven't."

"Where are you from?" Lorenzo asked. "You speak Italian better than some of our field hands."

"I grew up in New York City—the Bronx."

"Who in your family is from Italy? You learned our language from somebody."

"My mother was born in Sorrento. My father is from somewhere in Italy too, but I forget the name of the town. I think it is somewhere north of Rome."

"What is your last name?"

Before answering, Angelo noticed Isabella's eyes were twitching. She took a deep breath. He said, "Servidei. My last name is Servidei."

"What does your father do?" Bruno asked.

"He manages freight at New York Harbor."

"Do you have any brothers or sisters?" Lorenzo asked.

Isabella spoke up, "Why do you two insist on interrogating Angelo?"

Lorenzo smirked. "Interrogating? What are you talking about, sweetheart? They shot his plane down because he came here to drop bombs on us. We have mended his wounds and are now feeding him breakfast and asking him about his family. If you want to see interrogation, we can take him to—"

"The Germans," she interrupted. "I've seen what they do to downed airmen."

"I was thinking more of the Italians, but yes, the Germans would be even worse."

"It's fine, Isabella," Angelo said. "I don't mind their questions."

Addressing Lorenzo, Angelo said, "I have a brother, Mr. Leone. His name is Nino."

Isabella's fork paused halfway to her mouth. She tilted her head to the side. "Did you say your brother's name is Nino?"

"Si," Angelo said. "My brother's name is Nino. Nino Servidei. He lived in Italy for three years before returning to America. He was in Rome studying to be a priest."

* * *

Isabella tucked Angelo into bed. "You need to rest. I have to go to the monastery."

"I don't need rest."

"Rest anyway."

"Your grandpapa told me to walk more."

"So, after you rest, get up and move about. But don't leave the house."

* * *

Isabella entered the gate of the abbey, parked the truck, and made her way to Nino's quarters. Isabella knocked on the door several times.

"He isn't in there."

Isabella turned around to see Sister Maria standing behind her.

"Do you know where I can find him?"

He told Father Russo that he was going to the waterfall to pray.

* * *

After he washed them, Nino laid his cassock and clothes at the side of the pond to dry in the sun. He returned to the waterfall where he bathed nude in the waist deep pool, enjoying the cool, pounding water cascading on his head and body. Diving into the shallow stream, he swam a short distance before returning to the shower provided by the river. Although shivering, he submerged himself one last time, then made his way toward his clothes. When he got out of the water, he noticed movement behind a bush. He put on his undergarments, then his pants, before calling out. "Who is there? Come out."

Isabella rose and turned her back to him. "I'm sorry, Father. I didn't see anything."

Still shivering, Nino scrambled to put on his still damp clothes.

"How long have you been behind that bush, Isabella?"

"Only a short time. I'm sorry. I feel humiliated."

"What are you doing here? What can I help you with?"

"There's something I need to discuss with you. Are you free this afternoon? I need to take you to Bellissima Valle and show you something."

Nino, now fully clothed and standing behind her, said, "Isabella, look at me."

She slowly turned, looking at his shoes.

"Look at me, Isabella."

She tried to make eye contact with him but looked to her left instead.

"Look at me."

She raised her eyes. "I feel ashamed."

"You have no reason to feel shame."

She returned her gaze to the ground.

He touched her chin and lifted her face to see her eyes. "Don't let what just happened trouble you. It is not uncommon for a young…"

He paused, uncertain of the appropriateness of his comments.

"Isabella, temptation sometimes causes us to…"

Again, pausing. "Let me check and see if Father Russo needs me this afternoon. If not, off we will go to Bellissima Valle, and you can show me whatever it is you need to show me.

* * *

Nino watched Isabella shift the gears of the truck as she turned down a steep hill. She said little during their journey. He felt unsettled that she had seen him fully exposed at the waterfall and didn't want her embarrassment to strain their friendship.

Upon their arrival at Bellissima Valle, Nino noticed Lorenzo and Bruno on a hill clearing shrubs.

Isabella said, "What I want to show you is in the house, if you'll follow me."

Nino trailed her into the kitchen. Without hesitation, she made her way up the stairs.

Nino said, "Do you want me to follow you?"

"Si," she said, glancing over her shoulder.

When they entered the upstairs bedroom Nino could see a man standing at the window. He was turned away but looked familiar.

"Angelo," Nino blurted out.

His brother turned his head. Nino approached him.

"Nino!" Angelo called out, before pivoting on his cane. They embraced.

"Dear God," Nino said. "We thought you were dead."

"No, little brother, I'm still here to torment you, just like I always have been."

They laughed, released their embrace, then hugged again.

"Mama will be so happy. She was devastated."

"I was worried about her."

Isabella slid a chair from the corner so Nino could sit. Angelo rested on the bed, his back against the wall.

Angelo said, "What the hell are you doing here dressed like that? You didn't leave Hannah and the kids to go back into that priest bullshit, did you?"

Nino turned to see Isabella standing in the center of the room. She gazed at him, her arms crossed, and her eyebrows raised, curious about the question Angelo just asked.

Nino approached and faced her. "Isabella, I am incredibly grateful to you for bringing me here. But do you mind if I have a word in private with Angelo?"

She hesitated, then turned and left, closing the door behind her.

Nino returned to the chair.

Angelo said, "What the hell, Nino. Did you come looking for me?"

"It's not that simple."

"Why are you here?"

"The American government recruited me—the War Department. They sent me here to track down grandpapa DiVincenzo."

Angelo sat stoned faced. "Grandpapa? Why?"

"I can't tell you."

"Have you found him?"

"Yes, he lives outside of a little town called Ficuzza."

"What did he say when you showed up?"

"I've already told you too much."

"Can you get me to Grandpapa's? Maybe I would be safer there."

"No way. It's crawling with soldiers—both German and Italian. There is a German general and Italian major living in Grandpapa's house."

"So how the hell do we get out of here?"

"I have no idea."

THE SICANI MOUNTAIN RANGE

"You are a very mysterious man, Father Servidei," Isabella said as she swept her hair from her face. The wind from the truck's open window blew it back over her eyes, where she blocked it with her hand.

She looked down at Nino's cassock before returning her gaze to the windshield. "You aren't actually a priest, are you?"

"There is much I wish I could tell you, Isabella, but I can't. All I ask is that you trust me, tell no one of what you have seen today, and continue to care for Angelo. My family is grateful to yours."

"Does that include your grandfather? Is he grateful too? Will he stop his intimidation tactics to steal our land?"

Nino tilted his head to the side. "My grandpapa intimidates your family?"

"He has harassed us for years. Not just us, but dozens of other farmers and business owners."

"I'm sorry. I did not know. What has he done?"

"His men have burned our crops and shot at some of our field hands until they are too afraid to come to work. He has even ambushed our trucks, stolen them, removed the produce from the back, and returned the vehicles for a fee. He owns several farms in Sicily and obtained them from terrified farmers who agreed to sell them for a fraction of what they were worth. His men have murdered some who have fought back."

Nino looked out of the passenger window, remaining silent as he processed the wickedness his grandfather had inflicted on others, realizing that his own father practiced the same tactics in New York.

Isabella downshifted and turned the wheel.

"Where are we going?" Nino asked.

"I'm not ready to return to the monastery."

The path was narrow and, like most of the roads in the Sicani Mountains, the surface was jarring.

Isabella said, "Angelo referred to someone by the name of Hannah. Is she your wife?"

He glanced at her and grinned. "You are a curious one, aren't you?"

"Why shouldn't I be? Two Americans show up in my life while my country is at war with them, and I suddenly find out they are brothers. I then find out the ruthless tyrant Alfonso DiVincenzo is their grandfather, and that the brother who I thought was a priest is not really a priest but is married with children. Don't I have a right to some answers?"

"You do, Isabella, but not now."

As they made their way over the crest of a hill, Nino knew what was on the other side, for he had driven the Berline down this same road six days earlier and reported it via the wireless. In the distance a German fuel depot stood in the valley, under a modest canopy of trees. There was a wooden shack that served as an office and bunkhouse. To one side stood a fuel tank on a steel frame. It was covered in dark netting, stuffed with vegetation to camouflage it. Its height was twice that of the operator who was filling a canvass covered troop carrier with gas. Another troop carrier and two Kübelwagens were in the queue.

Isabella pulled to the side of the road. The soldiers near the fuel tank gave them a curious look, then returned to fueling their vehicles.

Nino asked, "Why are we stopping?"

"I want to know what's going on, Nino. Why are you in Sicily? You are a spy, aren't you?"

"Isabella, there is much going on in the world right now that you don't know about. It is evil, and it must stop. The world must fight back."

She glanced out of the windshield and shook her head. "My

papa and grandpapa have told me some of it but refuse to tell me everything. They too are up to something, but I don't know what. I sense it, but they won't tell me. I just know they despise Mussolini and Hitler."

"Lorenzo and Bruno are courageous men. You must trust them, and you must trust me."

Isabella stared at Nino and squinted her eyes. "When have you met my papa and grandpapa?"

"They have been by the monastery when I have been there."

"They go there and meet with Father Russo. It's all making sense now. That's why they haven't turned Angelo in. They are working with you, aren't they?"

"Isabella, you are very smart, and very special, and I don't want to lie to you, so I'll tell you nothing."

"I feel sick," she said as they heard the roar of airplane engines overhead.

Nino looked up to see American bombers flying low over the crest of a hill. They were approaching the fuel depot.

"We have to get out of here, Isabella," Nino said, as he pointed down the road from which they had just come. "Go! Now!"

"Why? what is happening?" she asked, as she frantically put the pickup in gear and accelerated.

She turned the wheel hard and performed a U-turn, the truck bouncing violently as her front tires went into a ditch, followed by the rear. Her wheels spun, slipping initially, then gripping the dirt surface and spraying debris from the rear tires. As she sped away, Nino peered through the rear window and watched soldiers sprint to the perimeter of the camp. The *Kübelwagens* sped away, leaving the troop carriers behind.

The bombs appeared as tiny pills from Nino's vantage point. A black and orange fireball erupted when the descending payload landed on the tanker. The troop carriers lifted off the ground and were soon engulfed in flames. As the trucks lay on their side, consumed in a blaze, the few soldiers who survived ran. Nino watched as their flaming arms and legs moved in desperation before diving to the ground and rolling in a futile attempt to save themselves.

Isabella stopped the truck, and they both leaped out. In silence they watched the inferno before them.

THE BRONX NEW YORK

Hannah knew she needed to pull herself together. It was late in the afternoon, and it would soon be time to dress Solomon and pick Lilia up from school. Salvador was paying for her to attend The Brearly School for Girls, one of the finest private schools in New York. Solomon was in the bedroom. She heard him stirring from his afternoon nap.

Hannah sat alone. She filled her glass with Nino's Scotch for the fourth time of the afternoon. After setting the bottle down, she took two sips and rested her head on the surface of the table. Her head was spinning. She closed her eyes wanting to sleep, for since her miscarriage, sleep had been her only escape from her deepening depression. Her mind often filled with fear, wondering if she would ever see Nino again. She bowed her head and wept. *Please come home to me, Nino. I need you.*

After another minute, she stood, approached the telephone, and picked up the receiver, hoping Maria would be available to pick up Lilia. Hannah heard Solomon crying. She returned the telephone receiver, took a deep breath and entered the bedroom to dress Solomon. She realized it was time to stop feeling sorry for herself. Her family needed her.

CHAPTER 16

"Someone is reporting our locations, I am sure of it," Generalmajor Richter said. "The targets they have hit have been well camouflaged. There is no way they could have been seen from the air, only from the ground."

General von Senger und Etterlin said, "I am aware of this, generalmajor. I have requested several wireless detection vehicles."

"When will they arrive?"

"General Kesselring's aide said there are two on the way."

"And in the meantime," Richter said. "I will continue to lose troops and equipment to Allied air raids."

"One thing we know is that these saboteurs are only targeting German positions, not Italian."

General von Senger und Etterlin approached a wall map of Sicily and picked up a wooden pointer. "We also know that other than Palermo, most of the targets have been here in the Sicani Mountain Range."

"That is until recently," Richter said. He pointed to the southern coast. "Last week they struck two ammunition storage facilities north of Gela. We had thousands of land mines in them."

Von Senger und Etterlin turned and crossed the room, his eyes staring down and both hands behind his back—fingers locked as he deliberated.

Richter spoke up. "I think we need to interrogate civilians. They must know something."

Von Senger und Etterlin turned sharply. "No! The Italians are our allies, not our enemies. That is a line we can't cross—at least not yet. I will get with General Guzzoni. I will speak to him about involving the *Carabinieri*. The Italian police have every right to interrogate Italian citizens as harshly as they need."

"But will they?"

"If it doesn't get resolved, there are always Mussolini's black shirts."

THE ABBEY OF SANTA MARIA

Nino knelt at the altar in the monastery's chapel. He heard the door behind him creak open, crossed himself and rose to see Father Russo behind him.

"You don't look well, Nino. What is troubling you?"

"Will you sit with me, father?"

They made their way to the front pew.

"Father, in 1938, I boarded a ship from New York. My destination was Rome, where I began my studies to become a priest. My plan was to serve God by caring for his children. Now, just five years later, I am here, tormented with guilt. I arrived here in early April—fifteen weeks ago. I have done what they have asked of me, understanding that somehow, I am performing a higher mission for God. Airfields, anti-aircraft placements, and weapons storage facilities have been destroyed because of our efforts. I know, because I have driven past many of them to confirm our success."

Nino got a lump in his throat.

"Go on," Father Russo said.

"Yesterday, Isabella was bringing me back to the monastery. There was a fuel depot on the side of a hill. I had reported its location days earlier. As we watched, American bombers few overhead, one of them flew directly above it and dropped its payload. It was a direct hit. A massive ball of black smoke rose into the air. Two troop carriers exploded. They were filled with soldiers. Isabella and I watched as a dozen Germans ran from the vehicles. Flames engulfed them as they traveled several feet before they dove to the ground and rolled in the dry grass. It too caught fire. Even though we were far away, we could hear their screams, until there were no more screams to hear."

Nino paused to regain his composure.

Father Russo lay his hand on Nino's shoulder. "Take your time, my son."

Nino said, "I don't want to keep doing this."

"You knew this wouldn't be easy, Nino. But it's a task that must be done. You mustn't lose heart now."

THE SICANI MOUNTAIN RANGE

Fieldwebel Arthur König adjusted his headset and twisted the dial on his wireless receiver. The Wehrmacht had recently captured a British radio operator in a shack on the southern face of Mount Etna. Yet, the bombings of sheltered targets in the west continued. With only two wireless detection vehicles on the vast island of Sicily, the searches were arduous. König and his driver parked alone, nestled in the woods near the peak of the Sicani Mountain Range. A second detection vehicle was six kilometers away, perched on the top of a hill.

"How long are we going to stay here?" *Obergefreiter* Wagner asked.

"Until the sun comes up. Last week *Feldwebel* Hoffmann said when his rig passed through here, they picked up a momentary blip. He said it could have been an anomaly, but I have a hunch."

THE ABBEY OF SANTA MARIA

There was more static in the air than during his previous transmissions, and Nino was frustrated as he adjusted the dials on his wireless in an attempt to make contact. After several minutes, he received the transmission from Neptune. Nino relayed the coordinates of a handful of new fortifications along the southern coast, as well as informing them of mechanized troop commands that had recently relocated on the island. The information he received in return was brief, but it emphasized the need to avoid his grandfather's compound and that it was critical that he stay away indefinitely. Nino inquired as to why yet received no clarification before the transmission ended.

After powering down the wireless and returning it to its hiding place Nino stood to exit the chapel. A sudden concern overcame him, for he sensed that the reason he had been instructed to stay away from *La Foresta*, was that it would soon be the target of air strikes.

THE SICANI MOUNTAIN RANGE

Fieldwebel König shouted, "We've got it." He pointed toward the rear of the van. "It's coming from the northeast. On top of that hill."

"There are only a few shanties up there," *Fieldwebel* Hoffmann said. "Should we search them ourselves?"

"There is also a monastery near the top. Call headquarters. Tell them we need two squads of men. Have them meet us there."

"At the monastery?"

"Yes, at the monastery."

* * *

With a broken right headlight, the 1928 Berline rattled down the road. It didn't drive out of the factory with much power, and after fifteen years of service, it had even less. Nino knew he would never make it to his grandfather's compound before the now setting sun disappeared completely. When he was three kilometers away from the monastery, he turned left. When he reached a crest, other headlights caught his attention. Making its way up the mountain was a convoy. The two lead vehicles were Wehrmacht vans with antennas on the roof. Following behind were two troop carriers, one German and one Italian. A Kübelwagen brought up the rear. They were headed in the direction of the abbey.

* * *

When Nino arrived, Father Russo was on his knees. Nino watched as they brought a rifle butt to his back, causing him to fall forward. Sister Catherine and the other nuns escorted the screaming children into a classroom.

An Italian officer hovered over Father Russo. "Where is the transmitter?" he shouted.

Father Russo was gasping for breath, and attempted to answer, but was still regaining his wind from the rifle blow.

"No!" Nino shouted. "It is not him. It is me. He knows nothing. I am who you are looking for."

The group of soldiers turned toward him as he approached from the Berline.

"Let him be," Nino said, while standing before them. He looked down at Father Russo. "I am sorry, father. I lied to you, and am not who I say I am. I was not sent from the Vatican. I am an American spy."

Father Russo looked up at him, shaking his head, still gasping for breath. Blood was trickling from his ear.

A German officer said something to the Italian, who said to Nino, "Where is your transmitter?"

He said nothing as he led them into the chapel and behind the altar. He knelt, slid the door to the side and removed the wireless.

They escorted Nino to the center of the courtyard. The German officer approached him. Holding his mother's rosary in his right hand, Nino prayed. The officer yanked the rosary, breaking the chain, causing several beads to fall at Nino's feet. The officer dropped the rosary on the ground and stomped on it with his heel, before backhanding Nino across the mouth. Another blow to the back of Nino's head caused him to stumble forward before he fell face first. With his cheek resting on the dirt of the abbey courtyard, Nino felt a swift kick to his ribs. Pain radiated through his body. The German officer pulled Nino to his feet. Dirt clung to Nino's cassock. With a swift blow, the officer punched Nino in the stomach. He hunched over and gasped for air. Again, the officer retracted his fist before slugging Nino across the face. Nino fell back, his head hitting the surface of the courtyard. He gazed up into the vastness of the heavens.

I will never see my family again.

CHAPTER 17

G eneral Eisenhower was up to two packs of Camels per day. When he wasn't smoking, he often rolled three coins in his hand: An American silver dollar, a French Franc, and a British Crown. He held them as he and British Admiral Andrew Cunningham entered the war room in the *Lascaris Bastion*.

Ike looked up at the forty-foot-tall ceiling and a twenty by thirteen-foot photographic mosaic of the 10,000 square mile island of Sicily.

"Welcome, general. Will this do?" An aide asked as he extended his arm to display a series of tables, desks, and telephones.

Ignoring the damp chill and the smell of mold, Eisenhower said, "I believe we can make this work."

In addition to Eisenhower and Cunningham, also in attendance were a half dozen American and British generals and admirals, as well as Army and Navy aides comprising low-ranking officers. A few enlisted men were also present to chart ship and troop movements on the map tables.

"General, if you will follow me," Admiral Cunningham said.

As they glanced at a map table, Eisenhower said, "What is our strength now, Admiral?"

"We will attack with 160,000 ground troops from three thousand ships and over 4,000 airborne troops from hundreds of aircraft."

"What's the latest on the defense numbers?"

"Our intelligence indicates around 250,000, with less than one third German, and the rest Italian. Our attacks on their airfields and our success with air-to-air combat has driven much of the Luftwaffe and the Italian Airforce to mainland Italy."

Eisenhower said, "Do we trust our intelligence?"

"As you have known all along, our eyes on the ground have been limited, yet the few agents we have in Sicily have been splendid."

The two men looked up at the photographic map on the wall. Cunningham said, "Our aerial reconnaissance has been superb. Those images that have not been clear we have instructed our agents on the ground to find specifics for us, and they have come through."

"Are we ready to go tomorrow?" General Eisenhower asked.

"I believe we are, general."

The DiVincenzo Compound

Her bath water had cooled. Gabrielle stood in the tub and reached for her towel. General Richter entered the lavatory and removed the cloth from the rack before she could grab it. He said, "It would be a shame to cover such a beautiful piece of art."

"Please, darling. I'm not in the mood to play right now."

He handed her the towel. "I am, but unfortunately, I must leave. I'm due in Gela this afternoon and will be home late. Perhaps you could wait up for me."

"Perhaps."

She wrapped the towel around her body.

"You don't sound enthused."

"I'm sorry. It's just that I have been in this compound for several weeks. I feel like a prisoner."

"That's understandable. This weekend I will take you to Palermo. We will dine at a fine restaurant, and I'll take you to the opera. Will that cheer you?"

She grinned. "I believe it would."

He kissed her cheek and smacked her bottom before turning. "I'll see you this evening."

She dried herself, entered the bedroom, and slipped a white dress over her head. She stared out of the back window, where she saw Alfonso approaching the house from the stables. He had his riding boots on.

When Gabrielle made her way to the bedroom door, she noticed Richter's briefcase on the desk.

She pressed her ear to the door, heard nothing, then opened it to confirm General Richter had gone. She approached the desk and the locked case. Looking for the keys, she opened the top center drawer, followed by each side drawer. After she found them, she opened the briefcase. Something caught her attention at the window. She looked up to see General Richter standing on the patio, staring back at her. He opened the French doors and charged at her.

"You little tramp, you have been using me to get information."

He crossed the room and slapped her face, knocking her off balance. He clutched her arms and flung Gabrielle against the wall, where she fell to the floor, before he lifted her to her feet and punched her across her jaw, knocking her to the ground once again. She looked up to see Richter standing over her with another closed fist. She raised her hands to block it. Before he brought it down, she saw a blur of Alfonso as he tackled Richter, knocking him against the nightstand, crashing a lamp against the wall. Richter removed his Luger from its holster, but Alfonso twisted his wrist. The gun fired into the mattress. Alfonso rotated Richter's wrist further, causing the weapon to drop to the floor. Gabrielle, still dazed, saw two German soldiers enter the room. One brought the butt of his Mauser rifle down on Alfonso's head. He dropped and lay unconscious.

Richter looked down at Gabrielle as he walked to the door. He said to the two soldiers, "Lock them in this room and guard them until I return."

* * *

Alfonso was lying in Richter's bed when he opened his eyes to see Gabrielle's bruised and battered face inches from his. Her lip and left eye were swollen. She was using a towel from the lavatory to wipe blood from the side of his head.

"Don't worry about me," he said. "You need to tend to your own wounds."

"I'll be fine. Do you think this is the first time a man has ever punched me in the face?"

Alfonso looked away, struggling with her question, for although it had been many years, he too had used his closed fist on more than one woman.

A German soldier guarded the locked bedroom door. Two more patrolled the patio, visible through the French doors, their Mausers slung over their shoulders.

"What do you think Richter will do with us?" Gabrielle asked, as she patted his injury.

"I don't know."

"Are you scared?" she asked.

He sat up and positioned himself next to her. "I'm too old and have dodged death too many times to be scared."

He looked around the room. "There was once a telephone in here. I had it taken out just to piss off Richter. That's why he left us in here, so I can't call my men."

"Where is Pierre?"

"I let him take Hercules into the mountains to visit a lady friend of his."

"What about your other men?"

"There are a few dumb ones still here, but the core group that have the brains to get us out of here won't return until tonight."

Gabrielle's lip quivered as she looked out the French doors. "Look," she said to Alfonso.

He turned his head to see a group of Wehrmacht soldiers throwing two ropes over a tree branch. Both ropes had a noose at the end.

Alfonso put his arm around her. "Don't worry, young lady. We'll get out of this somehow."

JULY 9TH, 1943
NORTHERN COAST OF AFRICA

The vast fleet spread across the curvature of the Mediterranean Sea. Seven Allied divisions were on board the 3,300 ships peppering the horizon. They comprised two task forces.

Task Force 545, the eastern taskforce, led by British General Montgomery consisted of the British Eighth Army. Among this group was the Canadian 1st Infantry Division. The objective of task force 545 was to gain control of the southeast section of Sicily, before moving north along the coast to Messina.

Lieutenant General George S. Patton led Task force 343, the American task force to the west. Their objective was to gain control of the southern beaches around Gela, then move to the northwest, with an ultimate objective of capturing Palermo.

At midnight, 4,600 American and British airborne troops would drop from the sky, only hours before the amphibious invasion of southern Sicily would begin. The bombing of Sicilian airfields, combined with Allied air superiority, had driven much of the Luftwaffe and the Italian Royal Airforce to mainland Italy, although they were still in range of the Italian southern coast if called upon.

LIBYA
AIN M'LILA AIRBASE

"When do we leave, major?" asked the B-25 copilot as he stirred his powdered eggs with his fork.

"This afternoon, captain. I'll brief the crew at 1100 hours."

"Where are we going? Are we bombing the hills north of Gela again?"

"Not this time. There's a compound hidden in the woods south of Ficuzza. There are reports that it is a lair for several mechanized units hidden deep in the forest."

"How many planes are with us?"

After taking a sip of coffee, the Major said, "Twelve. We are going to carpet bomb the shit out of that place with incendiaries. They have instructed us to turn those woods into a pile of smoldering toothpicks."

THE SICANI MOUNTAIN RANGE
INTERNMENT CAMP

With his hands cuffed behind his back, Nino jumped from the rear of the troop carrier. When he landed, his feet got entangled in the hem of his cassock and he fell forward, his bruised face scraping in the dirt. A Wehrmacht soldier reached under his armpits and jerked him to his feet, then shoved him forward where he fell again.

He hadn't slept in twenty-four hours. They had taken him to a different camp for an all-night interrogation. But he now knew the answer to the question Lorenzo had once asked him, "What if you get captured. Will you break?"

Nino didn't break. He insisted he was an American spy who acted alone.

"Ah...," Nino screamed as he took another rifle butt to his ribs.

"*Get up,*" the soldier shouted before jerking him to his feet a second time.

Nino hunched over, grimacing in pain. He scanned the camp. Others looked on. He stumbled. A tickle on his upper lip caught his attention. He looked down to see blood dripping from his face to the front of his cassock. As they marched him forward, he realized this must be a sight to the dozens of onlookers, as they watched what they believed to be a Catholic priest battered and beaten.

Not moving fast enough for their liking, two soldiers took hold of Nino's arms and, in a hurried pace, escorted him to a prison block. Having difficulty keeping up, Nino stumbled repeatedly, his feet dragging behind him.

* * *

"What the hell did that priest do to deserve that?" An Italian soldier said to Vito, who had just dismounted his motorcycle.

Looking on, Vito slid his goggles to the top of his helmet. "The world is shit and the Germans are bastards."

An officer standing behind Vito said, "Unless you want to join that priest, I would watch what you say, soldier."

Vito turned to the officer. "Is that what we have come to? Are we now tolerating the abuse of catholic priests just because we have allied ourselves with the Boche?"

The officer ignored the comment as Vito entered the office. A skinny clerk, not over eighteen, was behind a counter. His rank was *Soldato*, the lowest rank in the Italian army.

Vito said, "I'm here to pick up the weekly reports."

"Hold tight, *carporale*. Another prisoner just arrived. I need to add him to the list."

"You mean that priest they dragged across the camp? We better add him to the list. I'm sure he is a genuine threat."

The *soldato*, said. "Have a seat. You may be here awhile."

Vito sat in the corner and spit into the lenses of his goggles, then wiped them with a bandana he removed from around his neck.

Several minutes passed.

"Do you know how much longer it will be?" Vito asked. "I need to deliver this report to Palermo. I want to be back at my camp before dark."

Looking through the window, the soldato said, "I think they are bringing what I need now."

The door opened and an Italian soldier handed the *clerk* a sheet of paper before turning to leave.

"No wonder they were beating the crap out of him. This says he isn't a priest at all, but an American spy."

Vito approached. "How do they know he's a spy?"

"They caught him sending wireless signals from a monastery near here." The clerk lay the paper on the counter and spun it around so Vito could read it. "Here, see for yourself."

Vito studied the document. The name hit him like a jolt. *Nino Servidei?*

Vito asked, "This priest, where are they keeping him?"

"It says here 'cell block two.'"

"While you type that up, I need to go find the latrine." Vito said, before leaving the office.

* * *

With the shackles from his wrists now removed, the solitude of the dirt floor of his cell offered relief while he stared up at the ceiling. Nino's head, back, and ribs, and left hand were throbbing. He glanced down to see his fingers swollen and bleeding. The message of the last wireless transmission he had received played over and over in his mind, concerned that his grandfather's property would soon be bombed. His thoughts raced, thinking of the potential annihilation of the compound.

Grabbing his ribs and clenching his teeth, he struggled to sit up. He lay back down. With his head resting on the filthy floor, Nino's mind drifted to Hannah, Lilia, and baby Solomon. A tear rolled down his cheek as he realized he would never remember his papa.

Once again, he attempted to sit up, but his broken bones and spirit prevented him from moving.

* * *

"I need to see the Catholic priest you just brought in," Vito said to the guard at the outer door of cell block two.

"Who the hell are you? Why would I let you in?"

Vito reached into his pocket and pulled out a pack of cigarettes. "Here, I'll give you these. All I ask is a few minutes with him. I need his blessing. I just found out my mother is dying, and I need him to pray with me."

The guard turned his head to see that nobody was around. He then pulled out a set of keys and unlocked the door. "The priest is down that corridor, the fourth cell on the left—number seven. I can't let you in with him, but you can speak through the door. Don't be long."

Vito attempted to hand him the cigarettes. The guard said, "Keep them. I don't smoke. I'll be out here praying for your mother."

"Bless you," Vito said.

He made his way down the quiet passageway. To his right, faces stared back at him from two different cells. There was a smell of urine and feces. His heart raced as his mind filled with confusion. He missed his old friend and college roommate, but none of this made any sense. If this was Nino, and he was an American spy, they would execute him within days.

* * *

Nino woke to banging on the wooden door of his cell. A face stared back at him through the metal grid. He sat up, attempted to stand, then stumbled to his knees before finally rising to his feet. He approached the small opening in the door. It was at eye level. "Vito, is that you?"

"It's me, Nino."

Vito inserted two fingers.

Nino squeezed them. "I can't believe it's you."

"What the hell are you doing here? I thought you were in America. Why are you dressed as a priest? Don't tell me you were stupid enough to give up your life with Hannah and Lilia to return to the priesthood."

"No, of course not, but I need your help and don't have time to explain."

"The reports say you are an American spy. If that's true, they'll kill you."

Vito's words hit him worse than the rifle butt he took to the ribs. He had a brief vision of Hannah weeping, never knowing what happened to him.

He reduced his voice to a whisper. "You need to go to the DiVincenzo compound. Do you know of it?"

"I have been there."

"There are a handful of innocent people who must leave immediately."

"What the hell are you talking about? What is going to happen?"

"I don't know exactly, but I believe the Allies are about to bomb it."

"I know someone there. Gabrielle is her name."

"You mean General Richter's—"

"That's who I'm talking about. I love her."

"Then you must go now. I'll give you the names of the others you need to warn. They must leave."

Vito removed his helmet and ran his fingers through his hair while he looked down the corridor. He returned his gaze to Nino while he placed his helmet back on his head. He said nothing, then at a brisk pace made his way to the door he had just entered.

As Vito approached the metal door, he removed his Berretta from its holster, then knocked.

The guard opened the door. "I was just coming to—"

Vito placed the muzzle of the gun at the side of the guard's neck, then looked around to be certain nobody was in sight. "I'm sorry to do this to you, my friend, but you are going back with me to see the priest. Move—Now!"

Nino looked on as they returned down the corridor.

The guard strode at a rapid pace. Vito was shoving him from behind with the gun at his back. When they arrived, Vito said to the guard, "Open the door."

The guard fumbled with his keys until he found the one stamped with the number seven. He unlocked the door. Vito shoved him in, keeping the gun pointed at him.

"Off with the uniform," he said to the guard. "You too, Nino. I'll never get you out of here dressed as a priest."

Both Nino and the sentry stripped to their undergarments. Without hesitation, Nino dressed himself in the Italian soldier's uniform and was fully dressed, complete with gun belt and holster. Nino watched as Vito bent down and picked up the pants Nino had just removed, sliding the belt through the loops.

"Turn around. Put your hands behind your back." Vito said to the guard, still in his undergarments.

After Vito pulled the belt tightly around his wrists, Vito removed the bandana from around his own neck, placed the center in the guard's mouth, and tied the ends behind his head, to prevent him from shouting.

After Vito and Nino left the cell and closed the door, Nino peeked through the metal grill, addressing the restrained guard. "We are sorry to do this to you."

Leaving the cell block behind, they briskly made their way across the open courtyard, surveying their surroundings.

Nino said, "It's good to see you, old friend."

"It's been two years."

"The last time we were together, you helped me rescue Hannah. Now you're rescuing me."

"Hold your gratitude, Nino. We aren't out of here yet."

"Hopefully, we still have time to evacuate everyone at the compound."

When they approached the office, Vito said to Nino, "That motorcycle is mine. Stand by it. I need to go into the office and check out. Otherwise, they may realize something is up."

"Sorry it took me so long," Vito said to the clerk. "It must have been something I ate."

"Are you telling me I need to stay clear of the latrine for a while?"

"It won't be fit for man nor beast for at least an hour."

The clerk laughed as he handed the document to Vito,

who slid it into his leather shoulder pouch and exited the office.

Vito kick-started the motorcycle. As he had done dozens of times when they were together in Rome, Nino climbed on and sat behind Vito.

"Hang on tight, Nino. These mountain roads of Sicily aren't the streets of Rome. We will fly high and land hard."

Vito placed his goggles over his eyes, released the clutch, and twisted the throttle.

* * *

When they were a kilometer from *La Foresta*, Nino tapped on Vito's shoulder and pointed to the side of the road.

They dismounted. Nino turned, bent at the waist, and attempted to vomit. He hadn't eaten for a day and all he could do was heave air from his stomach.

"Are you going to be okay?" Vito asked.

"I'm fine. I don't know what overcame me."

"You've been through hell."

As Nino stood upright, Vito asked, "What is wrong with your fingers?"

Nino looked at his left hand. "They broke two fingers trying to get me to talk."

"What the hell? What did they want to know?"

"Who I was working with."

"Did you tell them anything?"

"I didn't tell the bastards shit."

Vito asked, "How well do you know the compound?"

"I'm familiar with the house and the stables in the back."

"If Richter is there when we arrive, this may be tricky," Nino said. "If not, it's just a matter of telling Gabrielle and my grandfather they must leave immediately."

"Did you just say, 'your grandfather?'"

"That's what I said. Alfonso DiVincenzo is my grandfather."

"No shit?"

"No shit, Vito. And to top it off, after we save Gabrielle and my grandfather, and a few others, I need to figure out how to get my brother out of Sicily. He is an American airman who was shot down weeks ago. A farm girl and her family have been hiding him."

"Jesus, Nino. You should have kept that to yourself. I love you like a brother, but I'm still an Italian soldier. We are on different sides of this war. You know that don't you?"

"You won't turn me in, will you? You just risked everything to save me."

"I have a problem with all of this, Nino. Besides now knowing about your brother, there are other Italian soldiers at your grandfather's compound. The Germans can burn in hell for all I care, but if I only go there to save Gabrielle, what does that make me if I just leave my fellow countrymen behind, knowing bombs may rain down on them?"

"So, what are you saying? Are you going to tell them?"

"I have to, Nino. Just like I view you as a brother, they too are my brothers. I won't betray them."

ABOVE THE MEDITERRANEAN SEA

"What's our ETA?" the captain of the lead B-25 asked his navigator.

"Forty minutes, captain."

"Brace yourselves, gentlemen. We are twenty minutes out

from heavy flak. Then we find that forest and rain hell down on it."

THE DIVINCENZO COMPOUND

Vito slowed the motorcycle as they approached the canopy of trees surrounding *La Foresta*.

At the main entrance, the Germans were to the right of the narrow road, the Italians to the left. Some vehicles were away on maneuvers, but most were in place. A few French tanks operated by the Italians were off to the side in various states of overhaul. Soldiers worked outside of their tents, cleaning weapons, and maintaining trucks. Some were kicking soccer balls or playing cards.

When the house came into view, they approached the front entrance. Richter's staff car was parked in the courtyard. Vito stopped. They both put their boots on the ground to balance the bike.

Nino said, "Drive around to the back near the stables."

Vito followed the dirt road around the house.

"Shit," Nino said.

Before them, Alfonso and Gabrielle stood on wooden chairs. Their hands were tied behind their backs and they each had a noose around their neck. Richter communicated with Brambilla, who relayed what he said to Alfonso and Gabrielle. Two armed Wehrmacht soldiers stood to the side.

The motorcycle engine revved, and the rear tire spit dirt into the air. Once adjacent to the small group, Vito braked hard, causing the bike to skid. Nino and Vito leaped off. With his hand resting on the holstered Beretta, Nino studied his surroundings, hoping a plan would reveal itself. His grandfather was stoic, as though he had accepted his fate. Gabrielle's eyes were locked on Vito.

Vito's breaths were shallow, and he was sweating when he approached Brambilla. "*Maggiore*, we need to get our troops out of here, "I believe bombers are on the way. The Allies are about to carpet bomb this compound."

"Who the hell are you, carporale?"

He pointed to his armband. "I am a messenger. General Guzzoni sent me here."

Brambilla relayed the information to Richter, who turned and in German shouted something to his two men. They ran toward the front of the house, leaving only Richter and Brambilla.

Richter said to Brambilla, "We too will leave, but first, we will execute two traitors."

He stepped behind Alfonso and Gabrielle, took hold of the back of each of their chairs and as he leaned back to pull them out, Nino and Vito stepped toward him, each man drawing his Beretta, and firing once. Vito's shot entered the general's side. Nino's entered Richter's face, causing a spray of red, before the lifeless body fell back into the pine needles that lay under the tree.

Startled, Gabrielle stumbled, and her chair tipped over, her body suspended as the noose tightened around her neck. Pouncing like a cat, Vito sprinted forward, lifting her onto his shoulders. Nino joined Vito. Together, they stabilized the unconscious Gabriele in mid-air to prevent the rope from going taut. Brambilla picked up the chair and leaped onto it, before using his knife to cut her down. Vito guided her to the ground and knelt, gently patting her face. "Please Gabrielle, don't leave me now."

Brambilla said, "Prop her feet up."

Nino said to Brambilla, "Let me use your knife."

He then stood on Gabrielle's chair, removed the noose from Alfonso's neck, and cut the rope from his wrists.

"Thank you, grandson."

Gabrielle's head turned from side to side, followed by a series of coughs. She sat up and embraced Vito. "I'm sorry I told you to leave. I've missed you so."

"I'm here now. But we need to leave."

Approaching Brambilla, Nino said, "Thank you for helping us."

"Thank you for killing Richter. He was a bastard."

Nino said, "I shouldn't tell you this, but I feel I owe you. What my friend here told you is true. Bombers are on the way."

As the words left Nino's lips, they heard the faint sound of airplane engines in the distance.

"I believe they are here. Good luck to all of you," Brambilla said as he turned and sprinted away.

"Vito, take Gabrielle on your motorcycle. Grandpapa and I will take one of his cars."

Vito yelled to Nino. "Where do you want to meet?"

"There is a monastery at the top of the Sicani mountains. It's called the Abbey of Santa Maria. Tell Father Russo I sent you. Wait for me there."

Gabrielle climbed on the motorbike with Vito.

Alfonso said, "Nino, follow me. My car is on the side of the house."

As Alfonso started the engine of the Fiat sedan, the ground

beneath them shook while a wave of explosions rumbled throughout the compound.

LASCARIS BASTION
THE ISLAND OF MALTA

Eisenhower climbed to the top of Lascaris Bastion. The wind was warm, yet swift, forcing him to cup his hand over the Zippo lighter he used to light his cigarette. The roar of the C-47s coming from the south prompted a glance at his watch.

Right on time.

They had left North Africa forty minutes earlier, and as instructed, banked toward the southern coast of Sicily after they passed over Malta. Eisenhower looked up, but the black night sky camouflaged the C-47's carrying the American airborne units.

May God be with them.

CHAPTER 18

FICUZZA

After leaving the compound, they drove to the center of Ficuzza. They parked in front of a café. Alfonso said, "Let me buy you an early dinner, Nino."

After being seated, Alfonso asked the waiter, "Do you sell cigars?"

"*Si*. I have an exceptionally fine Toscano."

"Bring us two. No make it four. I'll need some for later. And some cognac."

"*Si*. Mr. DiVincenzo."

Alfonso addressed Nino. "Toscanos aren't what they once were, grandson. Before the war, the Toscano cigar company imported their tobacco from the United States—Kentucky I believe. Now they use Italian tobacco. It's crap."

Nino's attention alternated between the burning forest engulfing his grandfather's compound and the strange conversation he was now having with that same grandfather.

Nino squinted and tilted his head to the side, "Grandpapa, do you see what is happening on that hill? Your precious home has been destroyed. It is burning before your very eyes."

He shrugged, "I own other property. Lots of it. I own a

beautiful apartment building in Palermo. It's three stories. I will be living there for a while. Come visit me."

Looking toward the inferno on the hill, Alfonso added, "I must admit, *La Forresta* was my favorite. But there is a beautiful citrus farm in the Sicani Mountain range I've had my eye on. It's called *Bellissima Valle*. That will be my next home.

"The Leone's farm?

"You know the Leones?"

"They will never sell to you."

"I have my ways, grandson."

"Leave them alone. They are fine people."

"Maybe they are, but I must have their property."

"You have another grandson."

"Your brother—what is his name? I have forgotten."

"His name is Angelo. He is in the U.S. Army Air Corps. He was shot down weeks ago. It just so happens that the Leones were the first to find him. They have been hiding him. He was badly injured from a shrapnel wound. They mended his wounds and probably saved his life."

"That was nice of them. But business is business."

Nino stared at Alfonso, saying nothing, as he studied this mysterious man.

Alfonso lit one of the cigars the waiter brought, then took a sip of cognac. "I'll make you a deal, Nino."

"What deal is that?"

Alfonso leaned forward, "You see Nino, as of yesterday, I was under the thumb of both Mussolini and Hitler. Now, if what I sense is true, help may soon arrive in the form of an Allied invasion, and I will have my island back, but I will need your help."

"My help. What do you need my help with?"

"Because I assisted you and your American friends, I believe I will be in a position to negotiate the release of my men who are currently in prison. Then I will be at full strength once again. I will just need you to vouch for me. Let the American government know how helpful I've been."

"Then what? You'll terrorize the people of Sicily even more than you do now."

He leaned back and laughed, "I will be King of Sicily once again."

"First of all, you assume I have more power than I do. I am just a pawn in this game of war. But if I try—if I 'vouch' for you as you say—will you leave the Leones alone?"

"My deal to you is this: I will give you a list of men. If you can get at least half of them free for me, the Leones will never hear from me again unless it is to buy their limoncello."

THE SICANI MOUNTAIN RANGE

Nino was still wearing the uniform of an Italian soldier. The hike from the bus station at the bottom of the mountain had taken him three hours and he believed he still had at least two more before he arrived at the abbey. There was limited light but enough to see the dirt road as he trudged. His body ached from head to toe, with a particular radiation of pain from his battered face, ribs and the two broken fingers on his left hand. At the café where he had eaten with Alfonso, he used the sink in the water closet to remove the dried blood from his face. He glanced at his wrist to see that his watch was missing. He remembered the Germans had removed it during his interrogation. He estimated the time to be around midnight. Other than dozing off for two hours on the bus ride, he hadn't slept in a day and a half. Taking a respite on the side of the road, Nino lay on his back, and looked up at the passing cloud cover, which occasionally opened to reveal a half moon.

After a few hours of sleep, he woke to a series of thundering explosions, then looked up to see antiaircraft fire and tracers dancing in the night sky. Toward the southern coast, the sky was inundated with flickers of light as though the beach was on fire.

Along the road to the abbey entrance, morning shadows were visible on the western side of the trees. The smell of pine was in the air. Airplanes passed overhead. Occasionally, they were German or Italian, but more often, Nino could see an American white star or British roundel on the fuselage. Nino heard birds chirping in the trees, oblivious to the war that was surely raging on the beaches to the south.

When he arrived, the gate was closed. Two German sentries ran from behind a row of trees. They said something he didn't understand. He wasn't certain of their rank, but they appeared young. With exaggerated arm gestures, Nino pretended to be agitated, demanding they let him in. Caving to his request, they pushed one of the massive wooden doors inward, just enough for Nino to squeeze through.

Parked in the courtyard were two German troop carriers and a couple of *Kübelwagens*. Wehrmacht soldiers were everywhere. They smoked cigarettes while chatting in small groups. They glanced at Nino when he passed, but were unconcerned, for he was nothing but another Italian soldier to them.

He entered Fr. Russo's office. It was empty. As he crossed to the Nun's quarters, he spotted sister Catherine and called to her.

She raised her eyebrows. "Father Servidei. Is that you?"

He pulled her to the side and whispered. "Shh... please don't use my name. I'm a wanted man. I escaped from a prison cell. Where is Father Russo?"

"He is in the infirmary with sister Anna. They are tending to a handful of wounded German soldiers."

"Where did they come from?"

"I don't know exactly. But they have an Italian interpreter with them. He said there is fierce fighting south of here. The Americans have overrun several coastal villages."

"I'm looking for an Italian soldier and a girl. They were to meet me here."

"I saw Father Russo escort them into your quarters last evening. I haven't seen them since."

Nino made his way to his room. When he entered, Vito sat in a wooden chair in the corner. Gabrielle lay face down, asleep in his bed.

Nino closed the door, Vito crossed the room and hugged him. They remained silent. The embrace of his old friend offered peace to Nino's tattered soul. The stress of the past two days suddenly overwhelmed him. He was beaten, battered, broken, and exhausted. He came to Italy on a mission to save the lives of Americans, yet in doing so, he killed countless Germans and Italians through airstrikes and more recently, a bullet into Richter's head. Now he was with his best friend, who had saved his life a day earlier.

They released their embrace.

Nino laughed, "Every time you get near me, you soon find yourself in trouble."

"I'm always at your service, *Mi Amico.*"

"God sent you to me yesterday, Vito. I have no doubt of that."

"What does God have in store for us now? We are both wanted men. You for being a spy and me for breaking you out of prison."

"I guess that depends on how this war goes."

Nino looked at the sleeping Gabrielle. "How is she?"

"She's been through hell. And I don't just mean the past few days. We spent last night in here and were up most of the night. I listened to the detailed stories of her life. She has had it rough since the moment she left her mother's womb. Her stories broke my heart."

"What's next for the two of you?"

"If I don't end up in prison, I hope to marry her and return to Milan."

"How is your family?"

"The past few years have been difficult for all Italians, including my family. They sent my brother to the Eastern Front and within a month, his entire unit disappeared. Captured by the Russians, it is assumed. My mother passed away last year. Papa's medical practice is surviving, yet few of his patients have money to pay him, and some have shunned him, because he still sees his Jewish patients."

"Your father is brave."

"Like many Italians, my papa has ignored the racial laws. Italians are good people, Nino. The support for Mussolini and his fascist ways is fading fast."

Gabrielle stirred before sitting up. Her face was swollen, and a rosy-red rope burn was visible on her neck. She stood and embraced Vito.

"Did you rest well, my lovely?" Vito asked.

"I don't feel lovely."

Vito kissed her forehead. "You are beautiful."

There was a furor outside. They heard German voices shouting commands intermingled with the sound of revving engines.

Nino and Vito entered the courtyard. Soldiers were loading gear into a troop carrier. They placed stretchers carrying wounded soldiers into the other.

In one of the *Kübelwagens*, the Italian interpreter sat in the passenger seat. He was communicating with the driver.

Nino and Vito approached him. Nino said, "Excuse us, Capitano. May we enquire what is happening?"

"How did you get here?"

Vito said, "On a motorcycle. We are messengers."

"Why are you here?"

Vito said, "We stopped here to see if the abbey had any gas."

"You better find some. The Americans are breaking through the beachhead. They may be here in a few days. We have been ordered to head to Messina. A defensive perimeter is being formed around the city."

The other *Kübelwagen* sped off, followed by the two troop carriers.

"We must go," the Capitano said. "Good luck to you."

After they watched the last German vehicle leave, they turned to see Father Russo standing behind them. He wore a white medical robe splattered in blood.

"Nino, it is so good to see you. When they dragged you off, I thought I would never see you again."

"Vito here rescued me. He saved my life."

Father Russo said, "And you saved mine, Nino. Had it not been for you confessing about the wireless, they would have killed me, I'm sure of it."

"What happens now?" Vito asked. "I'm a soldier with no home. I can't return to the Italian Army, or I'll be arrested. If the Americans catch me, they too will detain me indefinitely."

"This Abbey has always been a sanctuary for those in need," Father Russo said. "You and Gabrielle may stay here until Italy's future is made clearer."

Nino said, "Father, where can we get civilian clothes?"

"The Leones. Their son Aldo was an Italian soldier and was killed in Africa. He was about your size, Vito. And Nino, they may wear a little loose, but with the food shortages, everyone's clothes tend to sag."

Nino said, "Wouldn't that be a little forward of us to just go ask Lorenzo for his deceased son's clothes?"

"Maybe for you, but not for me. Let me clean myself up and I will drive the Berline to Bellissima Valle."

"Father, will you check on..."

Nino caught himself, realizing that Father Russo was unaware the Leones were harboring Angelo.

"Yes, Nino what is it?"

"Never mind, Father."

* * *

Six days had passed since the British and Americans landed on the southern coast of Sicily. Nino, Vito, and Gabrielle had stayed at the Abbey, and Father Russo did in fact return from

Bellissima Vale with several sets of Aldo's clothes for Nino and Vito. He also brought a sealed letter Isabella had given him. It was from Angelo, letting Nino know he was well.

Vito shared Nino's quarters, and Gabrielle stayed with sister Anna and sister Catherine. They had asked about her background, and she had considered lying, fearing they would judge her. Instead, she told them the truth, and they prayed with her and offered compassion to a young girl who had experienced little of it in her lifetime.

As they dressed for breakfast, Nino said to Vito, "If the reports are true, the Americans and Brits will occupy the entire island soon. What will you do then?"

"I don't know. I need to contact my father, but it sounds like all hell will soon break loose throughout Italy. And I'm sure by now that they know I helped you escape from prison. My hope is that in the chaos of war that arresting Caporale Vito Bianchi seems unimportant. What about you, Nino?"

"I'm just waiting for the Americans to show up. Then I'll walk up to the highest-ranking officer I can find, tell him why I'm here, then inform him of Angelo's whereabouts. After that, I'll figure out how to get home."

"I've missed you the past two years, Nino. Our time in Rome together was some of the happiest of my life."

Nino embraced him. "You once helped me rescue Hannah. Yesterday you saved my life. It may cost you your freedom. Depending on your punishment, it may cost you your life. They may execute you. You know that, don't you?"

"They have to catch me first."

"Where will you hide?"

"We'll stay here at the Abbey as long as Father Russo will

allow it. When I feel it is safe, we'll make our way to my father. How we get there is a mystery. But you know me. I'll figure it out."

"I can never repay you. But if you ever need me, I'll be at your side in an instant."

"Repay me by getting home to Hannah. Give her my love."

There was a knock at the door. It was Gabrielle. She said, "I'm going to go play with the children before breakfast. Will you come too, Vito?"

Vito held Gabrielle's hand. "We'll see you at breakfast, Nino."

Bellissima Valle

The sun was setting, and against Lorenzo's desires, Angelo and Isabella spent time together in the woods behind the house. Angelo still used a cane yet could manage without it if needed. They heard artillery fire in the far distance, and it appeared closer with each passing day.

"I'm frightened," Isabella said.

"Of what?" Angelo asked.

"The future. I don't know what's going to happen to my country. What's going to happen to you? Do you think you will go back to flying?"

"I hope to."

"So, you can drop bombs on Italians like me?"

He stopped and turned to her. The comment disturbed him. He opened his mouth to speak, then stopped himself.

Isabella asked, "What were you going to say?"

"You make it too simple."

"No, you make it simple. You Americans and Brits fly over our country and drop bombs on people you don't know, then fly back to base and have dinner. Meanwhile, we are left to bury our dead."

Angelo looked down, then into her eyes. "I would never want anything like that to happen to you."

"Because you know me. What about the Italians you don't know?"

"They are soldiers."

"Not all of them. And even if they are soldiers, that shouldn't matter."

"It's a war. Italians should have never joined forces with Hitler."

"Italians didn't. Mussolini did. We just got caught up in his politics."

"I don't want to discuss this. We may only have a few more days together."

"Will you think of me after you leave?"

"I'll never forget you, Isabella."

He leaned down and kissed her cheek.

Isabella said, "That day in Aldo's room, when I cuddled next to you in his bed was my first kiss."

"You'll find someone one day and have many kisses with them."

THE ABBEY OF SANTA MARIA

Nino stood on the top of a hill watching a cloud of dust on a distant valley road. Since hearing of the recent British and American breakthroughs, he had spent much of the day on the lookout for movement. His time in Sicily had made him proficient at spotting the difference between Italian and German vehicles. Like airplanes, they each had specific silhouettes and colors that were discernable from afar. However, today this convoy appeared distinctive. The troop carriers were larger, and the lead vehicles were smaller than the German *Kübelwagens* and Italian *Lancia Aprilia Coloniales*. With the assumption they were either British or American, he sprinted down the hill and toward the monastery.

Upon entering the gate, he ran to Father Russo's office where he found him sitting at his desk. Short of breath, Nino huffed, "Father, I believe the Allies are nearby. I saw them in the valley—a convoy. I'm taking the Berline. I'm going to intercept them."

"Be careful. They have no idea who you are. If they see your approach as a threat, the result might not be good."

"I'll be careful."

Father Russo reached into his desk drawer and handed him a white handkerchief. "Wave this as you approach."

Nino inserted it into his pocket and said, "Have you seen Vito and Gabrielle?"

"They are cleaning the kitchen."

Nino made his way across the courtyard. When he arrived, Vito and Gabrielle were in the corner kissing. "I thought you were supposed to be cleaning."

Vito said, "Everyone deserves a break."

"Vito, you must be careful. Be prepared to hide. I just spotted a convoy of military vehicles. They aren't Italian or German."

"Americans?"

"Or British. I have no way of knowing until I go meet them."

Vito stepped toward Nino. "What then?"

"Then I will tell them who I am and hope they believe me."

"When are you going?"

"'Now. I came to let you know."

Gabrielle said, "You won't be coming back?"

"No. If they believe me, they will want to debrief me. If I'm not believed, they may arrest me. Either way, I'm afraid this is goodbye."

They embraced. Vito said, "It has been so good to see you. Mi Amico."

Nino didn't want to release his old friend. "I owe you everything, Vito."

Vito kissed both of Nino's cheeks. "You owe me nothing."

Nino wrapped his arms around Gabrielle. "You have changed this man for the better. I have never seen Vito so in love. Take care of him."

"We will take care of each other."

"You will need to. The war has just begun for Italy. There will be a lot of uncertainty ahead."

* * *

The U.S. 16th Infantry division was traveling north. Nino approached them from the east and hoped the olive green Berline offered no threat to the convoy of trucks and American infantry snaking its way through the Sicani mountain range.

He was high on a peak and downshifted to a lower gear as he made his way down the steep slope, approaching perpendicular to the convoy and the dusty road they were traveling. His path leveled, the narrow road he was on forked, and he turned right, assuming the lead vehicles would carry an officer with a high enough rank to send someone for Angelo.

The soldiers marching beside the slow-moving vehicles glared at him and removed their rifles from their shoulders to have them at the ready. Others pointed their fingers and laughed at the ancient spoked-wheeled Berline.

Nino accelerated, passing the lead jeep, and waving father Russo's white handkerchief. After intercepting the convoy, he stopped in front of them, blocking their path. Nino leaped from the Berline and approached the front Jeep.

"I am an American. My name is Nino Servidei. I arrived in Sicily four months ago on an intelligence gathering mission for the U.S. War Department. There is a downed airman—U.S. Army Air Corps—at a farm near here. The family has been hiding him. His name is Angelo DiVincenzo, and he is my brother. I'm also aware of an internment camp not far from here where other American and British airmen are being held."

A tall, gangly colonel stepped out of the Jeep and stared intensely at Nino. "You sound like an American. But your story shouts of bullshit to me. He turned to a staff sergeant beside him. "Search him. His car too."

The staff sergeant patted Nino down, finding nothing, then approached the Berline.

Nino said to him, "You'll find a Beretta under the seat, but no other weapons."

Returning with the Beretta, the staff sergeant said, "He's right, colonel. This is all I found."

"Where are you from, Servidei?"

"New York—the Bronx, sir."

Addressing the staff sergeant. "What's the name of that medic? The one from New York. Didn't he say he was from the Bronx?"

"Sergeant Caputo."

"Go get him."

"Yes, sir."

Nino watched him run to the rear of the convoy, then studied the colonel who stared back at him. "I am who I say I am."

"We'll see."

Nino's nerves were on edge, concerned they might arrest him.

When the staff sergeant returned with the medic, the colonel said, "Sergeant Caputo, this man says he is an American from the Bronx. Interrogate him. Ask him questions to uncover any bullshit."

Caputo said, "Okay, buddy, what street did you grow up on?"

"Hoffman street."

"What was your address?"

"Twenty-eight eleven Hoffman Street. I lived on the seventh floor of Hoffman towers."

"Oh, so you were a rich kid?"

"That depends on your point of view."

"Where did you go to school?"

"Saint Francis."

"What is at the corner of third avenue and 188th Street?"

"A vacant lot, and across the street is a penny arcade. Four blocks down is Nickie's corner Market. Across from Nickie's is Ferraro's restaurant. What else do you need to know?"

"What is your last name?"

"Servidei. But I changed it to distance myself from my father. My father is Salvador DiVincenzo. Does that name mean anything to you?"

"Your father is Salvador DiVincenzo?"

"It is. My brother Angelo DiVincenzo is with the Army Air Corps. His plane was shot down and he is being hidden on a farm not far from here."

"My old man is a bartender at Luigi's Restaurant. He has met your father. He says he is a big tipper."

Caputo turned and addressed the colonel. "Sir, he is from the Bronx. I'm sure of it."

The colonel pointed to a vehicle behind him, whistled, then motioned for another officer to approach. When the Captain arrived, the Colonel repeated Nino's story. "Captain Davis, take two squads of men and go with Mr. Servidei. Confirm that what he is saying is true. If so, have someone bring his brother to me, then go to the internment camp. I need intel. See how fortified it is and report back to me."

BELLISSIMA VALLE

Two jeeps approached the edge of the courtyard, then halted. Lorenzo, Bruno and several fieldhands held rifles. A wireless antenna extended from the rear of the second vehicle. It carried two soldiers. Nino leaped from the passenger seat of the first jeep before making his way to Lorenzo and Bruno. "We came to get Angelo."

Lorenzo nodded his acceptance. Nino turned and waived Captain Davis forward. The soldiers in the second jeep stood pat. Nino introduced captain Davis who said, "Tell them we are grateful to them for protecting our airman."

Nino relayed the message, then followed Bruno into the house. The always suspicious Lorenzo brought up the rear of the small group as they entered his home, keeping his rifle at the ready.

Angelo sat at the kitchen table with Isabella.

"Sergeant DiVincenzo, I'm Captain Davis. We are here to take you home."

Leaning on his cane, Angelo hoisted himself to his feet before addressing Nino in Italian. "It's about time you got here, Nino. What took you so long?"

"I had considered leaving you here."

Lorenzo said, "That's not a good idea. It's time for him to go."

"Be nice, Papa," Isabella said.

Captain Davis said, "We need to get out of here. There are still Italian and German troops throughout these mountains. We are a bit undermanned to get involved in any firefights."

Once in the courtyard, Angelo shook Bruno's hand. "You saved my life. I'll always be grateful."

Bruno nodded his approval. "Keep using your leg. If you don't it will never heal completely."

"I will," Angelo said before turning to Lorenzo. "Thank you for everything, Mr. Leone."

Lorenzo shook his hand yet said nothing.

Angelo grabbed Isabella's hand and stepped away from the group. He got a lump in his throat. "If it were not for you..."

He bowed his head, then raised it before looking into her eyes. "If it were not for you there is no telling what would have happened to me. You risked your life to save mine."

She grinned. "And what did it get me?"

"A lifetime friend."

"Oh really. Once you drive off Bellissima Valle, I'll never hear from you again."

"That's not true. I'll never forget you. I suspect you haven't seen the last of me."

"I'll be waiting."

"No, you won't. Once the war is over and the young men of Sicily return, they will be lined up to be near you."

"Maybe."

He kissed her forehead. "Goodbye, Isabella."

"Goodbye, Angelo."

Angelo made his way to the jeep.

Isabella yelled to Nino, "Goodbye, Father Servidei."

Nino climbed into the jeep and waved. "Goodbye, Isabella."

Captain Davis said, "Mr. Servidei, the British have located the internment camp you told us about. The Italians and Germans have retreated. They left the prisoners behind. They have been liberated."

"What kind of shape are they in?"

"I don't know. But I have been ordered to take you to Gela."

Nino turned to see Angelo's jeep leaving the courtyard.

"Where's Angelo going?"

"He's on his way to a hospital ship in Palermo."

GELA SICILY

The journey down the winding roads to Gela had taken hours. They frequently passed American convoys making their way across Sicily, accompanied by the sound of distant machine gun and artillery fire. Twice, Captain Davis ordered the driver to steer the jeep into the woods for cover, only to find the threat to be an American troop carrier.

The center of Gela was a flourish of activity. U.S. soldiers bustled in the streets, avoiding merchants who were trying to sell them wine, citrus, and olive oil. The soldiers ignored them as they loaded provisions aboard trucks on their way to supply infantry units moving across Sicily.

Captain Davis instructed the driver to a seaside road where vessels of various sizes were tied to piers. Larger ships could be seen anchored in the harbor. They turned a corner and drove down a side street before being forced to stop. Nino felt ill as he saw two dozen bodies wrapped in canvas. One by one, he watched soldiers carry them across the street and into a small white building. Nino was tired of death. The stench, violence, and the coldness of it all was at times too much to bear. He had watched men die around him and he had experienced enough of it that he knew his life would never be the same.

The men carrying the bodies halted as they waved Nino and Captain Davis' jeep forward. After another four blocks, a large white building with a series of stairs and two double doors came into view. They parked in front of it.

"This is where I was instructed to bring you, Mr. Servidei," Captain Davis said.

Nino got out, shook Davis' hand and made his way up the stairs. Two MPs awaited him at the door.

"Apparently someone is expecting me," Nino said.

He followed one of the soldiers into a large foyer, then into an office to the right.

"Please wait here, sir. I will let Major Grayson know you are here."

Nino found three leather chairs in the corner. When he sat, it absorbed his aching body, and he found it soothing. He knew he should stay awake, but as his eyes closed, he made little effort to fight his exhaustion and soon the events of the past several weeks turned into a mixture of dreams and nightmares. He awoke to Major Grayson shaking his shoulder. "Servidei... Servidei. Wake up."

Nino's head turned from side to side before he opened his eyes to see the familiar face of major Grayson. The same major Grayson who had briefed him at the sand table at the Chopawamsic training facility in Virginia.

Nino sprang to his feet. "Major Grayson, I'm sorry. That is the most comfortable chair I have sat in since arriving here. I haven't been getting much sleep."

"That's fine, Servidei. Would you like some coffee?"

"Yes, sir. I need a strong cup."

They crossed the room where a stainless coffee pot sat on a large wooden conference table.

"Mr. Servidei, you will be here for a few days while I debrief you."

"How long before I can return home?"

"General Donovan will be here shortly. I believe he will share those details with you."

"General Donovan is *here*?"

"He came ashore with the first infantry division and was in the middle of the action for the first few days of the invasion."

"He was in the fighting?"

"He insisted. We had to drag him away from the front."

General Donovan entered the room. "Good afternoon, Mr. Servidei."

"Good afternoon, general."

"How's the hand? I heard what happened. The Germans are bastards."

"It could have been worse, sir. I'm grateful to be alive."

General Donovan directed Nino and Major Grayson to the three chairs in the corner.

Donovan said, "Mr. Servidei, your contribution to the success of the invasion was immense. Thousands of American soldiers are alive today because of you. However, history won't reflect that. The number of people who know you were here on behalf of the War Department are few and will remain that way. If anyone suggests the OSS played a role in the invasion of Sicily, we will deny it, as will you. Along with so many others, you will remain a silent hero."

"I understand, sir."

"Mr. Servidei, after your debriefing, you will be going home to recover from your injuries. However, we would like you to remain a member of our organization. You will continue to be paid by the War Department."

"I don't understand, sir."

"We have plans in the works, and we may need your services again."

"What do you need me to do? Where would you send me?"

"Several contingencies have been drawn up. However, until we take control of Sicily, those plans will remain flexible."

"How soon before you would need me?"

"We may never need you. But if we do, I would like you to be available."

Nino remained silent. His mind wandered to Hannah and his children. He didn't want to leave them again. He also thought of the dead soldiers in the canvas wraps, and how many more there might have been had he not come to Sicily? Not lost on him too, was how close he came to being in one.

Sensing Nino's hesitation, General Donovan stood and paced the room. "Mr. Servidei, I don't need your answer today. The people who work for me are all volunteers. It takes special people, both men and women, to go behind enemy lines and work clandestinely. Go home and recover from your injuries. I'll have someone contact you if and when we need you."

CHAPTER 19

THE ATLANTIC OCEAN

I t was their fourth day on board the hospital ship *USAHS Shamrock*. Although Angelo's bunk was in the rehabilitation ward, he spent his days walking, much of the time without a cane, yet with a severe limp. Today he was on the main deck.

Nino approached him. "How about a rest, Angelo?"

"Walk with me to the bow. Then we'll have a seat."

As they strolled, the wind off the Atlantic was swift. The salt spray stung their face. Angelo pulled Nino to the railing where they stood.

Nino said, "Do they think you will fly again?"

"If I have anything to say about it, I will."

"What if you can't?"

"I guess they'll find something else for me to do."

"How many missions did you fly before they shot you down?"

"That was my first. But I shot down a plane."

"On your first mission? Hell, that's impressive."

"You just said, 'hell.' I've never heard you swear, Nino?"

With a chuckle, Nino said, "Don't tell Mama. Or Hannah. She's never heard me swear either."

Angelo said, "So, this mission you were on, was it successful?"

Nino looked down. His mind went to the airstrikes he had ordered. Visions of the running men engulfed in flames filled his mind.

"Are you okay, Nino?"

He looked at Angelo. "I can't discuss this, nor do I want to. I never want you to bring it up again."

THE BRONX NEW YORK

It was late afternoon when the *USAHS Shamrock* docked at New York Harbor. They transported Angelo to a medical facility at Fort Hamilton in Brooklyn. The vast number of soldiers and sailors departing the vessel created a logjam at the bus and cab stations. It took Nino hours to get home, and when he arrived, the sun had already set. After paying the cab driver, he glanced up at his third-floor apartment. Only the kitchen light was on, and he hoped Lilia and Solomon were still awake. If not, he would wake them. It was the second week of August, and he had left his family five months earlier. From the time he first spoke to Father Morlion, to his time in Sicily, to this very moment had all been a whirlwind. It was as though someone other than he had experienced the recent events of his life, and he was nothing but an observer.

He exhaled a breath, crossed the street, climbed the stairs, and studied the locked door of his apartment. His knock prompted the scrape of wooden chair legs across the kitchen floor. Hannah's soft footsteps approached. The lock turned and the door opened. Tears flowed down his cheeks as Hannah wrapped her arms around his neck.

CHAPTER 20

A slight breeze contributed to a cool pleasant September evening. Nino had been home for three weeks and had spent much of his free time on the fire escape of their apartment. On this evening, Lilia sat on his lap. She proudly shared all the English words she had learned while he was away. During Nino's absence, Lilia occasionally reverted to Italian, but Hannah quickly forced her into English.

Nino said, "I'm proud of you, Lilia. You are the smartest little girl I have ever known."

"Grandmama says that I am smart like you."

He kissed her nose. "Your mama is pretty smart too."

Hannah stepped through the open window and onto the fire escape. She held the fidgeting Solomon. "What did I hear about mama being smart?"

"Papa said you were smart."

Nino said, "She's pretty too, isn't she, Lilia."

"She's the prettiest."

"I like this conversation. Keep going," Hannah said while sitting on the crate next to them.

As the evening passed, Hannah rested her head on Nino's

shoulder, while Lilia and Solomon slept safely in their parent's arms.

Hannah said, "Your mama has invited us over for Sunday dinner. I told her I didn't think you would go, and I wasn't coming without you."

"Will Angelo be there?"

"She said he would."

"I'll go."

"You *will*?"

"I need to speak to papa."

"About what?"

"Nothing specifically. Mainly grandpapa DiVincenzo in Sicily."

"Will you ever tell me what happened while you were there. You still haven't told me how you broke your fingers."

"Maybe one day. For now, I just want to forget the entire experience."

Hannah leaned over and kissed Nino's cheek. "I love you, Nino Servidei. You are a special man; do you know that?"

He kissed her lips. "I missed you. You and these two little angels are everything to me. I never stopped thinking of you."

"It's time to put them to bed," Hannah said. "Then you and I can return here with a blanket."

"You want to sleep here on the fire escape tonight?"

Hannah laughed. "Sleeping isn't what I had in mind, Nino."

OTHER BOOKS IN THE 'NINO' SERIES
J.D. KEENE

Nino's Heart
(Book I of the Nino Series)
A Novel of Love and Suspense set in WW2 Italy

Nino's Promise
(Book 3 of the Nino Series)
Return to Italy

ALSO BY J.D. KEENE

The Heroes of Sainte-Mere-Eglise
A D-Day Novel

Available now, in paperback and on Kindle,
from Amazon.

ACKNOWLEDGMENTS

I would like to thank the following individuals who contributed significantly to this novel. Their assistance was in the form of researching, technical expertise, advanced reading, editing, cover design our simply encouraging. Their support is vital and their suggestions are often brilliant: Andy Keene, Ben Garrett, Colin Fradd, Beth-Ellen Dolinsky, David Booker, Dawn Gardner, Elizabeth Gassoway, Evan Keene, Genevieve Montcombroux, George Harth, Gerri Adams, John Kruger, Joyce Schwarting, Katie Keene, Kayla Tucker, Mark Keene, Mary Alice Thomason, Mary Durr, Phyliss Sawyer, Sara Jane Lucy, Steve Feinstein, Tara White, Terry Gassoway.

ABOUT THE AUTHOR

Nino's War is J.D. Keene's third novel. He lives in Virginia, U.S.A. with his wife Katie.

To stay in contact with J.D. Keene, please visit his website:
www.jdkeene.com